Break Point

Also by Yahrah St. John

Her Best Friend's Brother
Her Secret Billionaire
Her One Night Consequence
Frenemy Fix-Up
Going Toe to Toe

Visit yahrahstjohn.com or the Author Profile
page at Harlequin.com for more titles.

YAHRAH ST. JOHN

Break Point

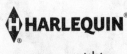

Recycling programs
for this product may
not exist in your area.

ISBN-13: 978-1-335-57492-3

Break Point

Copyright © 2025 by Yahrah Yisrael

Harlequin Enterprises ULC
22 Adelaide St. West, 41st Floor
Toronto, Ontario M5H 4E3, Canada
www.Harlequin.com

Printed in U.S.A.

To my best friend Kiara Ashanti for his support,
encouragement and assistance with
helping me, a tennis novice.

One

Teagan

Boss babe.

That's what everyone at Williams & Associates calls me. I don't know any other way to be but to go hard. Ambition and success are in my blood.

The last several years, I've been running my own brokerage in Phoenix, selling high-end luxury homes in Desert View, Foothills, Camelback East and Paradise Valley. Initially, I was the only sales agent, but when the real estate market blossomed, I added more. Now, I have a team of six. Yes, I'm good at what I do, but this is not how I expected my life to go.

Once upon a time, I was a bona fide tennis star, a Grand Slam champion. The next Serena Williams, my coach used to say. That's until I let Dominic Fletcher distract me from my goals. Losing a career I worked decades to achieve still stings, despite the passage of time. Thinking about the loss always makes me remember Dominic, the man I'd thought was my soulmate, because we shared a love of the game and each other. I was wrong.

Now I push aside these memories and stroll through the glass doors of Williams & Associates wearing my double-breasted suit by Sergio Hudson and favorite Balmain snake-skin leather slingbacks.

"Good morning, Teagan," says Amanda, my fresh-faced receptionist.

She's sitting behind a short white desk in the lobby. Her printed shirtdress looks like something I would wear. It's my motto that you have to dress for success, and I make damn sure all my agents and staff do the same. Appearances are every-thing in this business, in all business. I know from experi-ence because the tennis world and the press turned against me when I didn't live up to their image of what a tennis prodigy should be.

"Good morning." I sashay past Amanda and the offices of several of my agents. Everyone is in before me. That's a good thing. Today is our weekly meeting to go over upcoming sales and look ahead. I offer a wide smile and continue down the corridor, my heels clicking on the tile floors until I arrive at my office. Located in the rear of the building, it has bright walls filled with tasteful art, modern furnishings and luxuri-ous decor. It's my oasis from the storm. Part of the one-story building I now own outright thanks to an inheritance from my best friend's aunt.

Helaine Smith was like a grandmother to me, listening to my problems as I tried being a teenager, a tennis professional, a daughter and a friend. Her door was always open, and she allowed me and my friends—affectionately nicknamed the Gems—to be authentically ourselves. When she passed away a few years ago, we were all shocked. She was so full of life, having traveled the globe with my best friend, Wynter, in tow. What was more shocking was the fact that she left each of Wynter's friends a sizable chunk of change so we each could fulfill our dreams.

I try to make her proud every day.

Now, no sooner do I toss my Birkin on the sofa, sit in my white leather executive chair and turn on my Mac, than my lead sales agent knocks on my door.

"Hey, boss."

"What's up, Brett?"

At six feet, Brett Schwenneker has coal-black hair, a slim athletic build and compelling blue eyes that captivated me when we first met. However, his troubled look leads me to believe I won't like what's coming next.

"I hate to bother you before your morning cup of joe, but it's the Reynolds deal. They're backing out. Interest rates are too high, and they're going to wait it out."

Damn. My stomach drops. The Reynolds deal was a six-figure sale with a commission the agency needed to cover the next couple of months. Brett had been working the deal with me, so it's a hit for him too.

I motion him inside. "Is there any way to save it? Perhaps I can meet with them and allay their fears?"

Brett shakes his head. "I tried."

He's my top agent. If he can't convince the Reynoldses, then the deal is dead. I nod. "All right. Thanks for letting me know."

"Sure thing. Want me to get you an espresso?"

"Make it a double."

Seconds later, he's gone and I'm wondering what's next

when my cellphone pings. It's a message from Wynter in our group chat with details about the destination wedding of Egypt, a fellow Gem. There's been a lot of back and forth on locations. Usually, I'm all in for one of Wynter's fabulous vacations because our girls' trips are epic, but my money ain't right.

I haven't told the Gems or my parents about the brokerage being on the rails. Not that my father would care. He's never understood what it is that I do, not after my tennis career sank. Up until recently, I'd been killing it with real estate, but with the unpredictable market it's a struggle to keep everyone encouraged.

Paying for an expensive vacation to a destination wedding will set me back, but it's not like I *can't* attend. Egypt would absolutely kill me. If anyone can read someone the riot act, other than me, it's my girl Egypt. I don't want to be on the receiving end of that sharp tongue. I guess I'll be using my Amex for this one. I text back.

Tell me the day and time. And I'm there.

Only a small lie. I would rather be anywhere than watching another Gem tie the knot. First Asia married in secret, then Wynter and now Egypt. Each and every one of my five best friends has coupled up, leaving me the last single woman standing. But that's okay. I'm not looking for a relationship. The occasional date or hookup is fine with me. Ever since my previous relationship failure, I've told myself I don't need or *want* a man.

I plonk the phone down in my purse as Brett walks in carrying my double espresso. I accept the cup and slam the drink down like it's a shot. I need the hit of caffeine. Maybe my mind will start working on ideas of what to do next.

Instead of leaving, though, Brett closes the door and takes a seat in front of me. "What are we going to do?"

I shrug.

"C'mon, Teagan. You always have something up your sleeve."

In this instance, I don't, so I grasp at straws. "Do you remember Charity Wilson, one of our clients last year?"

"How could I forget her? Charity had so much work done, her face barely moved."

I can't resist a giggle. "Well…she invited me to come to the Phoenix Country Club. Said it might be a good place to drum up business."

"One of those memberships costs thousands."

"I'm aware." I lean back in my chair and let the jolt of caffeine do its work. "You know the old adage 'It takes money to make money.'"

Brett shrugs. "As long as you know what you're doing."

"I do." I don't, but sometimes you have to fake it until you make it. This is one of those times. "I'll reach out to her and set up lunch."

"Sounds like a good idea. I'll see you at the meeting." Brett rises to his feet, gives me a quick wave and heads out of the room.

Outlaying cash for a country club membership right now is not ideal, but I don't have many choices. I will do anything to keep Williams & Associates afloat until the market rebounds. I pick up my landline and reach out to Charity. She answers on the third ring.

"Hi, Charity. It's Teagan Williams."

"Teagan, it's been ages. How are you, darling?"

"I'm good. I was wondering if your offer for sponsoring

me at the Phoenix Country Club is still on the table." I hope it doesn't sound like I'm begging, but I need this.

There's a pause before she answers. "I thought you weren't interested."

"I can always use access to potential clients. PCC is known for catering to the elite." I stroke Charity's ego to ensure she's on my side.

"Of course the offer is still on the table. Would you like to come by for a tour? We have a fabulous tennis court on-site. If I recall, you used to play, didn't you?"

Mentioning tennis causes a knot to form in my stomach. I gave up the sport when Dominic broke my heart. When he abandoned me, he took not only my heart, but also my love of the game.

"Yes, I did, but that was eons ago. I doubt I'm any good."

"I'll be the judge. You should come out on Saturday and we can play a few games."

I want to say hell no, there's no way I'm getting onto a court ever again. But I need this opportunity to drum up new business. "I would love that."

She rattles off a time on Saturday and I put it in my calendar. When the call is over, I sigh and lean back, stare at the ceiling and tell myself, *You've got this!*

So what if playing tennis again stirs up old demons? There is no other option but success. My name is hanging on the door and I refuse to fail, *not again*.

I'm happy when the day is over and everyone has gone home. During today's staff meeting, I did my best to encourage the team, remind them economic downturns are part of the business. We will weather the storm and come out on top.

Yada, yada, yada. Brett looked skeptical, but he backed me up, and I appreciated it.

Now I'm in the office alone because it's less lonely than going home to an empty house. I have a beautiful four bedroom, four bath with panoramic mountain views. Lots of natural light, beautiful wood floors and beams, upgraded lighting, and a stone fireplace in the family room that overlooks a terrace and pool. *What more could a girl ask for?* When I saw the house on the market, I knew it would be a symbol of all I'd achieved.

On my own.

Without tennis.

My family, specifically my father, Russell Williams, was disappointed when I gave up the sport. However, after the injury to my meniscus and the blackballing after a personal moment was captured publicly, I had to go off and lick my wounds.

The Six Gems were there for me when I fell apart. Wynter, Egypt, Asia, Shay and Lyric have seen me through some of the best and *worst* of times. I need them now.

I place a video call to Lyric. The auburn-haired ballet beauty has a quiet softness about her that some people see as weakness, but that I see as her inherent strength. Lyric understands perseverance, working through pain toward a goal, only to see it fall apart—because it happened to her. She was the next Misty Copeland until an injury sidelined her ballet career.

"Teagan, how are you?" Lyric asks. "Wait a sec. Are you still at work?" She glances down at her watch.

"Afraid so. It's been a tough day. Hell, make that a tough few months."

I never shared with the Gems what's been going on with the real estate market. Everyone expects me to have my shit

together because that's my role. I'm the boss babe of the group.
Or at least I have been for the last decade. Plus, all the Gems
are happy now with their respective partners; I don't want to
be a downer with my financial woes. But today is just too
much.

"Why? What's going on?"

"All the economic uncertainty is negatively affecting real
estate," I respond. "Buyers can't get loans because home prices
and interest rates are too high. I started Williams & Associates when the market was booming and…well, now, I'm feeling the pinch."

"Oh, Teagan, I'm so sorry. Why didn't you say anything
before?" Her large almond-shaped eyes show true concern.
That's Lyric. She always has empathy.

"I didn't want to spoil the mood."

"Because we're all so happy and in love?" she offers.

I shrug. "Something like that."

"Just because I love Devon and Kianna doesn't negate the
fact that you're my friend and sister. You can *always* tell me
and the Gems what's going on. Even if we can't help, we can
sympathize."

"Logically, I know this, but I was hoping to turn it around.
Usually things go my way." *Except when they don't.*

Lyric chuckles softly. "You think you're a superwoman,
Teagan, but you're not. You're human like the rest of us."

"Are you sure about that? Because I could have sworn I
had supernatural powers. Didn't I help all of you find your
happily-ever-afters?"

"Oh, so you're gonna take the credit for that?"

I laugh. "Just a little." I pinch my thumb and forefinger

together. "I gave each of you a little push when the moment called for it."

"I think you gave us your two cents." Lyric snorts. "You weren't too keen on Egypt's fiancé, Garrett, or Asia's husband, Blake."

I nod. She's right. I was worried about my friends leaping before they looked. "True, but Garrett and Blake earned my respect. Besides, Asia made us both aunties—I didn't have much choice but to fall head over heels for Ryan."

"He is a gorgeous little boy."

"Yes, he is."

"I know you've always been focused on your career, but do you ever want a family someday?"

Before I met Dominic, my priority was tennis. He was slipping into my thoughts unbidden *again*. When we were together, I was happy and in love. I thought marriage and babies were a possibility, but not anymore. "I don't know, Lyric. Once, I thought I could have it all, but I gave up on those dreams long ago."

"You can still have them, Teagan," Lyric responds. "If ever you need a case in point, I'm it. Losing my ballet career hit me hard, but who lifted me out of my depression, *quite literally out of my bed*, and made me fight again?" She answers when I don't: "You. You told me, so what if that dream ended? I could make a new one. You suggested a dance studio where I could help other people find their dreams."

A tear leaks down my cheek. "I did do that, didn't I?" I give a wry laugh.

"Yes, you did. I know you'll figure this out. I've always looked up to you because you're such a fighter. Even when the world turned against you, you never gave up."

"Lyric…" Her name is a warning. To not go there. To not go to the darkest time in my life. When I lost my career and my man all in one fell swoop.

"I'm sorry. I won't bring it up," Lyric replies.

"Thank you." I've banned any of the Gems from talking about that time or even speaking his name out loud. It hurts too much to think about what a fool I was. I was duped, and I've vowed to never, *ever* be that gullible again.

"Of course. Maybe your parents could help?"

"Not a chance." There's no way I'm opening that hornet's nest or listening to my father say *I told you so*. Hear him wax on about how I should have never left tennis—as if I had a choice.

"Okay, okay. I know your relationship with them is strained."

That's putting it mildly. I barely see my mother except when my father is too busy to catalog her every movement. As for him, we haven't seen eye to eye in years, especially after I called him out for his controlling behavior toward me *and* my mother.

"I've got a meeting with a wealthy friend at the country club later this week. I'm hoping to drum up some business by joining."

"Can you really afford to do that?" Lyric asks.

"I'll manage."

"Should that change, please let me and the Gems know. We're your family, and we want your business to be successful, like each of ours. It's what Aunt Helaine wanted for all of us."

Thinking about the kind and generous older woman brings a smile to my face. It also puts fire in my belly. Wynter's aunt Helaine believed in us, and I can't, *won't* fail her, even in death.

After hanging up with Lyric, I feel encouraged. There's

nothing like unconditional love. I never had that until the Gems came into my life. With my parents, I felt like I always had to be the best—whether that was at home being the perfect daughter or on the court as a star athlete. It always felt like their love was conditional.

A long time ago, I decided I could live without their love *or lack thereof* and I wouldn't let it define me or who I wanted to be. I learned to depend on myself.

There's nothing I can't do when I put my mind to it, and this is no different.

Two

Dominic

There's nothing better than winning.

Or at least that's what I used to tell myself. *Once I get to the Grand Slam, I'll have arrived.* But that day has come and gone, many times over. I've been anointed the best player in tennis, ranked number one in the world. But with that comes pressure to stay on top.

No injuries.

Winning equals endorsements.

I'm the one keeping my family afloat. And have been since I was sixteen. In the early days, my mom worked hard and sacrificed to ensure I could go to tennis lessons and train with the best coaches, but that didn't stop her from making bad choices after I found some success. My mom always chooses the wrong man in her quest for love. Consequently, she had me at the ripe old age of sixteen, and three more children after me from different relationships—one brother and two sisters—without any fathers who would stick around. So, ever since I won that first championship, I've been taking care of her and my three siblings. Nothing got in the way of winning, and that included personal relationships.

"Dominic! You ready to go?" my assistant, Micah Strader, says, holding his iPad.

He's a foot shorter than me, with blond hair, brown eyes and an affinity for cardigans, but he's a godsend. Micah ensures I stay on schedule and I pay him handsomely for it as I do with my agent, publicist, accountant and lawyer. Everyone has their hand in a piece of my pie while I work my ass off day in and day out.

Should I complain? Maybe not. I have amassed wealth and privilege over the last decade. Not bad for a poor kid from Phoenix, Arizona, who somehow found himself on a tennis court with a knack for the sport. I can buy whatever I want, be it a multimillion-dollar mansion in Phoenix or a Caribbean villa. If I want the latest Rolls-Royce or Bugatti, it's mine for the taking.

"Yes, I'm ready."

Grabbing the handle of my Louis Vuitton suitcase, I roll it out of the suite and down the hall to the elevator.

It was another successful Australian Open, and I'm heading to Sedona for a couple of weeks to relax before heading home to Phoenix. Micah has me booked in a private wellness spa. The last several championships were brutal. I'm looking forward to recharging with a massage or two. Or three.

The elevator dings, signaling its arrival, but before I can enter, the woman inside screams, "Oh my god! It's Dominic Fletcher."

"May I come in?" I motion toward the elevator. She nods furiously, so Micah and I enter.

The woman stares at me shamelessly until finally whispering, "Can I have a selfie?"

"MaryAnne!" the man beside her protests, but she stares at me expectantly.

It's a hazard of the job, so I lean in and let her take the picture. Once she has her photo, she doesn't even bother saying thank you, just saunters out of the elevator when we arrive at the lobby.

I give Micah a what-the-fuck look and he shrugs. We head toward the exit. Being the excellent assistant he is, Micah already checked us out and a bellman quickly rushes to open the tall glass doors.

"Thank you," I respond, but the words are barely out of my mouth before the press swarms.

"Quite a match, Dominic. What's next for you?" one of them shouts in my face.

"A break." I have a love-hate relationship with the media. I need them to keep my name out there so I stay relevant, but then I have no peace.

"You're retiring?" another exclaims loudly.

No, you dimwit, I want to say, but instead, I clarify. "You have heard of a vacation, right? I think I've earned one after back-to-back championships."

There are several chuckles and Micah pushes past the press to the limousine waiting at the curb. I climb inside and Micah follows me and the door blessedly closes, sealing us away from intrusive questions.

Retire? I've given it some thought. I'm young and still in relatively good health save for the patellar tendinitis and rotator cuff injuries I've sustained over the years. I've put my body through a lot to stay on top. The endorsements help. I've planned for the future, not only for myself, but for my family. I've set up college funds for my siblings because I don't trust Mom not to give the money away to one of her many suitors. It's bad enough she flaunts my name to get ahead… She wasn't always like this. When I started out in the industry, Mom was humble and eager to see me succeed.

"Thanks for handling things." I look over at Micah.

"It's my job," he responds, and turns back to reviewing whatever is so important on his iPad. Sometimes being a celebrity is one of the loneliest jobs in the world. You can have people all around you and still feel alone.

Staring out the window, I remember someone long ago who understood, who shared my passion for the game. We could practice for hours and afterward have rounds of what I swear was the best sex of my life. *Was it just the heady feeling of first love or was it something deeper?* I'll never know because I was cut out of her life like I was a cancer she had to get rid of.

I don't know why I'm thinking about her. I haven't done so in ages. There have been many women in my life before and after, *especially after.* Winning brings out the ladies. Some are groupies who want nothing more than to be with a celebrity. I watch out for those types because I'm not looking to be anyone's baby daddy. However, I enjoy spending time with a woman who knows the rules of engagement. Tennis is my life. It's how I make my living, and those who get sprung are sent packing. I can't have drama messing up my game.

You see, we players all have our superstitions. For some, it's carrying their favorite penny or wearing the same pair of socks. For me, it's not having sex the night before a match. If I do, I'm sure to lose. And so I abstain. It's my practice. It's worked for me this long so I'm not about to change.

Eventually, we arrive at an airfield. A private jet is waiting to whisk me off to Arizona. I climb aboard the plane, which was built for my comfort in an elegant palette of grays and neutrals. There are four luxurious recliners with hand-stitched leather seats bearing my initials along with a private bathroom and a shower. After traveling commercial and being besieged by the general public, I quickly realized my privacy and peace of mind were tantamount. Once the multimillion-dollar endorsements started pouring in, the jet became a tax deduction since my work requires constant travel. It was a win-win situation.

No sooner than I'm seated, a beautiful, poised flight attendant asks if I would like a refreshment.

"Bottled water, please." After powering through six sets at the Australian Open, I'm exhausted and in need of hydration and sleep. In that order.

Micah sits across from me, tapping away on his tablet as if it holds the secrets of the universe.

Within half an hour, we're taking off and I find myself closing my eyes and trying to sleep. My cell phone buzzes in my pocket. I see it's my brother, Justice, and answer immediately. "Hey, bro, what's going on?"

"Hey, Dom. How was the match?" Justice inquires.

I sigh heavily. "It was a hard battle. Miguel Guinard is a young upstart from Spain who's been coming up the tennis charts to challenge me. It wasn't easy beating him." At thirty-two, I'm not what I once was.

"I imagine you have to practice harder and longer to keep up."

"You ain't lying. These challengers are at least a decade younger than me and much faster on their feet."

"So what's next?"

"I'm taking a few months off, until my next match. I told my agent no more championships until the French Open. It's a risk, but one I'm willing to take."

And more importantly, it'll give me time to think about what comes after tennis. I've been playing professionally since I was sixteen years old. Unlike some of my counterparts, I don't want to keep playing until I'm in my late thirties and besieged by injuries. I would like to go out on top with a legacy of being the best. Sometimes, you have to know when to fold 'em.

"I'm glad you have some free time," Justice says, interrupting my thoughts. "I was hoping I could run a new idea by you, one I have for a business."

"Is that so?" I rub the signature goatee I've been rocking for years.

Ever since Justice graduated from Howard University, my kid brother has been on a quest to build his own wealth without working for "the man." I want to support him, but I won't waste money on a venture that's not profitable, even if he is family.

"Have you put together a prospectus?" I ask.

"I have. Can I send it over to you? Could make for an entertaining read on your private jet."

"Or put me to sleep," I respond wryly.

"Ha ha. So, is that a yes?"

"Go ahead and send it. I'll take a look, but I'm not making any promises."

"I know, I know," Justice replies. "Meanwhile I'll keep toiling away at this nine-to-five."

"That you happen to be making six figures at," I add.

"Whatever."

"How's Mom? Anything I should be aware of?" I ask, holding my breath, hoping she hasn't gotten herself into yet another relationship on the train to nowhere.

"Naw, same ole, same ole," Justice replies. "I stay close by to ensure Ciera and Bliss aren't a victim of her bad decisions."

Justice and I bore the brunt of Mama's poor choices in men. Several years older than him, I tried to shield Justice, but once I moved on to play professionally and travel the globe, it was a lot harder to do from a distance. Justice took over as man of the house.

"I appreciate you, bro," I say. "I'll talk to you in a few days." I end the call.

I love my family, I do, but it's never been easy being the oldest or the sole provider. Mama stopped working when I turned pro, and I get it. She worked hard to help me achieve my dream. I owe it to her to give her the very best, and I've done that.

She wanted to stay in Phoenix close to her friends. I bought her an expensive house in prestigious Paradise Valley. She wanted a luxury vehicle; I got her a Porsche Cayenne and gave her a sizable monthly allowance. Yet it seems like it's never enough because Grace Fletcher has a knack for finding all the Mr. Wrongs, who only use her because of who I am. To combat this, my accountant handles all the house bills, credit cards, and Ciera's and Bliss's private school tuitions and other expenses. Who knows what would happen if I left Mom to her own devices?

Sometimes I wonder, where is the strong, independent woman who raised me and fearlessly fought for me to have a place on the tennis courts? I want that woman back.

Maybe someday I'll brave her waterworks and share my feelings. For now, I keep them to myself.

"Dominic, would you like anything for lunch?" the flight attendant inquires.

"No, I'm good. Thanks."

And I will be. I have to learn how to deal with my mother's shortcomings and not internalize them. The next couple weeks of vacation will be good for me. I'll recharge so I can deal with my family and figure out what's next for me professionally.

Three

Teagan

By the weekend, my stomach is in knots, and not just because my business is on the cusp of financial ruin. My lunch with Charity Wilson at the Phoenix Country Club is today, and she wants us to play a game of tennis. I hung up my racket years ago. Feeling the solid handle and taut strings reminds me I vowed never to play the sport again. I had every intention of keeping that promise—until now.

My tennis dress is classic and unlike my former fashion choices of bold and graphic colors. It's white with a built-in bra and a semi-fitted skirt made of breathable Dri-FIT material. I'll fit right in with the country club crowd. However, putting it on feels constricting; I can't breathe. I bend over, take in big gulps of air and give myself a pep talk. *You can do this, Teagan. You have to. Everything you've worked for since reinventing yourself over a decade ago is on the line.*

Be the boss babe.

I stand up straight and stare at myself in the mirror. But the reflection staring back at me is not one I recognize. I'm used to being calm, confident and sure about my actions. Today, I'm the opposite. I'm scared of opening up a part of myself I closed off and buried. Playing tennis again leaves me fraught with anxiety. Instead of wearing my hair feathered, up and away from my face with hairspray, I've slicked it down with gel until it frames both sides of my face. Other than arching my brows, mascara and a swipe of lipstick, I keep my makeup to a minimum. In the past when I played, I never wore any, but I can't go without, not today. I need armor.

I snatch my new racket bag, sling it over my shoulder and head out of the bedroom. I got rid of all my tennis paraphernalia years ago and had to purchase new gear earlier this week. Within minutes, I'm in my Benz and headed to meet Charity. I try not to let anxiety get the best of me, but it feels as if a large elephant is sitting on my chest. I push through, driving into downtown until I reach the sprawling eighteen-hole golf course and pull up to the valet stand outside the entrance of the Phoenix Country Club.

After we take care of preliminaries, the attendant quickly picks up my bag and follows me inside while another valet hops in my Mercedes and pulls away.

"Will you be playing tennis or racquetball today?" the first attendant asks.

"Tennis," I respond in a clipped tone. "I'm meeting Charity Wilson."

"Follow me." He leads me through the main club until we arrive outside. With each step, I feel my anxiety level rise. Eventually, we stop at the tenth court.

Charity is already there with who I can only assume is her tennis coach, a blond fellow in shorts a bit too short. Meanwhile, Charity is rocking a two-piece tennis ensemble that shows off her svelte figure complete with the new boobs she raved about getting last year. Her red hair and bright emerald eyes easily stand out on the hard court.

"Teagan!" she screams when she sees me. She rushes over to give me air-kisses. "Omigod! I can't believe you're here."

Neither can I. It's the last place I want to be. "Thank you so much for the invite."

"Of course, anything I can do to help a former champion." Charity circles her arm through mine. "When I told the ladies you were coming, they were all so eager to meet you. No one's ever met a Grand Slam winner."

Why does she have to bring up my former glory? I didn't have time to luxuriate in being a champion. I'd won only a few Grand Slams before the rug was pulled out from under me.

"That was a long time ago," I respond politely.

"True, but no one else here has those kind of credentials. Trust me, it'll go a long way with this crowd. Appearance is *everything.* Would you like some refreshments before we get started?" I notice a small stand with an attendant next to a large cooler. "There's Evian, Fiji, smartwater, Gatorade... Or if you need something stronger," she whispered, "I can arrange that also."

"Water is fine."

"Cole, do be a dear and bring me over two Evians, please." Charity pulls me over to a bench outside the court.

"Yes, ma'am."

Were all the attendants young men in their late teens or early twenties? I'm sure that's no coincidence. I bet some of the married women have indulged in trysts. I try to be cordial so the day isn't completely about me. "How's your husband and the boys?"

"Ben is working like always," Charity sighs. "He's trying to make partner at his law firm so it's all about clocking the hours, but that means I spend a lot of time alone with our three- and five-year-old. It was driving me bonkers until I joined the club and made some friends."

"I'm sorry to hear that. It sounds difficult."

"Sometimes I feel like a single mom." Charity sighs again. She tosses her red hair as if she's indifferent, but I sense she's lonely. "I doubt you came today to talk about the woes of being a housewife. How can I be of assistance?"

"I'm always an ear to listen," I respond, touching her hand. "As for helping, if you know of any friends who might be in the market to sell their home, that would be a start."

"Of course. Ann Marie Walther mentioned the other day she and her husband might be relocating to Texas. She's horrified to have to move to the Lone Star State."

"I can put their house on the market *and* I lived in San Antonio during my teens before I went pro and can help them find a new place."

"Sounds great. I'll make the introduction."

The attendant brings over our refreshments. Immediately, I'm unscrewing the cap and downing mine as if my thirst comes from being in the middle of the desert. My heart is loud in my chest. *Can Charity hear it?*

"Are you ready to get started?" Charity inquires.

I nod and finish off my water, tossing it in a nearby recycling bin. "Sure." I attempt levity when I feel the exact opposite.

We stroll back to the court and I'm awed at the beauty of it.

The hard rectangular surface with a low net stretched across the center ruled my life from the time I was eight years old until my forced departure at nineteen. I learned to play on different surfaces: clay, grass and hard court, but my favorite was always this one, the acrylic-topped hard top, because it's faster and the balls bounce lower.

My hands are sweaty as I grab a ball from my bag. I was known for my serve, but I feel as skittish as a first-timer. I rub my hands down my dress and then lift my racket into the air and let the ball go. Everything else happens in slow motion, as if I'm watching myself play. Despite the years that have passed, tennis comes naturally to me and when Charity swings the ball back at me, I let my racket rip and topspin the ball cross-court. She's unable to hit it.

The score is 15–Love.

Charity puts her hands on her hips. "I thought you told me you haven't played in years."

"I haven't."

"Then you're as gifted as everyone said you were," Charity replies, "but I'm pretty good too and I'm not going down without a fight." She crouches down into position for my next serve.

"Bring it on, Charity." I send another serve her way.

We continue rallying. She gets several past me and has me on the run because I'm a little rusty, but with practice I can get better. *If I want to.* I'm not sure I do. This is a means to an end. A way to get in front of the wealthy and elite. After we play a set, I take a water break.

"Everyone at the club will want to play with you," Charity says, dabbing her forehead with a towel. "Having you here will make everyone want to step up their game."

"Honestly, I didn't think I still had it."

"You more than have it, Teagan. You never lost it."

"I beg to differ. In the past, I would have slayed you."

By the end of the match, I've won two sets and Charity's won a set. Given I haven't seen a court in over a decade, it's not a bad outing, but I would definitely have kicked her ass if I'd been at the top of my game. Being back here brings up old memories.

"Everything all right?" Charity asks, coming over when she sees me in distress.

I shake my head to jolt myself out of the past. "Yes, yes, sorry."

"Does being back here hurt?" Her green eyes peer into mine. "I would have thought after all these years it was behind you."

I thought the same, but apparently, I was wrong. Some hurts run so deep they never heal.

Four

Dominic

My goal was to go to a Sedona spa for a couple weeks before coming back to Phoenix for the rest of my hiatus. Unfortunately, my mom blew up my phone on the jet so I made an immediate diversion home instead.

As usual, there are several cars I don't recognize at her Paradise Valley five-bedroom estate. But am I really surprised? Mom likes to entertain and brag about her multimillionaire son, the tennis champion. Micah decided to go on to Sedona without me and start his vacation early. I don't blame him. If I could afford not to come, I would have, but I'm her son.

Exiting the SUV Micah arranged, I head inside. Sure enough, there's a full-blown party underway with music loud enough the neighbors are sure to complain. People roam about the spacious open living room, kitchen and terrace that overlooks the mountains.

A waiter walks around carrying canapés and comes toward me. "Goat cheese croquette?" he inquires.

I shake my head. "No, thank you."

"Darling, there you are," Mom screeches when she sees me, and several heads turn. I can see the minute most recognize me. Meanwhile, Mom is walking toward me wearing a flowy silk caftan and looking like she's the queen of all she surveys.

Grace Fletcher doesn't look like the mother who raised me. Her cocoa brown skin is much like my own, but her short bob has been replaced by a long, straight weave, which hits her shoulders. The extra weight she carried from having Ciera and Bliss is gone thanks to some work she had done.

She envelops me in a quick hug and stands back to admire me. "You're getting more and more handsome each time I see you, Dominic."

"No need for flattery. Why am I here?"

Her mouth quirks into a frown at my exasperated tone. "Is it too much to ask for you to visit your mother once in a while?"

I sigh. Of course she would make this about her, like she always does, which is why I never share my frustrations about her spending. She forgets I've had a brutal and exhausting two weeks winning the Australian Open and want to rest.

"What's going on?"

"It's your sister," Mom replies. "Bliss is being a terror."

I frown. "How so?" I've never known my fifteen-year-old baby sister to be anything other than circumspect. She's on the track team and always gets good grades. I'm proud of her.

However, my younger sister Ciera, I worry about. Right now she's conversing with one of Mom's adult friends and thinks she's grown. Ciera likes being in the spotlight and every time I look up, I find one of her posts about makeup or what she's wearing on social media. She already has fifty thousand followers. How is it possible a seventeen-year-old has that many people interested in her lifestyle posts?

Mom pulls me away from the crowd and into the corridor so no one can hear us. "She's downright disrespectful," Mom replies. "She's told me I need to stop relying on a man."

"I agree with her."

Mom rolls her eyes. "Not you too. Are you and Bliss in cahoots or something?"

"No, Mom, but I happen to think all of this—" I spread my arms wide "—is over-the-top."

"Can't I celebrate my son's win with a party for all my friends?"

I rub my bald head. "I don't know any of these people, and I suspect you don't either. Why are you always posturing and vying for position? Just be who you are."

"That's easy for you to say, Dominic," Mom says, gesturing wildly with her hands. "The world loves the ground you walk on. Some of us have to work at it."

"Seriously? Are you telling me about working for something? What do you think I've been doing over the last fifteen years? I've been working my ass off so you can live a life of luxury."

"Don't you dare talk to me like that! Not after everything I sacrificed for you to be in the position you are."

"I've repaid you for everything and then some," I snipe. I know I'm being petty and shouldn't get into this conversation with her here, *now*, where anyone can see, hear or record us. But I've been feeling so much lately, it slips out.

Mom's eyes well up with tears and one escapes her lids, falling down her cheeks. "Why do all my kids hate me? Have I really been that bad a mother?"

I immediately regret my words and pull her into a hug. "I don't hate you, Mom." I softly caress her back. She always has a way of making me feel guilty, as if I'm in the wrong.

"Yes, you do." She sniffs. "Bliss does. Only Ciera is on my side."

"Is everything okay over here?" a deep voice asks from behind Mom.

I glance up to see a beefy-looking guy, about six feet with salt-and-pepper hair and wearing a Hawaiian shirt and khaki pants. He's staring back and forth between us.

Mom quickly stands upright and pulls away from me.

"We're fine." She wipes an errant tear from her cheek and puts a fake smile on her face. One I've come to recognize as her trying to impress people. "Miles, I'd like you to meet my son Dominic Fletcher. Dominic, this is Miles Crawford."

Neither of us offers the other a hand to shake. Instead, we glare at each other.

I turn to Mom. "Where is Bliss? I'll go have a chat with her."

"That would be great. She's upstairs in her room. She hates parties."

As do I. I leave Mom and Miles and turn in the direction of the floating stairs. I take them two at a time until I reach the second floor and make my way to Bliss's room. The five-bedroom estate has four bedrooms with en suites upstairs while the primary suite and bath are on the main floor.

I knock when I reach Bliss's door. It swings open with such force, I take a step back, but when Bliss sees it's me, she flings herself into my arms. "Dominic!"

I hold her tightly. "Hey, baby girl."

"I'm so happy you're here," she says when she finally releases me and looks up at me with ebony eyes that match my own. "I can't stand those insufferable people downstairs. All they do is prance around in overpriced clothes and try to one-up each other."

At five foot six, Bliss has what they call a brickhouse physique thanks to her running track. Her beautiful honey-blond braids are in an elaborate style I see on other young girls and she's wearing small dangling gold earrings and a tracksuit.

"Well, you look beautiful."

She smiles broadly and then flops onto her oversize bed. "You're saying that because you're my older brother."

"No, I'm saying it because it's true," I reply, sitting on the edge of the bed next to her. "So, tell me, what's going on with you and Mom?"

Bliss rolls her eyes. "Same as always. She's got another sorry asshole." She catches herself and apologizes. "Sorry, Dom. You're not here all the time to see the men she brings around. Why can't Mom see she deserves better?"

I shrug. "I wish I knew. I suspect Mom has self-esteem issues. She's always looking for love in the wrong places. I don't want that to happen to you, Bliss. Or to Ciera. I don't want you to feel like you need a man to validate you. I want you to love yourself."

"I do," Bliss states emphatically. "I don't want to be anything like her. I'm determined to stand on my own two feet and use my brain—" she points to her head "—instead of my looks to get ahead because those will fade."

I nod in agreement. "I'm glad to hear it, Bliss. If you ever need reinforcement, your big brother will always give it to you. You're a beautiful Black queen."

"Awww, Dom, who knew you were such a softy." She

gives me a playful nudge with her shoulder. "Why are you still alone? You will make someone a good husband."

My mind drifts to the one woman I ever considered having a future with. Five foot nine, hooded dark brown eyes, long toned legs and a tight ass. I move from where I'm perched on Bliss's bed and walk over to her bedroom window. When I look out, there are still people flowing in and out of the house.

"I'm not interested in getting married, Bliss," I finally respond to her earlier comment.

"Why not?"

Spinning around, I face her. "In case you haven't noticed, I haven't retired. I'm still out there winning championships, keeping bread on the table."

"Ha." Bliss stands up and folds her arms across her chest. "C'mon, Dom, I'm not stupid. You could quit tennis at any time. You're rich. You continue to play because you love it. Admit it. You love the thrill of *winning*."

How can my fifteen-year-old sister be so wise? Maybe she's too smart for her own good. I change the subject. "I didn't come up here to talk about me. I came to discuss that despite you disagreeing with how our mother chooses to live her life, you still need to show her respect. You can't be talking back."

"Respect is earned," Bliss replies hotly.

This girl won't let up. "Bliss…" My tone is a warning and she rolls her eyes.

"Fine. I'll do my best," Bliss responds. "Why can't I come live with you?"

"You know why." I sigh. "We discussed this. I'm always on the road. I can't give you a stable home."

"Whatever. How long are you staying this time?"

"I'll be at a spa in Sedona for a few weeks, but I'll be back for the rest of my hiatus."

"Thanks, Dom."

I walk toward her and pull her into my arms. "You don't have to thank me. I love you. I'm your big brother and I'll always be here for you."

Afterward, I make my way downstairs. I'm heading toward Ciera to say hello when the man Mom introduced me to earlier steps in my path.

"Can I help you?" I inquire.

"Yeah, you can stop upsetting your mama," Miles replies.

Is this motherfucker seriously going to tell me about my own mother? "I suggest you stay in your lane, my friend. You might be sleeping with my mom, but I'm her son and the one who pays for this lifestyle you're enjoying. Best not to bite the hand that feeds you."

I push past him and head to the front door, where my driver waits for me. "Mr. Fletcher." He opens the passenger door and I climb inside.

I'll have to check on Ciera later. I can't stay in this environment where I might blow a fuse. I have to get my head right; the French Open is in a few months and it's going to take everything I have to win it.

Last year, I was beset by an injury and barely managed to eke out the win at Wimbledon and keep my ranking as number one. The Australian Open was even tougher. It's why I've been thinking about what happens after tennis. I'm not getting any younger. But for now, I'll close my eyes and allow my mind to rest, but when I do, visions of the past and a brown-eyed beauty cloud my mind.

Bliss mentioning marriage and a family makes me remember the dreams Teagan and I shared. Why have I never been able to move past her? What will it take for me to finally make peace?

See her again, an inner voice whispers.

Five

Teagan

Having tennis back in my life is a game changer. Charity and I play again on the following Saturday. After years of feeling as if I'd lost a part of myself, it's finally back. I'm having fun again. A feeling of thinking anything is possible returns. I know it's not true; I'm not invincible. However, it's given me the pick-me-up I need to tackle a dinner with my parents on Sunday.

Typically, I limit my interactions to the holidays and the occasional birthday. And wouldn't you know, it's my father's birthday and I've been summoned to dinner at their four-bedroom, three-bath house in Camelback East. It's not our family home in San Antonio where I grew up and where I met the Gems. Instead, my father received a promotion to his company's headquarters in Phoenix, and he and Mom moved here after I decided to play tennis professionally.

To state Russ Williams is controlling is an understatement. My mother can't do or spend anything without running it by him first. He's got to be in control of her every waking minute. When I lived under their roof, it was the same way. Once he realized I was good at tennis, he had to control what I ate, what time I went to sleep, how long I practiced and who I practiced with. I had to do exactly what my father said.

Went I went pro, I took control of my life and called the shots. It was thrilling and exciting—until it wasn't. When I was injured, my father went back to taking care of everything *again*. My father never let me forget that I should have listened to him and stayed the course. Instead, I got enthralled by a man and look what happened.

His words haunt me as I drive to his home with a bottle of his favorite bourbon. It set me back several hundred dollars, but you can't come to Russell Williams's house with anything but the best. It's unacceptable in his book.

I pull into the driveway in my Mercedes-Benz GLE. With the financial straits Williams & Associates is in, the monthly payments are kicking my ass. But I refuse to show up on my father's doorstep driving a used or low-end vehicle. I park the SUV and climb out. As always, I'm immaculately dressed even though it's a family dinner. I'm wearing a single-breasted brocade buttercup Dolce & Gabbana blazer with matching button-down vest over fitted black slacks and Gucci slingbacks.

I arrive to the front door with the bourbon in hand. I don't have a key to my parents' house because that would mean my father giving up control. I ring the doorbell like everyone else.

Mama arrives in a beautiful studded long-sleeve top over a pencil skirt. She looks positively elegant. "Hey, Mama," I say, and kiss both of her cheeks. Her sleek jet-black hair hangs like a curtain down her back.

"Teagan." She accepts my embrace, but then steps back to

inspect me. "Couldn't you have worn a skirt or dress? Your father won't be happy."

"Sorry, I had a work engagement earlier." It's a lie. I wear what I want, but I'm trying to keep the peace. "Surely, this will do. It's designer."

"Of course, darling. C'mon in. Your father is waiting in the living room."

I grab Mom's arm. "How are you?" I inquire. Although my father has never physically touched her as far as I know, she doesn't call me often because he tracks her calls.

"Is that you, Teagan? Come in here so I can get a look at you," my father's voice booms out.

I glance into her brown eyes and implore Mom to speak openly, but she doesn't and motions me toward the living room. I paste on a smile and walk inside. "Happy birthday, Daddy," I say, walking toward him. He's seated in a chair that, if I'm honest, resembles a throne while the rest of us are relegated to a mere sofa in the king's presence.

"Teagan." His dark irises assess me, glancing me up and down. I've made sure not a hair is out of place. My father gives me a smile, which means I pass muster. "You're looking well."

"Thank you." I incline my head and hold out the bottle of bourbon.

"My favorite brand, good girl. Please sit down and join your mother and I." He inclines his head, indicating Mom and I can both sit down on the sofa. So we do.

"Tell us, what's new with our favorite daughter?"

Their *only* daughter. Much to my father's chagrin. He'd hoped to have a large family to lord over, but my mother had trouble conceiving and they were only able to have one child. Me.

"All is well."

"That's not what the news says. The real estate market is on the decline."

I suck in a deep breath and remind myself to stay calm. "I'm staying afloat."

"Staying afloat isn't thriving. We Williamses thrive."

"I know, Daddy, and..."

"Don't interrupt me, I wasn't done."

My ears burn at his harsh tone. I want to rebut because he interrupted *me*, but my mother shakes her head.

"What are your plans to weather this storm?"

"Do we really have to talk business at dinner?" my mother asks quietly.

"I wasn't talking to you, Olympia."

I should have been ready for Daddy to rain hellfire down on me. Yet each time he does, I keep hoping things will change. "I'm working my contacts and I recently joined the Phoenix Country Club, which has led to some prospects."

"Sounds like a waste of money if you ask me. You should come with me to some of my business meetings and let me introduce you around."

"Thank you for the offer. I'll think it over."

"I heard the Phoenix Country Club has some lovely tennis facilities," my mother adds.

"They do. I recently played with a friend."

My father takes immediate notice of that statement. "You're playing tennis again? Do you think that's wise after your injury?"

"They never said I couldn't play. Just not professionally."

"All that money and time down the drain." My father rises from his throne and heads over to the wet bar at the far side of the room, bourbon in hand. He pours himself two fingers in one glass, one for him and then another for me. Mama doesn't drink, but since I was old enough to drink, Daddy always gave me one. Maybe because he wanted a son, but he only had me.

He brings over the tumbler and I accept. I take a measured sip, needing the burn of the liquor to help get me through the night.

My mother helps me out by saying dinner should be ready. We head into the adjacent dining room, where there's an elaborate setup with three arrangements. I don't know why Daddy insists on these grand affairs, but I play my part and take a seat while Mom brings out the first course.

Conversation is stilted during the four-course meal. I'm hoping to get out unscathed, but my father must have been waiting until dessert to end the evening with a real bang.

"Speaking of tennis, that young fellow you were so enamored with, he won another Grand Slam, the Australian Open."

Damn. Why did he have to bring up Dominic now? Lately, my mind has been so caught up in the past. Ever since I started playing again, I keep thinking about everything that went wrong and how I could have done things differently.

"Is that so?" I ask, reaching for my wineglass.

"You sound surprised. You don't follow him?"

"Why would I? Dominic dropped me like a hot potato when I tore my meniscus."

"Yes, he did. It was an unfortunate injury to a promising career."

"Do we have to rehash the past?" I inquire, eager to move on to another subject, any subject. This is downright painful.

"If you're destined to repeat it, yes," he says. "My advice

would be to steer clear of tennis. Listen to your father and let me help you shore up your little agency."

My little agency. My father has never respected my real estate business. The situation I'm in isn't helping matters.

"Look at the time," I say, glancing down at my Cartier watch. "I really need to go. I have an early showing tomorrow."

"Do you have to go?" my mother asks. "Surely, you can stay for dessert?" Her eyes implore me to stay, but after talk of tennis, Dominic and my failures, I've lost what appetite I had. "I'm sorry, no, Mom. Next time?"

"Very well." I can see she's upset, but I beat a hasty retreat. I pass by Daddy long enough to kiss his cheek and I head for the door, but not before my father can land one more blow.

"And next time, Teagan, do try and wear a dress or something. It's bad enough you persist in having that short haircut like a boy, at least a dress will make you appear more feminine."

I don't look back at his barb. Instead, I rush out and quickly stride to my car. Once I'm in my Mercedes-Benz, I release a loud scream. Why, why, why do I put myself through this and let him get to me? Because my mother is there. Caught in a web of her own making. I've promised to help her get a fresh start, but she is too afraid to leave him. I start my car and drive off, but I can't escape the memories.

Maybe my father was right for once. I should never have gone down this path of playing tennis again. All I'm doing is opening up old wounds I thought had healed and leaving myself vulnerable to my father's scrutiny.

Once again, I let him push my buttons, but I won't follow his advice. If I do, he'll take over my life, like he did previously. I have to listen to my intuition even if it's digging up a hornet's nest. Tennis once brought me so much joy, and playing again has sparked something within me. I can't let it die. I won't.

But the past is dead and buried and can no longer hurt me.

The rest of the week at Williams & Associates proves promising. One of the women I met at the country club, Joanne Cobbs, contacts me to sell her home in the Biltmore area. It's a win. Her husband is getting transferred and she needs my help. If I sell her house, the commission will be a quarter of a million dollars. That would be the pickup the agency needs.

I happily show up to the country club on Saturday to meet with Charity. She is secretive about the meeting's purpose, but I don't care. I owe her one.

When I arrive, I find myself in a meeting with several other women.

"There you are!" Charity comes up to me in a sleek white tennis dress with contrast trim along the side that screams couture. "Everyone, I'd like you to meet my newest recruit to join our charity tennis tournament, Teagan Williams."

"Tournament?" I glance at her wide-eyed. Why do I feel like I'm being ambushed again? First my father at dinner and now Charity. The hits keep coming.

"Of course, with your history in the sport, you're a natural choice to help," Charity replies.

Several pairs of eyes land on me. I have no choice but to ask, "What can I do?"

"This year's Phoenix Desert Smash is supporting the Foster Alliance, formerly called Arizona Helping Hand. Their programs provide care for children in foster care. We're hoping to garner some celebrities to help lend authenticity to the tournament," Charity explains.

"We've already recruited a couple of Hollywood actors to join our effort," one of the ladies adds.

"That's awesome," I say.

There is continued talk about sponsorships and how we can increase participation. I raise my hand in an effort to endear myself to the group. "I know a lot of businesses in the area. I would love to help out."

"Way to pitch in, Teagan," Charity says.

"What we really need, though, are some ATP or WTA pros on the circuit," adds Mitzi, another brunette and the tournament cochair. "My husband says he'll snag a big tennis star for us, but won't tell me who. He's pretty good friends with their agent. But I don't want to solely rely on him. What if they are blowing smoke up his ass?"

I wonder who she's referring to when her blue eyes land on me. "Charity mentioned you used to play professionally, Teagan. Perhaps you might have some contacts?"

Anyone I used to know wouldn't dare answer a call from me. I'm persona non grata in the tennis world after my meltdown, but none of these women appear to know that.

"Of course." I smile politely. "I'll reach out to some folks."

"Great." Charity gives me a wink and the group continues talking about the event. Meanwhile, my mind races. How the hell am I supposed to come up with a tennis star?

Thankfully, the meeting ends within the hour, and Charity takes me aside to speak with me privately.

"Are you okay?" Charity inquires. "You seemed a bit flustered during the meeting."

"There's a lot in my past that you don't know," I reply. "Didn't you look me up?"

Charity shrugged. "I know what I need to. We all have pasts, Teagan. I'm sure if you looked into mine, there might be some unsavory things I'm not proud of, but it's made me into the person I am today, so I have to own it. The good and the bad."

I stare back at her incredulously. "That's pretty insightful."

"I have my moments. If you ever want to talk to me about it, I'm happy to listen."

"Thank you. I appreciate that." And I do, but when it comes to business, I've learned to play my cards close to the vest. If I want to confide in anyone, I talk to the Gems, but instead of contacting them by phone, I feel like a trip is in order. Calls are great, but it's been a long time since I've seen my girls, and I could use some reinforcements.

They will understand how impossible it will be for me to find anyone in the tennis field to accept my call. My entire world changed after my blowup with Dominic was publicized. I was ostracized by everyone I knew, players and coaches. It hurt knowing everything I worked so hard to achieve went up in a puff of smoke.

And there's only one person to blame.

Dominic.

Six

Dominic

"I've set up something great for you," my agent, Scott Barr, says when he walks inside my home in Paradise Valley. It's in the same area as my mom's place, but in a more exclusive neighborhood.

I'm feeling relaxed after my month-long sabbatical at a Sedona spa and ready for the rest of my hiatus. Micah is on an extended vacation. The young man was excited about the break and stated he planned to bum around Europe for a couple months.

"Hello to you too." I roll my eyes as Scott walks inside.

I close the door and follow him into the living room. As usual, Scott is dressed immaculately in cut trousers, a silk button-down shirt and leather loafers sans socks. There isn't a hair on his head that's ruffled or out of place. Scott prides himself on his appearance.

"I hope it's not another match on the tour. I told you I need a break."

"It's what you always say," Scott responds, and takes a seat on the plush sofa. "I know you. I've been your agent for over a decade, which is why you're going to thank me for this."

"Ya think?"

"Hear me out. Yes, you would play tennis, but it's only for fun. A charity tournament called the Phoenix Desert Smash. It would be great press for you. Not to mention it's a cause near and dear to your heart, foster children."

Dammit if the man's not right.

Do I want to play right now? No. I've enjoyed the last month. Sleeping in rather than getting up at the crack of dawn like I usually do when I'm training. At the spa, I relaxed with long walks on the hiking trails and wonderful ninety-minute sports massages.

When I'm quiet, Scott stares at me. "Well?" he asks. "What do you think?"

"How much time would be required?"

"As much or as little as you want to give," Scott replies. "They've only asked you to play in the one tournament, but if you lend your name and efforts to help raise more cash, I'm sure the country club's tennis committee would be thrilled."

I rub my goatee thoughtfully. When was the last time I played for fun? Too long. Plus, it is for a good cause. "All right, I'm in."

"I thought you would be." Scott reaches inside the briefcase he brought with him and pulls out some legal documents. "I took the liberty of negotiating the contract and one appearance."

I laugh out loud at his high-handedness. "Am I really that predictable?"

"No, but you pay me well to know what you will and will not take on."

"Yes, I do." Scott is one of the top agents in the business, and he's worth every penny. He negotiated the highest endorsement I ever received, one hundred million dollars, when I was twenty-two years old. It was no small feat and everyone wanted to sign with him, but Scott doesn't accept just anyone. He wants consummate professionals. Divas need not apply.

"When do I need to show up?"

"The event is at the end of April, which works perfectly with your hiatus. You'll be gearing up for the French Open at the end of May. It's up to you how much or *little* you wish to practice beforehand."

"Sounds perfect."

"Now that you're committed, they have asked if you'd be willing to come to their cocktail party event for sponsors next weekend. You absolutely don't have to do this, but my friend's wife, Mitzi, is chairing the event and it would mean a lot if you could do me a solid."

"Scott Barr is asking for a favor?"

"Yeah, don't get used to it." He chuckles. "Can I depend on you to pull through?"

I smile good-naturedly. "Of course I'll come. You don't usually ask for favors so it must mean a lot to you."

"Darren and I go way back. He spotted me the money to help set up Barr Sports Management. I wouldn't be where I am if he hadn't given me a chance."

"You're a good man, Scott." I lean across the short distance and shake his hand. "I've always appreciated your loyalty."

"I'll always have your back, Dominic, even if I don't always agree with your choices. I'll text you the details," Scott says.

I chuckle. Scott didn't want me to come on this sabbatical. He wanted me to stay focused on the tour and prepare for the French Open, but it's months away and I need downtime. After the injury last year, I clawed my way back to the top. I've realized over the last month that my time with tennis is nearing its end. Although I love to win, it's getting harder and harder to push my body to compete against my younger competition.

I walk Scott to the door and then head back to my brother's prospectus for his new business. I need to get prepared for the next phase of my life.

The following weekend, instead of driving myself to Manuel's, the upscale restaurant where the Phoenix Country Club is holding their event, I hire a driver in case I want an adult beverage. Rather than wearing jeans and a T-shirt, my normal attire while on vacation, I settle on a black silk shirt and trousers with Gucci loafers. I read through the info Scott gave me about the tournament, which is nearly twenty years old.

When I arrive at the restaurant, a valet opens my door. There's a small red carpet and backdrop for the event, but I don't pause for photos. I hate the whole song and dance that's part of being a celebrity athlete. For me, it's about the game. I walk to the entry and am greeted by a brunette in a slinky dress.

"Omigod, you're here!" she squeals as I step inside the lobby. "My husband told me he could make things happen."

"I take it my presence is a good thing?" I inquire. I glance around. The restaurant exudes sophistication and timeless glamour. There's a lush dining room with crystal chandeliers, a floating fireplace and a cobblestone terrace with mountain views.

"Oh, absolutely. You'll lend authenticity to the tournament. Having someone of your caliber is a godsend. You're a legend."

I smile. "I don't know about all that."

"You're a Grand Slam winner. You've won five Wimbledons, five Australian Opens, two French and five US Opens."

"Keeping score?" I ask with a smile.

She shrugs. "I love tennis. I've been following you a long time."

"I appreciate the support. And your name is…?"

She smacks her forehead. "I'm so sorry, my name is Mitzi Jones. I'm cochair for the event tonight. My fellow cochair is over there with a former player you might know, Teagan Williams."

Hearing her name with no warning, after thinking about Teagan earlier, leaves me shell-shocked. "P-pardon?"

"They're over there." Mitzi points to a crowd of women across the room, but all I can see is the spotlight beaming on Teagan, making her shine brighter than any other woman. *Bright like a diamond.* Seeing her is like a punch in the solar plexus. I don't know if I want to rush over and take her in my arms or rail at her for giving up on us so easily.

I need a moment. "Where is the restroom?" I ask quickly, desperate for some purchase.

"Across the hall," Mitzi advises. "Whenever you're ready, I'll introduce you around."

She walks back inside the restaurant, giving me time to move into the shadows and get a better look at the woman who has haunted me for years.

Teagan is more stunning now than when she was the teenager I fell in love with, on the cusp of womanhood. Even from where I'm lurking, I can see her beautiful peanut-butter-colored skin is clear and bright. Her deep-set dark brown eyes are alight with merriment as she chats with the other cochair of the tournament. She's got the same short haircut she rocked when we were young, but now the style is chic, slicked back and coiffed to surround her face. As for her figure, the years have been good to Teagan. Her curves have filled out in all the right places, and she looks divine in a beaded strapless black dress. Is she taller than the five foot nine I remember? I glance down to her feet. She's rocking some killer stilettos.

She's fascinating.

A woman I've never forgotten. Teagan Williams knew me inside and out. We shared the same passion for the sport that brought out our competitive nature. At times rivals. At times lovers. No woman has ever come close to comparing to Teagan. She knew exactly how to kiss me, touch me, love me.

She's the one who got away.

I know she thinks I let that happen, but there were more circumstances at play, ones she has no idea about. I've never told her, not that she would have allowed me. Teagan was so angry with me after she was injured. I could continue to play the sport we both loved and she might never play again. I would have been there for her, but she didn't seem to want that. Preferred to believe I *didn't want* to be there for her.

And I was angry at her for thinking so poorly of me. I'm not the kind of man to walk away from the woman I love for money. But that's who she thought I was. A spineless coward in love with the almighty dollar. True, I had a family to support who needed my income and the endorsements I was bringing in, but I would never have given up on us.

She gave up on us first.

Seven

Teagan

"Did you hear?" Charity asks when we're standing at the bar at Manuel's waiting to be served. I ordered an old-fashioned while Charity opted for prosecco.

"Hear what?" I ask absentmindedly. I would give anything not to be here, putting up a front. I don't want to be any more involved in the tennis world than I already am, but I'm here for the business connections.

"Our special guest has arrived. It's a big get for Mitzi. She's over the moon."

"That's awesome! I'm glad her husband pulled through." I hadn't exactly gotten around to making those calls to my old tennis colleagues, which would have gone nowhere. So this special guest, whoever they are, had better have real star power.

"Pulled through?" Charity laughs derisively. "Teagan, she shattered the glass and if you don't think so, I invite you to set your eyes on Dominic Fletcher."

Dominic?

My stomach plummets as if I'm on a high-octane roller coaster.

No, no, no, I must have heard wrong. Surely, the man who is the reason my tennis career blew up isn't here tonight at the event where I'm trying to rebuild my real estate agency?

This can't be happening.

However, when I spin around, I see Dominic at the edge of the crowd. My eyes aren't deceiving me. Exactly how long has he been here? Does he know I'm part of the tournament? If he does, he had the advantage of time to assess me without my knowing. I hate that because I haven't been able to do the same.

I blink several times and when I do, he's gone.

Where did he go?

"Isn't it insane?" Charity asks. "*The* Dominic Fletcher. He's a Grand Slam winner and he'll be playing at *our* country club for the Phoenix Desert Smash! This will give us so much cred."

Charity leaves me to share the great news with others. Meanwhile, my eyes scan the crowd for his tall, dark frame. Dominic is head and shoulders above the rest.

I don't have to wait long because our eyes make contact from across the room, and he comes straight for me.

It doesn't take him long to reach me. He does so with several easy strides. Seeing him again almost brings me to my knees, but I catch myself. I close my eyes, hoping it's a nightmare, but when I blink them open, he's standing right in front of me. His smoldering ebony gaze pierces through me, making me lose my breath. No one since Dominic looks at me quite like he does, or makes me want to drop my panties. I find myself standing taller despite the wetness forming between my thighs. My nipples tighten of their own accord and push forward in my strapless bra.

"Teagan." Hearing my name on his lips again makes me think of the times he growled it out when my tongue swirled around his dick.

I find my voice and give it as much levity as I can. "Dominic."

"You look good."

"Wish I could say the same."

His mouth quirks into a grin. "Still bristly, I see."

"I have a right to be," I say. "We didn't exactly end on good terms. In fact, it was quite the opposite."

He nods as if recalling the horrible argument the entire world heard, and how afterward I was labeled as the stereotypical angry Black woman.

"I had no idea you were going to be here," Dominic says. "I'm doing my agent a favor."

"Lending your star power?" My words drip with sarcasm. I'm angry. Dominic got to live the life I wanted—that I deserved—while I had to pick up the pieces and figure out a new game plan.

His eyes narrow. "Can't we be civil, Teagan? It's been over a decade."

"That's easy for you to say, Dominic. You didn't lose everything. I did."

"Teagan—" Dominic wants to say more, but Charity interrupts us.

"Dominic Fletcher, as I live and breathe. It's so great to have you here with us," Charity gushes.

Dominic gives her a cursory nod.

The tension is palpable and Charity looks back and forth between us. "Wait a second. Do you two know each other?"

"Something like that," I mutter.

"Well, I'm sorry to interrupt," Charity replies, "but I need to steal Dominic away so we can introduce him."

"Of course," I respond. "I wouldn't dream of stealing the spotlight from our illustrious guest."

Dominic's eyes spark at my words. "We'll speak later, Teagan."

As if. I don't want to talk to him, much less see him or hear his praises lauded by Charity or Mitzi. Having him here, seeing him again, reminds me of all my old failures. How I let myself down, let my parents down. Intellectually, I know the accident wasn't my fault. I had no idea when I did that backhand that I would lose my footing, fall and injure my meniscus.

What I should have done after the injury was focus on my recovery and rehabilitation. Instead, I was too focused on me and Dominic. I worried that not being present in our tennis bubble would make me lose him. I acted out because of fear and insecurity. I blamed him for winning and being what I couldn't be. How was I to know he still had his microphone on and everyone heard my plea for him to stay and see me through my injuries? They heard a desperate, clinging woman who became angry when he wouldn't stay. Who became even more irate when she realized the audio and cameras were rolling.

Dammit!

I hate these old feelings of not being good enough. I was made to feel that way my entire life. My father always pushed me to succeed, to be better than the rest, and when I finally wasn't, he felt vindicated that he was right. I would never amount to anything. And now having Williams & Associates on the rocks has me on edge.

I force myself, on wooden legs, to walk out of the restaurant and outside onto the terrace with a beautiful view of the mountains, but not before grabbing a glass of champagne. I want to down it like a shot, but instead, I sip on the crisp drink. If Dominic is around, I need to keep my wits about me. No one here seems to know about my past with him, at least not yet. Fortunately for me, the terrace is empty because everyone is inside, no doubt eager to rub shoulders with Dominic.

With his popularity, if anyone sees us together, they are bound to get suspicious. The last thing I want is to remind the press about that old footage of our fight because it's still out there. I don't want to become viral or a laughingstock with memes made about me. Cancel culture is real. I remember how hurtful my last scramble with the media was and I don't want a repeat.

Pull it together, Teagan!

This tournament is not about Dominic. It's about schmoozing and socializing with the higher echelon to garner business for my brokerage. *You're not here to revisit a past love or go down memory lane.* After I give myself a good pep talk, I'm about to go inside, when a large presence blocks my path.

Glancing up, I see Dominic. I allow myself a moment to take another look at him. His features have sharpened over the years, emphasizing the square cut of his chin and the fullness of his lips. A long-ago memory surfaces, of me kissing him, my fingers clutching his head as I arched my naked hips toward his.

I jerk myself backward, away from him. "Not now."

"When?"

"How about never?" I respond sarcastically. "I mean, do we really have anything to say? We share a past, big deal. Everyone has one." I sound poised and together. Score!

"Not like ours," Dominic states. "If we're going to work together in this tournament, don't you think we should hash this out?"

"Can't you pull out and say something has come up?"

"That would be unprofessional. I keep my commitments."

My brow rises. "Do you really?"

His ebony eyes sharpen on me with cold intensity. It makes me feel as if I'm being examined under a microscope. "Teagan—" my name on his lips is coated with icy disdain "—your question is the precise reason why we need to clear the air."

My head snaps back. "I think not."

I walk forward and attempt to push past him, but his body is hard and unmovable. His hand touches my bare arm and sparks ignite in my nerve endings. I let out a sharp breath that to me sounds surprisingly loud. Dominic's gaze fixes on me, on my mouth, and his eyes glimmer like molten lava. I hate myself for feeling the horrifying thrill of being alive for the first time in years.

I've been with other men and enjoyed it, but I was first introduced to unbearable heights of pleasure with Dominic. The fact that my body is having a tingling response means I've been too long without sexual contact. I'll need to remedy that because I refuse to accept that this feeling is the excitement of Dominic's touch.

I glance down to where his hand still grasps my arm, and he yanks it back. "I'm sorry, but I disagree. If you want, we can do this right now where anyone can hear us or we can go someplace quiet."

His comment reminds me of how my life blew up over a decade ago due to curious ears. "Fine. Where?"

Dominic reaches into his pocket and pulls out his wallet, producing a business card. "Tonight, my place. I'll meet you after the party."

I snatch the business card from him, and this time he steps aside, allowing me to pass. As I do, I catch the intoxicating scent of cedarwood, which always made me horny.

I won't be there tonight. Nothing will come of our meeting later. I know exactly who he is.

He's the same callous bastard who left me when everyone turned against me. He can burn in hell for all I care.

Eight

Dominic

I watch Teagan, the woman who broke my heart, walk away. I get it; she's angry with me because she thinks I left her, but there were so many more variables at play.

Yet seeing her again after all these years leaves me unsettled.

Blood rushes through my body and my heart speeds up at the sight of my former lover. Never in my wildest dreams would I have imagined Teagan would come strolling back into my life, and certainly not at a tennis tournament. She vowed to never pick up a racket again.

When the final doctor told her she might never play professionally again, she crumbled. I understood. Like me, she was a tennis prodigy and the sport was her whole world. Instead of turning to me for comfort, she railed at me, all because I could play. Her accident wasn't just the end of her career; it was the end of us.

Despite my churning feelings, I carry on with my appearance because I'm a consummate professional. I push down my emotions and focus on being Dominic Fletcher, the All-American tennis star with the heart of gold.

My trajectory started when I was six years old and continued until I went professional at the age of sixteen. It was necessary to help support my family. Going pro brought in a constant flow of cash, and once I started winning Grand Slams, the endorsement deals kicked in. From shoes to athletic gear, I became the face of tennis. My mug was everywhere. Talent was a given, but it has always been my personality that propelled my star status. Since then, I've prided myself on my well-thought-out strategy of saving, investing for myself and my family, and creating a foundation to help underprivileged children. It's my way of giving back to the community.

I make the rounds of the party, connecting with several large supporters of the Phoenix Desert Smash, but I never lose sight of Teagan. Like me, she's working the room, weaving in and out of the crowd. I wonder why.

What's her agenda? Why is she here? What has she been doing all these years?

After our breakup, I blocked her from my social media, from my world. I couldn't bear to see her moving on with her life, possibly with someone new. I'd willingly given her up, but that didn't mean there was no pain or heartbreak. I threw myself into my career, practicing and training rigorously. I never thought I would achieve the success I did. The level of wealth I have now ensures my family and I will never experience poverty again. My success is why I want to help my brother. He too has big dreams, and if there's anything I can do to assist Justice, I will.

But first, I have to get through tonight, get through the reckoning coming with Teagan. It won't be easy. She has a lot of animosity toward me, because she jumped to conclusions about me. I've always wondered if she knew the truth, would she feel differently?

As if she senses me watching her, our gazes connect across the crowded room. She tears the card into little pieces and throws it in a nearby trash can. If we ever hash this out, it won't be tonight. My chest tightens; this woman still has power over me.

I remember the first time I saw her. Teagan's dark brown hair had been plastered to her face as she chased a ball down center court. The force with which her racket slammed the ball was nothing short of epic. I got hard instantly. It didn't help that the curves of her young body were clad in a bright pink tennis dress with stripes down the sides, which emphasized her great ass.

I wanted to know more about her immediately. At the time, she was lauded as the next Serena Williams. She didn't let it go to her head. Instead, she was focused and confident, and that was a turn-on. Her father, Russ, was always by her side and never seemed to let up or allow her to take her foot off the gas. I steered clear of him because he was intense, and I didn't want to be in his crosshairs. It wasn't until Russ had a medical procedure requiring bed rest that Teagan had some freedom.

Consequently, I discovered another side of her. A fun, carefree side. She was competitive and when I found myself on the opposite end of the court, she sometimes beat me. We had a camaraderie and love of the game that spurred our affection for one another. One day, I acted on it.

Our first kiss was fiery and all-consuming. I can still remember the way she'd tasted of strawberries. So sweet, so innocent. When we finally made love, it was real and raw.

It didn't matter that she was a virgin. I craved her and she craved me.

I'm so deep in my memories of what we had that I don't hear Mitzi until she repeats my name. "Mr. Fletcher?"

I blink her back into focus. "I'm sorry, what was that?"

"I asked if you would be willing to come to some of our practices at the country club. I know it's not part of your contract, but your appearance would certainly help rack up sponsorships."

I wonder if Teagan will be there. *Is she playing tennis again?* I always hated she gave up something she loved. With her skill set, she could easily have become a coach and commanded high earnings. "Sure, I'll come if you think that will help."

Mitzi's cherubic face lights up with a large smile. "It absolutely will. Thank you so much."

I try not to give too much thought to why I said yes when the entire point of this sabbatical was to breathe and relax without commitments. But deep down, I know why.

It's because of the possibility Teagan might be there.

I have never been able to resist her.

"Teagan is here in Phoenix?" Scott inquires when I ask him to drop what he's doing and come back to town ASAP. Since I did him a favor, Scott didn't mind the inconvenience of a pit stop between clients.

"Yep." I nod as we sit on my terrace drinking bourbon, neat. The burn of the dark brown liquid is exactly what I need.

"How did this reconnection come about?" Scott asks, placing one leg over the other.

"Because of you," I say, sipping my drink. "If you recall, you asked me to attend Phoenix Desert Smash's cocktail party.

Well, imagine my surprise when I stumble across Teagan after all these years."

"I can't imagine," Scott responds. "The way things ended between you was far from pretty. In fact, I would say it was downright ugly."

"The press was brutal in their treatment of her. They painted her as a down-on-her-luck tennis star when in fact she was the best of her time."

"I remember. You tried to be there for her, but she pushed you away. You refused to listen or give up on her and continued to call and text."

"I did. At least until her father told me to back off, that I was doing her more harm than good by coming around. Teagan and Russ blamed me for what happened. Russ told me she lost focus on the game because she was too wrapped up in our romance. I felt guilty about what happened and took everything he said to heart like a dumb schmuck."

"You were young and Teagan was your first love."

Only love, I want to say, but don't.

"Yeah, well, Russ preyed on my naivete, made me think the best thing I could do for Teagan was walk away."

"Did you ever tell her what he did, what he said?"

I shake my head. "How could I, Scott? It would only make me appear weak and spineless that I didn't stand up to her father. She used to tell me how Russ had a way of making you do what he wanted, but I didn't believe her until it happened to me."

"But now that you're older, surely you can reveal the truth?"

I've thought about it countless times, but the outcome would still be the same. "What purpose would that serve?"

"It might get you out of the doghouse," Scott says with a smirk, taking a sip of his bourbon.

"Yeah, and it could also cause tension with her father, and I don't want that."

"What do you want, Dominic?" Scott replies. "Because your voicemail made it seem as if it were life or death that I hightail my ass here. So do you want to get back with her or what?"

I rub my head. "No, I—I just want..."

"Another run at her?" Scott asked. "I looked her up. Teagan Williams has turned into one fine-ass looking woman."

"Hey..." I may not be ready to go down that rabbit hole again, but I sure as hell don't want Scott talking about Teagan like that. I know I have no right to feel this way because she hasn't been my woman in a long time, but I feel a little territorial.

"See?" Scott points to me puffing out my chest. "There's still something there. Maybe something unfinished between you."

I can get down with what he's saying. "Yeah, I suppose. I feel like it's a chapter I haven't completely closed."

"Maybe this tournament will be a way for you to close the door on the Teagan chapter. You need to figure out what's going on up here—" Scott points to my head "—and here." He points to my heart. "Tell her whatever you need to say and get it off your chest. Fuck her brains out if that will give you the closure you need, but either way, you can't keep straddling the fence."

"I'm not." But as soon as the words come out of my mouth, I know they're a lie. I'm conflicted about Teagan. On the one hand, I'm angry at her for believing I would ever walk out on her, for not giving us a chance to work. On the other hand, I do *want* her.

"You're a bold-faced liar," Scott calls me out on my bullshit. "I don't know if you've ever fully gotten over Teagan."

"I have. I've been with other women. Lots of them."

"You have, but I've never seen you like you were with her."

"What do you mean?" I inquire. I've always treated the women I've dated with kindness and respect. "There's never been anything negative in the press."

"That's not what I meant." Scott stares at me for a long time. "When you were with Teagan, you were happy. There was a lightness about you that I've not seen in a long time."

"I'm happy," I respond, but the words ring hollow even to me. "But I admit after Teagan I became more disciplined and focused on my success, on being the best. You don't have any idea, Scott, how hard it is day in and day out to push yourself to outdo your best. And I'm competing with boys and men younger than me."

"Yet you do it and make it look easy."

I laugh. "I doubt that, but I am proud of everything I've achieved. But I would be lying to you if I said something isn't missing. I feel like I've achieved everything I need to."

"You're aren't having an existential crisis and thinking about retirement, are you? Because I won't hear of it. You've got a good five to ten years left in you."

"I know retiring would be bad for your business," I reply.

"Hey, hey, you know I love you, man, and have always wanted what's best for you. You helped make me a multi-millionaire."

I laugh. "I did, didn't I?" Scott receives 15 percent of my

endorsements, but he's always worked hard for me, and not just with tennis. He's been a friend and confidant.

"You did. If you said you wanted to retire today, I would make it happen."

I nod and smile at him. "Thanks, Scott."

"You don't have to thank me, but what you do have to do is figure out what's going on with you. I know you've got some family issues to address, and now you've got the added element of Teagan reappearing in your life. Figure out your shit." He raises his glass.

"To figuring out my shit." I tap my glass against his.

I know Scott is right. I feel unsettled with my career, my family and now my love life. I lied when I said I was happy. It's been a long time since I was. I don't know if Teagan will make things better or worse. I just know that one way or another, I need to resolve things with her; only then will I find true happiness again.

Nine

Teagan

The Phoenix Desert Smash cocktail party did wonders for Williams & Associates. I networked with several movers and shakers and consequently picked up two new assignments. My gamble on joining the country club is paying off.

But isn't that life? When one thing goes spectacularly, the rest falls to shit. Or at least that's how I feel after Dominic Fletcher strolled back into my life as if he had a right to be there.

I was happy and going about my life as if he never existed, as if the year we spent together wasn't the best I ever had. But now all those old wounds are reopening and I see the scabs never truly healed. He *hurt* me so much I've never let another man get close. I've not had a serious relationship in over a decade.

I enjoy men casually, will even fuck them if the mood is right, but none of them have ever rocked my world like Dominic. I'm angry because he took away something priceless, my ability to trust, and I'm not sure if I'll ever get it back. I've only trusted the Gems. I know they'll never hurt me. They pull through in the clutch and are there when the going gets tough. They pushed past reporters and even my father to get to me. And that's no easy feat. The Gems are who I need now to make sense of the madness.

It's a good thing I already had an appointment in my calendar, flying to North Carolina to help Egypt try on wedding dresses. It's hard to believe another Gem is headed down the aisle. Nonetheless, I'm here to do my bridesmaid duties. It's not Egypt's fault I've got problems.

To save on costs, I didn't fly in the night before like the other Gems and instead chose to come directly for the fitting, have a one-night hotel stay and head back to Phoenix tomorrow. When I arrive to the bridal shop, everyone is already there. The ladies squeal in delight when I walk in wearing torn denims, a white tank and a blazer.

"Ooh, I love the greeting, Gems," I say with a smile.

"Come on over here and give us a hug," Egypt commands. She's always been headstrong, much like myself, which is probably why we occasionally bump heads.

"Hey." I rush over and give her a warm squeeze. "Congratulations!"

Her beautiful brown face spreads into a smile. "Thank you, girlfriend. It's good to have you. We couldn't get this party started until the last Gem arrived."

"That's right!" Lyric pulls me into her embrace. "I've missed you."

"Same," I respond. Whenever I get together with my girls, I feel like I've come home. The outpouring of love I receive from them I can't find anywhere else. "Let me have a look at you." I hold Lyric's hand and spin her around. "Happiness looks good on you. How's Devon and Kianna?"

"Absolutely wonderful," Lyric responds with a wide grin.

"And the living situation?" Asia sashays her petite form in between us so Lyric can spill the tea. "Are you enjoying being a mom? 'Cause, girl, had I realized having a toddler was going to be this difficult, I would have kept my legs closed."

Several of us chuckle. Trust Asia to keep it real. She's always been a spitfire, but it's what we love about her.

"Actually, it's been better than I ever imagined," Lyric answered. "I always wanted a family of my own and now I have that."

I reach across the distance between us and squeeze Lyric's hand. "And you, Wynter?" I lean my head so I can get a look at our travel influencer, who's lounging on a chaise. "How's the baby-making coming along?"

Wynter shakes her head. "Not a word from me until we get this one—" she winks at Egypt "—in some dresses."

"Aw, Wynter, you're such a softy," Egypt states, "but yes, today is all about me, so we'll dish later. Find me some dresses, ladies."

We each rush off to different parts of the store and riffle through the racks. In the end, Egypt decides on the crepe chiffon dress because it will travel well.

"You look stunning!" I say. The dress hugs her ample behind while the sweetheart neckline shows a touch of bosom and the slit reveals her toned thighs.

"You look hot!" Asia announces. "I'd fuck you." Asia's no-nonsense answer makes us all break out into laughter.

"Thank you, darlin'," Egypt replies. "But the only person I'm interested in fucking is Garrett."

"Oh, lawd!" I roll my eyes. "Can we get on with it?"

Sharing this moment is bittersweet because I'm nostalgic about a time when I saw a future with Dominic, even dreamed we might get married one day with me in a dress as beautiful as Egypt's. I haven't been sleeping because visions of him are breaking free from where I bottled them up to be ignored and forgotten. And now I can't forget him.

Why can't I let him go?

Once we're seated at Flame later that afternoon for cocktails, I plan on telling the Gems everything that's happened. Everyone is giving updates on what's going on in their lives. Shay catches us up on the latest expansion of her studio, Balance and Elevate.

"Memberships are up," Shay states. "We had a slow start with the cycling studio but once word got out about B&E and our fabulous instructors, classes are packed. I even have a waiting list."

"That's amazing," Egypt responds. "And you, Asia. How's Six Gems doing?"

Asia named her jewelry store after our group. I was proud to see her handmade rare gemstone pieces on display when she first opened. "Business is strong and steady," Asia replies. "I'm not expanding like Shay, but my customers are a lot different. They aren't coming for a service. They're buying one-of-a-kind pieces that can only be found at Six Gems."

"Do you still love designing now that you have Ryan?" Wynter asks.

Asia smiles and takes a sip of the fruity concoction Egypt's bartender made while the rest of us sip on wine. "Actually, I enjoy it more because it reminds me I'm not just Ryan's mom or Blake's wife, though I love both my Coleman men to the moon and back."

"So profound, Asia." Lyric chuckles. "Who knew you had it in you?"

"Are you giving me shade, Red?" Asia calls Lyric by a nickname only she uses because of the auburn shade of Lyric's hair. "Because you know, I'll give it right back."

"Bring it on, Asia. I ain't scared of you," Lyric responds with an affectionate grin.

"Girls, girls, do I need to step in?" I inquire.

"Maybe you should." Egypt swivels and turns to look at me. "'Cause you been awfully quiet tonight. You usually have an opinion about everyone and everything."

I roll my eyes. "I'm listening and giving everyone a chance to talk."

"Since when?" Egypt asks incredulously. "Earlier at the bridal shop, I sensed you had something on your mind. So spill the beans."

I glance around at the beautiful, strong, independent women sitting at the table. "Well…if you must know, Dominic is back!"

"You've got to be joking!" Egypt stares at me in disbelief.

"We need deets," Asia replies, "like where, when and why would the man who ruined your life suddenly return out of the clear blue sky?"

"It's because of the tennis tournament, isn't it?" Lyric asks.

"What tennis tournament?" Wynter inquires, looking back and forth at me and Lyric.

"I needed to drum up business for Williams & Associates because of the current real estate market. I decided to join the Phoenix Country Club. My thought was to schmooze with the wealthy and hopefully get some leads. Instead, I've ended up not only playing tennis, but getting talked into being on the tennis tournament committee."

Asia's mouth forms an O and even Wynter sits back farther into her chair, flabbergasted.

"Y'all know what a big deal it was for me to pick up a racket again."

"Yeah, you vowed never to play again," Shay states.

"And I meant it, *at the time*. I never assumed joining a country club meant opening up Pandora's box. And so with a door opened to tennis, Dominic walked right through it. The co-chair of the committee recruited him as a tennis star to lend authenticity to our charity tournament. Imagine my surprise to see Dominic at one of the fundraising events."

"How'd he look?" Asia asks.

I glare at her. "How do you think? Fine as hell and as sexy as I remember."

"Did you speak? Did you confront him? What did you do?" Wynter peppers me with questions.

"Not exactly. We spoke, but got interrupted. He asked me to come back to his place to talk later, but I chickened out. I didn't think we had anything to say. I refuse to be a victim on the Dominic Fletcher train ever again."

"It's not his fault how the press portrayed you," Lyric says quietly.

"Whose side are you on?" I snap. My brown eyes burn into hers.

"Yours, of course," Lyric responds. "Always yours, Tee."

"Then you have to know how hard it was seeing him again." My voice cracks when I speak. "He—he's the only man…"

Egypt reaches for my hand and squeezes. "You don't have to say it. We lived it with you." Her kindness makes tears trickle down my cheeks.

"He ruined me," I say weakly. "I've never been the same after him."

"No, no, no. You're not going to give Dominic Fletcher that kind of power," Egypt responds. "You're Teagan Williams, an unstoppable force of nature and a Gem. You're precious and worthy of so much love and when the right man comes along, he will recognize it, *fight for it.*"

I love how Egypt boldly defends me, no matter what. She sweeps back my tears with her palms. I mouth, "Thank you."

"I love the girl power, sista souljah, I do," Asia responds, looking at Egypt, "but what is she supposed to do with Dominic in her tournament?"

"What do *you* want to do?" Wynter asks.

"I want to show him who's fucking boss!" I say loudly.

"That's right!" Shay stands and starts clapping. Wynter, Lyric and Asia rise to their feet and join her.

"I want to show him I'm still standing and he didn't break me," I continue, feeling the fire. "I want to show him what he missed out on!"

"There's my girl!" Egypt shouts. "I knew the real Teagan was lying underneath this self-doubt. Despite losing a career you worked toward and the man you loved, you still came out standing. I'm proud of you."

"I'm proud of me too, but what if I get hurt again?"

"And what if you don't?" Asia responds. "You used to love tennis and were one of the best women in the sport. It's still there. Believe in yourself. If you want to play again, do it for yourself and not because you have something to prove. Because you don't."

"See, us Gems have pearls of wisdom," Egypt states. "And if you need us, really need us, ask. No ask is ever too small, ya feel me?"

I nod.

This trip was exactly what I needed to remember who I am and how much I've grown. Asia is right. I don't have anything to prove to anyone, but maybe I need to prove to *myself* that I still have what it takes on the court. And if Dominic is a witness to my triumphant return, then that's the icing on the cake.

Ten

Dominic

To keep myself in shape for the French Open coming up in a couple of months, I do the workout routine my coach created. A mix of agility work, cardio and strength exercises helps me maintain muscle and stamina for those long matches. It's not easy staying strong and fit as I get older, but I try. I like running because it helps me clear my mind of anything that's been troubling me, and lately I've been troubled.

By unsettled feelings in my career. *Am I done with tennis? Do I need something more to fulfill me?*

By my family. I don't like the company Mama keeps or her outrageous spending habits.

By Teagan and her resurgence into my life.

I've always looked back on that period in my life fondly because it was one of the few moments that I allowed myself to be happy, to *feel*. My world didn't revolve solely around a tennis ball or the racket in my hand. Instead, it was about me and Teagan allowing ourselves to have something for the two of us.

When it fell apart, I've always held a self-righteous belief that I did the right thing. Teagan's father demanded I leave her alone and allow her to recover in privacy after the sports world turned on her. It was the safe thing to do, the *easy* thing. It allowed me to be off the hook while still pursuing my career.

Teagan blames me for leaving her—and maybe she's justified—but she gave up on us too. She pushed me away, making my decision to listen to her father easier than fighting for her. Teagan didn't believe in us, in me, that we could weather the storm. She's quick to judge and blame me, but there were two of us in that relationship. We share equal blame for its failure.

I push myself to run harder and faster on the track, trying to beat my previous time. If I don't continue striving to be the best, the players rising in the ranks will best *me*. Right now, my strength and endurance will help me keep winning. And don't get me wrong, I like the public's adoration and all the people screaming my name. However, none of it has ever brought me the same peace, the same joy, as when Teagan Williams told me she loved me the first time.

Damn, why do my thoughts keep coming back to this woman?

Maybe because I'd never been in love until I met her. Quite frankly, I'd never had the time. Like Teagan, I was a tennis prodigy and my life was all about the training. When I wasn't in school, I was on the court with my coach, which meant my afternoons and weekends were pretty much taken up.

It's no wonder when I laid eyes on the beautiful Black queen that is Teagan Williams, I was smitten. She was ferocious and fearless. She was blazing a name for herself, and I admired her. Admiration turned into respect, which turned into competition, which turned to lust. We shared a passion so electric, anyone standing in the room could feel it.

And the other day at Manuel's, it was like nothing had changed. The energy between us was palpable.

I stop running and take a moment to catch my breath. I'm not perfect, never thought I was, but I stand behind my actions. Teagan can hate me as much as she wants. I'll take the hit, but it won't change the situation. We'll be working together on this tournament for a charitable cause whether we like it or not.

Who knows how we'll fare on and off the court? But I look forward to the challenge. She might try to deny it, but the chemistry between us didn't fade with time.

"Bro, I'm so glad you're here," Justice states when I stop by to visit his bachelor pad in Scottsdale later that day.

With a tapered, closely cropped haircut, smooth dark brown skin, bushy eyebrows and full lips much like myself, Justice Fletcher has turned into a fine-looking young man. Once upon a time, he was much shorter than the average boys in his class, and I never thought he'd get any taller. Then in his sophomore year, he sprouted to five foot ten.

I'm immensely proud of everything Justice has accomplished. At twenty-nine years old, he doesn't need my financial assistance. He's working at a company handling investments and making six figures.

"I'm sorry it took me so long to come by, but I wanted to talk to you about your prospectus and helping student athletes."

Justice nods. "I see how hard it is for top high school and college athletes to get by. Their families spend tens of thousands of dollars per year for coaching, entry fees, equipment and clothing. I want to be able to help them reap some rewards in the form of endorsements."

"For a small portion of the profit," I add.

Justice nods. "It's what other sports management companies do, except my focus will be junior and college athletes. I can help them build their brand, see their value and give them a vision for their future career."

"I'm intrigued and would love to help you get your company off the ground."

My brother's eyes go wide. "You would?"

"Don't sound so surprised. I believe in you, Justice. You've always had a good head on your shoulders, from going to Howard University to getting your MBA from Wharton. I wish Ciera had the same, though it does look as if Bliss is following in her big brother's footsteps."

"Ciera wants to be the next big influencer. It takes time and a little blind luck to find a video that goes viral."

"Exactly!" I point to Justice. "I've tried to get through to Ciera about school, but she's adamant she won't be attending college."

"She has to blaze her own way, Dominic. We—" he points to me and him "—may not agree with her choices, but it's ultimately her decision."

"Yes, but I won't foot the bill if she wants to do something so frivolous."

"You're cutting her and Mama off?"

"Not entirely, but I need to have some discussions with them on their spending. I work hard to provide for them, but at some point, I have to hold them accountable."

"Sounds fair. Let me know when you intend to have that discussion with Mom because I intend to be far, far away."

I laugh. "Definitely. When do you need the investment?"

"Soon. I have my eye on a location in Scottsdale, but I want to take another look. Now that we've got work out of the way," Justice says, "what's up with you? I've sensed a restlessness with you of late."

"You have?" It's very intuitive of Justice, but then again, we're closer in age than my other siblings.

"You've had a tough couple of years after your second injury tore your rotator cuff."

I nod. "I had to fight my way back to a number-one ranking."

"I knew you would, Dom," Justice replies. "Whenever you put your mind to something, you stop at nothing until you achieve it. It's what I admire about you and why I've tried to emulate you."

"You don't have to be like me, Justice. Forge your own path. Whatever it is. There was a lot of pressure on me to succeed because it was our way out of poverty."

"I know, Dom. We owe you a lot for the sacrifices and hard work you've put in. It's why I'm shooting my shot with this new business venture, but I know you paid a cost."

"What do you mean?"

"It's always been about the work for you, bro. You've never allowed yourself a world outside of tennis, to have a relationship. Over a decade ago you were with Teagan. I know we've been forbidden to ever mention her name, but I never saw you as happy as you were with her."

I frown. Why would Justice bring up Teagan now? I haven't spoken about her in years, but suddenly her name, her presence is everywhere in my life. "You wouldn't know this, but recently I ran into Teagan at a tennis tournament fundraising event."

Justice's eyes grow large with surprise. "Wow, how's that for a blast from the past!"

"Don't I know it, and what's worse is I'll have to see her over the next couple of months while I prepare for this event."

"Do you, though?" Justice inquires. "You're Dominic Fletcher. You can go anywhere you want. Maybe there are still some things unresolved between you. Perhaps you need closure."

"And when did my little brother become so insightful?" I ask, rubbing my goatee. Scott said the same thing.

"I won't bill you for this therapy session," Justice replies, "but next time…"

We both chuckle. But hearing another person offer the same advice gives me pause. Perhaps Teagan and I can rewrite the end of this tale and at the very least part ways amicably.

But knowing Teagan, the answer is probably no. Given she refused to meet with me or call so we could talk like grown-ass adults, that's a hell no. And maybe that's fair, but we're going to be in each other's orbit during this tournament.

She'd better buckle up and get used to my presence because I'm not going anywhere.

In fact, I'll make sure she can't ignore me.

Eleven

Teagan

I pushed thoughts of a six-foot-three chocolate tennis star out of my mind and focused on business the rest of the week. Although the Gems offered to help me out financially, I don't want their money, not if I can avoid taking it. I hate failing. It reminds me of when the choice was out of my hands and I had to walk away from tennis, something I loved, something I was good at. It broke my heart as much as losing the man I loved.

Speaking of Dominic, I've not heard anything from or about him. I'm sure that will change when I attend today's tennis tournament committee meeting. How did I let Charity talk me into agreeing to help? Having to play the game once in a while to schmooze is one thing, but a full-blown tournament? It's for a good cause, but it's putting me in Dominic's path. If it was up to me, I'd put a wide berth between us, but it's not my decision. He's the star they've hired to promote the event.

I put on a maroon Nike tennis dress and a pair of matching sneakers. I slick my hair back with a headband and I'm ready for battle. I'm hoping for zero drama, but now that Dominic has signed on, all bets are off.

"Are you prepared for all the hoopla that will accompany having someone of Dominic's stature at the tournament? Tickets will sell out," I warn Charity when I arrive at one of the country club's meeting rooms mid-Saturday morning.

Her eyes gleam with excitement. "That's what we want. We'll be sure to retain enough tickets for the committee and country club members, but having Dominic is a game changer."

Several other committee members arrive and Charity calls the meeting to order. I learn they've set the date along with a fundraising goal of two million dollars, which is quite ambitious. The event will be open to country club members, friends and members of the Phoenix community. I try to be enthusiastic. My sole goal is to garner business for Williams & Associates. I push my feelings about Dominic aside and focus on what's important.

When Charity and Mitzi ask for volunteers, I raise my hand. "I'll help."

"That's great, Teagan. We appreciate you, as a new member, stepping up to the plate."

The rest of the meeting continues with discussion about weather contingencies, players, attendance, streamlining the sign-up process and stepping up efforts to recruit sponsors. Somehow, without my agreeing to it, my name has been offered up as a player.

"But I haven't played in years," I respond quickly. I don't want to be in front of a crowd again where my every move is assessed.

"C'mon, Teagan," Laura Ragans, one of the other committee members, says. "We saw you the last couple of weeks and you're better than most of us."

I sigh with defeat. "I think my efforts would be better served behind the scenes."

"Don't worry," Charity replies. "You'll be great."

And just like that, my worst fears about playing again are realized. You can't give candy to someone with a sweet tooth and not expect them to eat. Tennis was my life. My entire world revolved around that court. If I have to play in the tournament, it means I'll have to play my best. I'm scared of another injury, but the doctor always told me I didn't have to give up tennis entirely. He'd said I could play recreationally. But I hadn't wanted to. It was all-or-nothing.

I chose nothing.

It scares me to get back on the court. I'm an athlete, or at least I was. I only know how to aim for a win, which means I'll need practice and lots of it.

After the meeting is over, I head down to the courts. I need to practice my footwork, timing and serve. After checking the schedule, I find my favorite, court seven, and head over to practice.

After lining up the ball machine, I walk to the baseline. I'm not worried about my stance or my grip on the racket, which come naturally, but when I played with Charity a couple of weeks ago, I didn't always connect with the ball. Typically, I like to hit big, with a spin inside out. I also need to make sure my backhand is in an open stance with my shoulders parallel to the net. I hit the on button to begin.

An hour in, I feel encouraged and move to turn off the machine when I'm interrupted by a masculine voice that says,

"Your backhand has never been the prettiest. I always told you it makes you flat-footed."

The hair on my nape rises and a shiver races through me. I don't have to turn around to know the owner of that voice. I'd hoped to avoid hearing it after I failed to meet with him. Apparently, that's not to be.

I swing around and see Dominic Fletcher standing on the court. He's wearing a bemused expression and looking quite dapper in Nike shorts and a white polo while I feel drenched in my tennis dress. A ball swings by my face and I quickly rush across to the other side of the net to turn off the machine.

"What are you doing here, Fletcher?" I ask, glancing up from my task. I ignore the butterflies swarming in my belly.

"I'm here to practice, same as you."

I roll my eyes. "You don't need to practice. There's not another Grand Slam for months."

"Still keeping up with the sport?"

"I'm not deaf and blind," I respond.

He snorts. "Would it hurt you to play nice in the sandbox?" He walks closer and stops several feet shy of me, but that doesn't mean I'm not affected by him.

I tell myself he has no power over me. He can't have it unless I give it to him. "Why are you really at the club?"

"Maybe I'm here to see if the edge you once had is really gone. I mean, if you're going to play in this tournament, you'll need some pointers."

I roll my eyes. "I don't need them from you."

Since I allowed myself to look him up recently, I devoured his stats and know all his averages, including who he's beaten and who's beaten him. Dominic is a formidable player.

"I'm the number-one player in men's tennis, Teagan. You could learn a thing or two from me."

"On how to run when the going gets tough?"

Dominic sighs and rubs his bald head. "There you go again. Still stuck in the past. We don't have to be enemies."

I glare at him and move away. "We're definitely not friends."

"Agreed," he says. "I extended an olive branch, which you snubbed by tearing up my card, by not calling or meeting with me."

"Can you blame me?"

He rolls his eyes. "Whatever. I'm trying to help you so you don't look like a fool, but if you'd rather not be up to snuff…"

His words make my back stiffen. "This—" I point to him "—is precisely why I didn't want to play in this tournament to begin with. I wanted to be behind the scenes."

"You and I both know you love the spotlight."

"Same as you," I respond, and notice the edges of his mouth tighten. "If you recall, having all that attention didn't turn out too well for me. I was once the darling of the media until I wasn't. I don't wish to relive that again."

"Then why come back here?" he asks, motioning around the courts.

"I don't owe you an explanation." I turn away from him, pick up my racket and grab my tennis bag. I'm not about to tell superrich Dominic about my money troubles and that my membership at the country club is a last-ditch effort to save my fledgling real estate brokerage.

His dark eyes narrow, and I can tell I've struck a nerve. "No, you don't owe me anything, Teagan, but I'm here and I'm not going anywhere. Your tournament needs a star, and I'm it. Unless you have someone else up your sleeve, I suggest you deal with the fact I'm here to stay." He surprises me by walking past me to the ball machine.

"What are you doing?"

"If you don't want to play, then I guess I'll practice alone."

I sigh. I don't want Dominic here because his presence reminds me of who I used to be and never will be again. It's hard to forget everything I lost, but he's right about one thing. If I intend to play in the tournament, I've got to improve. My serve is not what it once was. Back in the day, I hit a 125-mile-per-hour serve, but those days are long gone.

"Fine!" I say, tossing down my bag. I've always had a competitive streak when it comes to Dominic. "I'll play."

He raises an eyebrow. "With me?"

"Is there anyone else on the court?" I ask, cocking my head.

He chuckles. "I love it when you're feisty, Teagan." He tosses the tennis ball at me. "Your serve."

"Why do I have to go first?"

"Because you're the one who needs practice."

I hate that he's right. I watch him saunter across the hard court to the other side of the net. Dominic has a confident stride that lets anyone looking know he's sure of himself and who he is. His swagger is one of the things that attracted me to him in the first place.

And apparently, nothing has changed. He still makes my heart go flip-flop.

Twelve

Dominic

I didn't expect to see Teagan at the country club. My thought was I'd come in, play a few sets, no harm, no foul. But as I walked down to the courts, my eyes caught sight of a backside I'm very familiar with. I told myself it couldn't be. As far as I know, she'd never picked up a racket since her career ended. So imagine my surprise when I discovered I was right. She is on the court. My first inclination is to turn and leave, but I've never been one to avoid a fight and I'm not about to start now.

As I suspected, Teagan isn't happy to see me, but she also can't resist bantering with me. We always had a friendly competition between us and now is no different. Actually, I would say it's heightened because she sees me as an enemy not a lover.

"Let's get it started," she says, and directs the ball my way.

Her serve is solid, but I easily send the ball in her direction. We continue a steady pace of back and forth until I win and it's the start of a new game. When it's finally my serve, she's unable to run it down.

"Damn!" I hear her mutter. "Again."

I like it when she orders me around, but only on the court. When we were in bed, she wanted me to take charge because she was new to lovemaking. I enjoyed learning ways to please her, and she had no guile or shame in allowing my discovery. The way her mouth fell open on gasps as she reached her peak, or the way her muscles gripped me, quivering as I pounded into her... And the way she moaned, sighed and screamed my name when I feasted on her... Her responses were heady.

"Earth to Dominic!" I hear Teagan say, and blink to remember we're still on the court and not back in a hotel room after one of our competitive matches.

"Sorry." I lift my racket and slam the ball across the net.

This time, Teagan reacts quickly and manages to clip the ball, volleying it back to my side, but I'm right there waiting because I'm faster on my feet. I swing my racket and hit it square on. Teagan rallies, running toward the ball, but she's too late and it hits the court.

"Dammit!" she yells in frustration.

"Easy, Tee."

"Don't call me that!"

"You used to like it."

Her eyes narrow into thin slits. "That was before you ripped my heart out and left it for the vultures to eat."

Shit. I don't like being on the receiving end of her well-targeted barb. I was enjoying the game and for a moment forgot the past.

"That's not fair, Teagan," I respond, using her given name. "You act as if what happened between us is all my fault. You played a role in our demise too."

"You're blaming me? I was bedridden, watching the career

I loved bleed out like a loose tourniquet while you stood by and let it happen. You didn't fight for me."

Fury roils through me, and I reach for my Nike bag, tossing my racket inside. "We're not getting anywhere. I'm leaving." I turn on my heel, but Teagan races in front of me, blocking my path.

She might be five foot nine, but I tower several inches over her. She folds her arms across her bosom and I watch her breathe heavily. "Of course you would run. That's what you do best. Leave when the going gets tough. You know what that makes you—"

I don't let her get another word and lower myself until we're eye to eye. "You'd do well not to poke the tiger, Tee." I purposely use her nickname to vex her. "I bite, and if I recall, you couldn't get enough of my love nips."

Her eyes grow wide, and I see the moment she remembers being in my bed, unabashedly naked. It was the first time we'd stayed in bed all day because neither one of us had matches. I nipped at her dark brown nipples and took love bites out of her deliciously round ass. There was no place I didn't explore and she let me have my way.

She steps aside and I chuckle. "Chicken," I whisper in her ear, and then walk away.

I don't bother looking behind me because I want her to remember how completely obsessed we were with each other, *about each other.* She was a fire in my blood.

Has she always been there just waiting to be reignited?

Thirteen

Teagan

I can't believe Dominic said that.

He is trying to get a rise out of me and remind me of the passionate connection we shared. Of course, I haven't forgotten. He was my first love, my first *lover*. I let down my guard and allowed him to see inside—to the Teagan who wanted to be loved.

Intellectually, I know my parents loved me, but my father never showed it. When my mother tried, my father told her not to coddle me. *I'm raising a champion not a coward*, he would say. He would have been happier if I'd been a boy, but instead he got a girl. When I wasn't interested in baseball, softball or basketball, my father put me in tennis. He was thrilled when I took to the sport like a fish to water. I never imagined my love of the game would cause him to withhold his love entirely.

"Teagan, was that Dominic Fletcher?" Charity asks as she steps onto the court.

"One and the same."

"Were you guys playing? How do you know each other?" Charity fires off questions.

"We knew each other when I played professionally," I offer. I don't want to say too much, but if she wanted to, she could look up the awful headlines online. More than once, I've searched for myself. None of the articles or video clips are flattering.

"And?" Charity's shoulders go up in inquiry. "Was there something more? I mean, Dominic is one fine-ass looking man."

A giggle escapes my lips. "Um, yeah, he is, but..."

"But what? You wouldn't tap that if the opportunity presented itself?"

If she only knew. I not only tapped that, but his touch brought me to life and took my drab, beige world and made it fully Technicolor. Dominic showed me what passion looked like—how luxurious and powerful it could be. And I fell head over heels in love only to have it blow up in my face. But I'm not prepared to share that heartbreak with anyone who isn't one of the Gems.

"I have to get going," I say. "I have a showing later."

"Has being a member of the club helped? Are you seeing improvement?"

I appreciate Charity showing interest. "In the velocity of clients, absolutely." I nod. "Now it's a matter of getting them to the finish line and closing the sale. Thank you for making those introductions."

"That's wonderful news," Charity replies. "I'm glad I could help. We'll talk soon."

I rush off as quickly as I can because I don't want to talk about Dominic. Though, our battle on the court was invigorating. Maybe having him around isn't such a bad thing. Playing tennis again has reminded me of my love for the sport, and I could improve my game while helping the brokerage.

On the other hand, playing again with Dominic is risky. My competitive streak could lead me to reinjure my knee. Then there's the close proximity to Dominic. I'm not immune to him. When he mentioned love nips, it took me back to a place, a day, where I pleaded with him to fuck me every conceivable way. He made me his, and I've never been the same since.

The next morning, I drive to Papago Park, not far from metropolitan Phoenix, for a long walk on the west side. Although the east trail has better views of the Sonoran Desert flora and fauna and the popular scenic view point of Hole in the Rock, I'd rather stay on a more accessible, paved pathway. It has a series of loops around the big and little butte that are great for walking.

I used to do a lot of sprints and running when I played tennis professionally, but after I injured my meniscus, my rehab doctor told me to do less impactful cardio. Walking became my thing, and I can easily complete several circuits of the Double Butte Loop in an hour.

Today, it's a bit cool out with a high of sixty degrees. I've dressed in an African-print sports bra and leggings that fit me like a second skin, with a sweatshirt over them. Once I get warm, I can abandon the sweatshirt and tie it around my waist. I place my smartphone in the pocket of my leggings, insert my earbuds and I'm off.

I'm listening to my favorite workout playlist, which has a mix of current pop and R&B tunes, while maintaining my stride. I'm nearly done with two laps around the loop when I feel someone by my side.

Turning around, I give a start because Dominic is jogging beside me. I snatch my earbuds out and glance around. "What are…? How did you know where I'd be?" The impact of seeing him makes my skin flush and my heart beat erratically.

He shrugs. "I didn't. I came out here to exercise, same as you, or rather run in my case. Since when did you start walking?"

"Since I ruptured my meniscus," I respond hotly.

"I'm sorry, that was insensitive, I wasn't thinking. And you don't have a monopoly on the park—it has a great running path."

"Well then, don't let me keep you," I reply.

A flash glitters in his eyes and his jaw tightens. "Are you afraid for me to join you, Teagan? Do I unnerve you that much?"

"Not in the slightest. But I'm walking not running. I imagine it's beneath you."

"The only thing I want beneath me is—" He cuts off his sentence, but I know exactly what he'd been about to say.

The only thing I want beneath me is you.

He used to say things like that when we were together to elicit a response, but I'm not giving him one. "Do whatever you want. I'm finishing my workout." I immediately start walking briskly, but Dominic doesn't take the hint. Instead of running, he joins me walking, matching my brisk stride.

I glance in his direction and see the stubborn determination on his face, which he wears when he's intent on winning. He's not going to win with me. I ignore the breadth of his shoulders in the tank top he's wearing, the sexy goatee that makes him look like a dangerous predator.

"I imagine this must be pretty boring for you," I say after minutes tick by with no conversation between us. "Running is high-octane."

"I don't mind walking if I have company," Dominic replies.

Unwilling company, I want to add, but I don't dare get caught up with tit for tat. The passion between us always sparked from pushing each other's buttons. If I want to get through this walk, I have to act like he's not here. But how can I do that when I feel his pulsing energy?

"How's your family?" Dominic surprises me by asking, and I find myself pausing midstride. He does the same.

"Why do you want to know?"

He sighs and shakes his head. "I'm making conversation, Tee. Does everything have to be a battle?"

Yes! I want to respond like a petulant child. He wants to sweep our past under the rug like it never happened.

But I can't forget. Our past had a lasting effect on me, from my career to my personal life to my relationships.

"They're fine," I finally answer his question. "And your mother and siblings? I imagine your brother and sisters are all grown up now or close to it."

Dominic nods. "Yeah, Justice graduated with his MBA from Wharton and is working for a financial services company. Ciera is a senior in high school, but I'm afraid she's more interested in TikTok than anything else. Bliss, she's the all-around kid. She runs track and is smart as a whip."

I can see how proud Dominic is of his siblings. When we were together, he talked about making enough money to take care of them. "I'm glad to see they're finding their way in the world."

"They are," he responds. "I do my best to show up for them when my schedule permits. It's not easy, but they're a priority so I make the time."

"I'm glad to see that hasn't changed."

He smiles and it's like the sun shining. Dominic always had that effect, but I have to minimize it. I resume walking and he follows suit.

"So what have you been up to all these years?" he inquires. "I've always wondered."

"I doubt that," I reply sarcastically, "but if you must know, I became a real estate agent. I own my own brokerage and have a team of agents."

His face splits into a grin. "That's wonderful, Teagan. I'm glad to see you've become a success."

"Not like you," I mutter underneath my breath.

"What was that?" he asks.

"Oh, nothing." I want to get back to my car, but Dominic doesn't let up with the questions.

"And the Gems? What are they up to now? After we broke up, they all blocked me on social media."

I can't resist a knowing smirk. My girls will always show their solidarity.

Dominic continues, "I did manage, during my off time one year, to catch Lyric when she was a principal dancer for the San Francisco ballet company. She was breathtaking and so talented. I was saddened to hear about the fall ending her career."

"I commiserated because I'd been where she was. I understood her pain and devastation."

"And now? Is she better?"

I nod. "Lyric started her own ballet studio. Wynter is a big-time travel influencer, Shay has her own yoga and cycling studio, Egypt's restaurant, Flame, is a huge hit in North Carolina and she's thinking of expanding. And big news, Asia not only owns her own jewelry store, but she's a mom to two-year-old Ryan."

Dominic's eyes grow large. "Get out. Of all the Gems, I would never have guessed it."

"It was an unexpected surprise, but Asia is a great mom who happened to fall in love along the way."

"You sound wistful, Teagan. Do you envy her?"

"Me?" I laugh wryly. "I wasn't meant to procreate let alone live a normal life. It's never been in the cards for me."

"Why not?"

Because of you, I want to say. *Because you ruined me for any other man. You made me believe in love, but as soon as the going got tough, you left. You weren't in it for the long haul. You made me see how foolish I was to believe a man could complete me. I learned to depend on myself.*

"Oh look," I say, noticing we've come to the end of the trail. "I've completed my walk." I tap my Apple watch to log my exercise. "I should get going."

"So that's it?" Dominic asks. "Our friendly ceasefire is over."

I regard him warily. "Who ever said it stopped?"

Dominic leans toward me, crowding my personal space. I have to crane my neck to stare up at him. The connection between us is still there, burning bright. My eyes grow wide when his pupils flare and he bends toward me. The warm scent of his skin fills my nostrils, and I can feel long-forgotten desire build in the space between us. As he draws closer, my lips open in what, preparation for a kiss?

Is that really what I want?

Of course not. I can't forget the hell I endured after this man left me and went on with his career. At the last moment, I turn my head and his kiss lands on my cheek. Immediately, I step away.

His dark gaze burns, and if I'm not mistaken, there's a hint of disappointment there, but just as quickly it's gone and his expression is inscrutable.

"I have to go."

I rush away as fast as my Nike sneakers can carry me. I don't look back, but I can feel Dominic's eyes on me, or rather on my ass. He was always a booty man. He might as well enjoy the view because he's never getting another chance to touch me.

Fourteen

Dominic

I wanted to kiss her.

And Teagan wanted it too. I saw it in her eyes.

But then she thought about what a kiss would mean—that this living, breathing thing between us isn't over. It never was. It's been buried by years of anger.

I don't want to be angry at Teagan. It takes too much brainpower, but I'm also not going to stand by and let her put all the blame on me for the failure of our relationship. I could have handled things differently, but in the moment, I thought I was doing what was best. What her father asked for.

But you didn't ask Teagan, my inner voice reminds me.

And there's the rub.

I can't go back and undo what I did. I can only move forward. I've been hired to be the face of the Phoenix Desert Smash and that's what I'm going to do. Teagan's animosity or wishy-washiness can't get in the way of that. However, that doesn't mean I don't want her either, or that I don't remem-

ber how explosive we were together. I could hardly keep my
hands off her; today was no different.

She was in a sexy getup of leggings as tight as a second skin,
molded to her soft curves. The top wasn't any better. As we
moved on the path, she'd abandoned her sweatshirt to reveal
a sports bra, which showed the swell of her fantastic cleavage. I tried to make sure my tongue wasn't wagging like a
dog ready to pounce.

I rub my hand across my face and inhale sharply. Teagan
has a way of getting under my skin. I acted unaffected when
she pulled away and my kiss landed on her cheek. If that's the
way she wants to play it, I'm determined to do the same in
the coming months before the tournament. It will be up to
Teagan to change the rules.

Instead of focusing on our interlude, I visit my mom. I
haven't swung by in over a month. However, since I'm on
hiatus, I'm making a determined effort to spend quality time
with her and my sisters.

After leaving the park, I take my Bentley Bentayga SUV
over to the house. When I arrive, I find my mom's Porsche
Cayenne sitting outside. Once I started making millions, I
told her she didn't have to work anymore. I give her a generous allowance. However, of late, my accountant has told me
she's been asking for more. I want to ask her what's going on.
I couldn't do that when she hosted a crowd of people, but I
can now. Besides, now is a good time; Ciera and Bliss should
both be at school.

Turning off the ignition, I exit the vehicle and ring the
doorbell to give her a heads-up before I use my key to enter
the house.

I'm barely through the corridor when Mom comes from the direction of the kitchen. Her hand flies to her chest. "Dominic? What on earth are you doing here, and so early?"

"Good morning, Mom. Didn't you hear the doorbell?" I walk over and press a kiss to her cheek. She's dressed casually in yoga pants and a fitted short-sleeve shirt. "I finished a run at Papago Park and thought I'd come over and have a cup of coffee with you, if you're free?"

"For you, of course!" she replies. "I'm not due at the spa until later this afternoon."

I'd heard about her monthly spa and salon visits. Mom is racking up quite a tab. It's one of the things I intend to talk to her about. I follow her to the kitchen with its white cabinets, contemporary lighting and a sleek waterfall island that spans the entire length of the kitchen.

Mom goes behind the counter to a built-in espresso machine underneath a stainless-steel microwave. "What are you in the mood for? Do you want an espresso or would you like a cappuccino or latte?"

I prefer my coffee black. "An espresso, please." I take a seat on one of the suede bar stools at the island.

"Coming right up." She pulls out a cup from an upper cabinet, places it under the machine and, after pressing a couple of buttons, the aroma of coffee wafts through the air.

"I'm happy you're here. You're always welcome, of course, but you could have called," she says, sliding the cup of espresso my way.

I purposely wanted to catch her off guard. If I'd given her notice, she might have come up with an excuse as to why I couldn't come over. This way, she's forced to deal with me.

"Sorry about that," I lie. "Are you having one?"

"No, Dominic. I'd like to know why you came. Because you're not stopping by unannounced without a reason. You've always been about schedules, ever since you were little."

I take a sip, savoring the taste before diving in. She's right. I like everything being on point, which is why I hired my assistant, Micah.

"All right then, I've found out about your spending. Micah and the accountant informed me you've racked up quite a credit bill lately, with trips to salons, spas and designer boutiques. It has to stop."

"C'mon, Dom. You're being unreasonable. I have expenses that aren't much different from anyone else in the neighborhood."

"So all of this…" I motion around the house, which she's redecorated since the last time I was here. It cost a quarter of a million dollars; I have the receipts to prove it. "This is all to keep up with the Joneses?"

She sighs dramatically. "You have no idea what it's like, Dominic. People are always looking at me as if I don't belong."

"Seriously, Mom?" I ask incredulously. "Have you forgotten how hard it was for me to break into tennis as a Black man?" I motion down to my dark chocolate skin. "The stares, the whispers I endured to get to where I am. I'm beloved now, but that's only because I had to earn it."

"Of course I remember," she replies. "I was right there with you, making sure they saw how good my son was. I busted my ass to ensure you got all the training and practices you needed, had the best coaches. Is it so much to ask to enjoy the fruits of the labor I helped you achieve?"

Why does she do this? Turn it all back on me. I know what she sacrificed. The late nights, the double shifts to ensure food was on the table for me and my siblings.

"No, it's not too much to ask, Mom," I say, "but I have done right by you all these years. As soon as I made my first million, I bought you, *not me*, a house. So you, Justice, Ciera and Bliss could have a home."

"Yes, but—"

"No buts. You won't make me feel bad. I've supported you since I went professional. You haven't had to work. I pay the mortgage on this house, Ciera and Bliss's private school fees, and you have a very generous allowance for personal expenses, but they are out of control. I can't let it continue. I won't be pro for much longer."

Mom frowns. "What do you mean, are you retiring? You can't! You still have several more years in you. Serena Williams played until she was nearly forty."

"I'm not Serena, Mom, and *I'll* choose when I'm ready to walk away."

"I know, baby." Mom's voice softens. "I'm saying, don't give up so soon."

"I'm not, but I would be lying if I told you I'm completely fulfilled with tennis. I'm proud of my achievements and records, that I broke boundaries and allowed others to come behind me…"

"But you need something more?"

"Maybe." I hadn't intended on sharing my thoughts about leaving tennis with anyone, much less my mom. I feared she would push me to stay because she doesn't want to give up the lifestyle she's grown accustomed to.

"Is there, uh, a problem financially…?" Mom leaves the sentence dangling.

Just when I think she's on my side and wants what's best for me and how I feel emotionally, she brings this back to money.

I want the mom I had growing up, who was a fearless protec-
tor. "No, Mom. I'm not running out of money. I've invested
well and I've diversified, but that's beside the point. I'm not
being unreasonable asking you to curb your spending. You
need to live within your means. My team knows I will not
pay for anything beyond what you're allotted each month. So
you can stop asking."

Her face mars into rage. "You would do that? You would
leave me hanging when I have bills to be paid?"

"Yes," I respond, finishing the rest of my espresso and setting
the cup on the table. "You have everything you need. You've
got this house, three cars, both Ciera and Bliss have their own
vehicles, not to mention the vacation house in the Caribbean."

"It's where I take the girls on spring break. Are you going
to stop supporting your sisters too? We're in the last half of
Ciera's senior year, she's going to have expenses from gradu-
ation pics, yearbooks, prom dresses, a school ring and more."

I point my finger at her and rise to my feet. "Don't you dare!
You know I have always taken care of my sisters."

Mom has the good grace to lower her head in shame, but
when she glances up, there are tears shimmering in her brown
eyes. I was wondering when the waterworks would turn on.

"I don't know why you're so angry with me, Dom. I've been
a good mother. I've always been there for you. I show up to
all your matches when the girls' schedules permit."

She does. Many times I've looked up to see Mom in the
stands cheering me on. I walk over to her and pull her into
my arms. I kiss the top of her head. She always gets me in
knots. I love her, but I don't want Ciera to get into these bad
habits either.

I lean back so I can peer down at her. "You know I love

you, right? And I've appreciated all your hard work and support all these years, but you know as well as I do that money doesn't grow on trees. There's not an endless supply."

She sniffs and nods. "Fine."

"You'll agree to stay within budget?"

"You have the purse strings," she responds, stepping away from me.

"Mom…"

"It's okay, I'll review my expenses and dial them back."

"Thank you."

"Was that the only reason you came?" she asked, glancing up at me.

It was, but now I feel bad, as if I've mortally offended her. "No. How about I take you to breakfast?"

Her face brightens. "I would love that."

I know Mom isn't perfect, but she's all I've got. I never knew my father. He was out of the picture before I was born, and she raised me by herself with blood, sweat and tears. I take care of her because it's a privilege to do so. Life has afforded me opportunities I never had growing up. Yet in the back of my mind, there's still a niggle of discontent.

A feeling of wanting more.

Something that brings me purpose.

I'm hoping this time away from tennis competition brings me peace and the space to discover what comes next. But is that possible when the woman I've never been able to forget has resurfaced, when the passion between us hasn't been extinguished?

I don't know, but I suspect I'm about to find out.

Fifteen

Teagan

"Hey, boss." Brett knocks on my door at the office on Monday morning. After my inauspicious meeting with Dominic on the trail yesterday, I came in early to clear my head. He's been invading my thoughts far too much lately, so I'm perusing the latest financials. They are still abysmal, but at least there's hope for the future.

"C'mon, Brett." I wave him in. "What's going on?"

"I have some good news," Brett replies. "The Walthers have signed the contract for the North Scottsdale. They want to close in thirty days."

My eyes widen in surprise. "Really?"

He nods enthusiastically. "Given the state of the company, would I lie?"

"Omigod, Brett," I sigh, leaning back in my chair. "I'm so excited to hear this. I was worrying about how much longer I could keep up at this rate. This commission will definitely help."

"Hell yes, it will," Brett says. "I think your gamble with the membership at the country club is paying off. I got another call from a couple who was referred by Mitzi."

I clap my hands in glee. I wasn't sure it would yield dividends, but I'm glad to see I was right. "Now you just have to close the sale."

"I'm your number-one sales agent," Brett replies with a huff. "Do you doubt my abilities?"

"Absolutely not." If anyone can close, it's Brett. It's why I hired him. He has charisma in spades and, having been born and raised here, he knows Phoenix real estate. Brett graces me with one of his signature smiles.

After he leaves, optimism fills me. Right when I'm feeling defeated, a spark of hope comes through. It hasn't been easy keeping up this facade, but the nature of the real estate business requires it.

It's not the first time I've been down and out and unsure of the outcome. When I lost tennis—the thing that brought me joy and success and garnered me independence from my father— I was devastated. *How would I support myself?* Others suggested I could become a coach, but the thought of being unable to play professionally was too much. I know I'm the pot calling the kettle black because I suggested Lyric teach ballet after her injury, but we're different people with different experiences.

Despite being adopted, Lyric always had two loving parents who supported her no matter what while I, on the other hand, felt as if my parents' affection was conditional based on if I won or lost. Maybe it wasn't that way for my mother, but it was certainly the case with my father. Russ Williams made his displeasure known if I failed.

And when my injury meant I could no longer play tennis,

and the thousands of dollars he'd spent making a champion was taken away, my father was angry. While I was battling my own demons, fears and insecurities, and dealing with my crumbling relationship with Dominic, somehow I found the inner courage to pick myself up by my bootstraps and start over.

A colleague of my father's, Lou Payas, had a real estate business and offered to take me under his wing. Since I didn't have other options and was staying at my parents', I took Lou up on his offer of employment. He taught me the ropes and I blossomed. I found I didn't just have a knack for hitting a ball across the net. I was a people person and skilled at the art of negotiation. Soon, I was one of Lou's top sales agents, until eventually it was time for me to branch out on my own.

I saved up money and leased my office, but I wanted to own the building where my brokerage would be located. My inheritance from Wynter's aunt Helaine was a godsend and gave me the remaining collateral I needed. I would never want to lose this place—because of her my new dream was realized.

But I never forgot about my old dreams, which have resurfaced because of the club and Dominic's reappearance. Everywhere I look, he turns up. It's disconcerting. I don't want to think about how gaga I was over this man. How he made feel not only important and *seen*, but beautiful and *sexy*, without even trying. Most men saw me as a tomboy because of my short hair. But Dominic, he saw me, and I *noticed* him too.

Still do.

And that's the problem.

I feel vulnerable with Dominic. Yesterday, when he drew closer, I wanted him to kiss me. I know how Dominic kisses. He passionately uses his lips, tongue and teeth to spark a flame.

And for a moment, I was tempted to have a taste of him.

★ ★ ★

On Saturday, I show up to the country club in a new out-fit. Did I go to Lululemon to *buy* a new outfit? Maybe. Does this Cascadia Green, collared tennis bra with open back and a deep V cup my breasts and show a hint of cleavage? Maybe. And so what if my high-rise, pleated tennis skirt happens to show my toned thighs and the firm shape of my legs. I'm proud of my body. It has nothing to do with the fact that when I called earlier to check if the courts were free, I learned Dominic had been on-site since 7:00 a.m.

What is he doing here so early? He's supposed to be on break. I'd hoped to get in a few sets because the wealthy housewives aren't quite up this early, so most of the courts are empty. Get in early and be out of the country club before Dominic arrived. No such luck.

With my tennis bag over my shoulder, I head to my lucky court seven, but who is there? Dominic. He knows it's my lucky number and that we tennis players are superstitious. He could have chosen any other.

Did he come here on purpose?

My eyes can't help but stare as his lean, solid frame glides across the court as if he owns it. Dominic's hitting partner is trying his best, but Dominic doesn't know how to lose. Even-tually, they take a break and that's when Dominic leans down to grab a bottle of water. He's chugging it when he notices me ogling him like a teenager with a crush.

"Teagan, good morning."

His eyes pierce mine and I feel my cheeks heat at having been caught. A knowing smile stretches across his beautiful face. It's electric and dynamic and the sensation drenches my skin like it did all those years ago when he used to look at me like I was the only woman in the world.

I tremble. *Can he tell?* Our gazes clash and his seems to me to glint with amusement. He finishes off the bottle and tosses it into the empty recycle bin.

"You're on my court," I say defensively when I come to stand in front of him.

He glances behind me. "I don't see your name on it."

My eyes narrow. "You know it's my lucky number."

"And you weren't here to claim it first—I was. I guess you'll have to find another one."

"Not necessary," Dominic's opponent replies, stalking toward us. "If you feel brave enough, you should practice with our champion here. I, for one, have had my fill." He salutes Dominic. "Should I say thank you for the ass kicking?"

Dominic chuckles. The two men shake hands, leaving Dominic and me alone.

"Guess I'll find another court," I say.

"Why? Scared to practice with me again? My offer to help is still on the table."

"I don't need you."

"Maybe not, but I can help you rise to the occasion and finish strong at the tournament. And the Teagan I know always loved a good challenge."

I toss my bag down and grab my racket. "You don't know me as well as you think you do, Fletcher. Bring it."

A lazy smile crosses his lips. "Game on."

I let my mouth run away with me when I agreed to play Dominic again, but in actuality I'm dying inside. I won the first game. It was a fluke. I managed to stay afloat by a stroke of luck, but Dominic is a master of the long game. He knows about the pressure, the expectations of having the crowds, the world watching and waiting for you to win or lose. I haven't had that kind of pressure in a long time, but I can feel it bubbling inside of me. The need to live up to what I once was.

I lose the remaining games because I'm out of shape, and it pisses me off. It takes stamina and endurance and I'm out of practice. I'm going up against one of the best players in tennis. Dominic can easily go round for round in extreme weather conditions and on different surfaces. That used to be me. Not anymore—I'm drenched in sweat. My once-cute outfit is sticking to me like a second skin. Meanwhile, Dominic barely has a light sheen on his brow. He used minimal to no effort to best me and it grates on my nerves.

"Good job, Teagan," he says at the end of the fifth set when he's demolished me 6–2. Dominic offers a hand, which I begrudgingly shake. I've never been a sore loser; it's unsportsmanlike. It is one of the few things I learned from my father. He wouldn't tolerate childish antics.

"I feel like your hitting partner. Should I thank you for that smackdown?"

"You'll get better," Dominic replies. "You rely too much on your forehand. You always did and now you don't have the speed you once had."

"I didn't ask for your advice."

He shrugs. "Well, you're getting it. Can I interest you in a cold beverage inside?"

"All I'm interested in is a hot shower."

I want to go in a corner and lick my wounds in private, but Dominic won't let up. Why does he want to spend time with me anyway? I'm not the young ingenue or child tennis prodigy I used to be.

"C'mon, Teagan. You were willing to spar with me on the court and now you're running with your tail between your legs? I thought you had more grit."

Fury sparks and I walk right up to him and poke him in the chest with my index finger. "You don't get to judge me, not after what you did."

"Christ!" He rubs his hands over his bald head. "Don't you ever get tired of fighting?"

"With you, no," I say, deadpan.

"Bullshit. I think there's a part of you that still misses what you had before."

I raise a brow. "Tennis?"

"No, being in my bed."

"You smug son of a—" I don't get to finish my sentence because Dominic's hands close around my upper arms and pull me to him. "Wh-what are you doing?"

Suddenly, my sweaty bosom is pressed against his hard torso and my legs are between his, allowing me to feel the heat of his groin against my belly.

Lightning arcs through me and I feel soldered to the ground.

"Don't you think it's time we stop playing this game?" Dominic's voice is a low whisper as he tips my chin up to meet his hungry gaze. "I know what you want, Teagan. It's what we both want."

I swallow hard and I lick my dry lips. This can't be happening. I can't still *want* him. I sway, desperate to get away, but lose my balance and my palms flatten on his broad chest. I should push him away, but instead I feel the steady beat of his heart. It's in time with the thud of mine. The air between us is thick with sexual chemistry.

Don't overthink it, Teagan, my body says. *Take what you want. Don't be afraid.*

I grip Dominic's T-shirt in a tight ball and pull him down to me. Our mouths are within centimeters, but we don't kiss, not yet. It's as if we're preparing each other for what comes next. It seems he's as uncertain as I am, but like a moth to a flame, I slide my hands up to his face and cup it between my palms—that's when Dominic finally brings his mouth down on mine.

It's a soft caress at first. His lips brush mine, once, then twice, but then he settles in. His tongue glides across the seam of my mouth, and I open for him. That's when everything changes. The kiss turns erotic, all-consuming, carnal. Our heads angle for better access, our hands grasp and our bodies press together. I shake with the force of need that erupts within me and wiggle myself between his thighs until I register the long column of Dominic's thick, hard dick.

Dominic grips my ass and draws me to his erection. With only damp fabric between us, I feel his hardness against my softness, but that's all I can think about because I'm straining against him. I circle my hips and heat saturates me from my hairline to my toes, but most especially my core, where an ache is starting to form from the friction.

I want more. I devour his mouth and he lets me, then devours me right back. He rams his tongue deep inside me with unbridled desire. My entire body arches to meet him, eager for him to possess me as he once did. I rake my hands across his back. Moans of pleasure escape my lips and Dominic groans, burying his face in my neck and planting hot, wet kisses on the sensitive skin. It feels so good to be in his arms again that I momentarily lose time and place. It's Dominic who finally lifts his head, his ebony eyes trained on me. How can he be this coherent after those earth-shattering kisses?

"Teagan...we need to find someplace more private than, uh, the tennis courts."

Reality hits like a Mack truck and I give him a shove, pushing him away. Anyone walking by could have seen us making out. I'm mortified. What the hell was I thinking?

I wasn't.

I was carried away by Dominic's passionate, hungry kisses. The way I rubbed myself against him was unconscionable. I'm supposed to be angry at him for the way he treated me and I still am, but somehow one kiss is enough to make me forget about all the nights I cried myself to sleep because I felt lonely and abandoned.

"We're not finding someplace private. That shouldn't have happened."

His brow furrows, and he moves closer to me. "Like hell it shouldn't. Every time we're within a few feet of each other, there's sparks, Teagan. You know it and I know it. What's wrong with acting on the attraction we obviously still feel?"

I shake my head and let out a deep breath. "No, no. I can't... We can't." I turn away from him, desperate for some space to think.

"C'mon, Teagan. I've seen the way you look at me."

Appalled, my head whips around to stare at him. "And how do I look at you?"

"Like you want to touch me. And I don't mind because I want to touch you." His words are bold, but I'm humiliated by my behavior. I need to escape and think about why this happened. How I can stop it from happening again.

"I have to go." I find my tennis bag on the ground, lift it over my shoulder, but Dominic is already to me in two seconds flat.

"Dammit, Teagan! Don't do this. Running away won't change things. We have chemistry. Always have."

I glare at him. "It doesn't mean we have to act on it. That kiss was impulsive and a mistake. One I deeply regret!" I move as quickly as I can without breaking into an all-out sprint. I don't look behind me because I don't want to be brought back into a sensual haze. He's only been back in my life for a couple of weeks and I'm ready to drop my drawers because he looked at me with those fuck-me eyes.

I'm deep in trouble because, lord help me, he's right. I do want him. But going to bed with him will only muddy the waters. I know that alienating him, I run the risk of ruining his participation in the charity tournament and consequently my chances of resuscitating Williams & Associates, but I can't think clearly when I'm around him.

I have to get away while I still can.

Sixteen

Dominic

"Dominic, over here!" several reporters yell as I exit the limousine at the Atlanta headquarters of my clothing brand, *Dominic*. I'm here for the debut of the new menswear collection. It's a happy reprieve from Arizona after the encounter with Teagan went sideways a few days ago. Coming to this party is what I need to get my mind off the siren.

Besides which, *Dominic* is a labor of love. It's a luxury line for the discerning buyer who wants to look fashionable in tailored men's clothing. I started it a few years ago when buzz about me was at a fever pitch after I won four consecutive Grand Slams. I could do no wrong in the public's eyes, and I decided to capitalize on it.

I stop for pictures and give my profile in several directions. I'm considered one of the greats so the media are still eager for a photo. I came prepared, wearing one of my signature *Dominic* looks in a blue single-breasted suit with notched lapels and a crisp white shirt open at the collar. I've never been one for ties. After the photo op, I depart the red carpet and head inside.

The event tonight will be relatively low-key. The designer, Ian Palmer, a gregarious young fellow who I've pretty much given carte blanche to design as he sees fit, approaches me. With dreads down his back, a complexion the color of short-bread, he wears a fitted blue tuxedo but no bow tie. He looks like classic *Dominic*. We shake hands and I head to my seat, but I see Justice is already there with my agent, Scott.

"Hey, Dom." Justice rises to his feet and gives me a hug. He was already in town visiting friends and decided to come to the show. "Thanks for the invite."

"You're welcome, but it was also to help your business. Tonight will give you access to several athletes. Isn't that right, Scott?"

My agent is seated to my left while Justice is on my right. "Absolutely. You'll have male and female athletes attending tonight's show. They're all eager to see if *Dominic* is still on the pulse of what's relevant with the next generation."

"So they can take his spot?" Justice asks.

"It's a dog-eat-dog world," Scott says. "Lucky for you, you're only interested in college and junior athletes. The professional arena is a lot more ruthless and we'd be competition."

"You told Scott about my idea?" Justice asks accusingly.

"Bro," I begin, and wrap an arm around his shoulder. "In a good way. I was telling Scott what a great idea it was, and if you gave me half a chance, I was going to tell you that I'm very interested in your new venture."

"And willing to be a silent investor?"

I chuckle. "Not so silent. I can give you valuable insight as a former child athlete," I respond, "but if you don't want it…"

"No, no." Justice shakes his head. "I absolutely want and *need* your help. And I'm sorry for jumping the gun."

I nod. "It's fine. Let me introduce you around."

The next half hour consists of me taking Justice to meet several current tennis professionals who I'm friendly with on the ATP tour. They always come out every time I have a show. There's also a couple of football players from Atlanta, a handful of NBA stars and some up-and-coming tennis and women's basketball players. Justice not only takes the introductions in stride, but collects a few names on his own. I'm impressed with his business savvy. He's always had a good head on his shoulders. With his big brother to back him up, he's going to do great things.

The lights blink, indicating we should take our seats, and I prepare to be impressed by seeing the models in what Ian created this season. There's applause and cheers as piece after piece crosses the runway. The line is stylish and luxurious.

After the show, everyone buzzes about how they can't wait to purchase the clothing. While Ian soaks in the adoration, I go in search of my brother. He's deep in conversation with a WNBA star, so I decide to head out but Scott stops me.

"Leaving so soon?"

"You know I don't like the dog-and-pony show," I reply. "I do it for the brand."

Scott chuckles. "Of course you do. I was curious how things were going in Phoenix with Teagan."

"Not great."

"So you haven't hashed things out?"

Talking isn't what I had in mind the other day. I wanted to fuck her.

"I'd like us to get along," I respond, not revealing my

innermost thoughts. "She's a member of the Phoenix Country Club and on the tournament committee, not to mention
she's playing again."

"Is she?" Scott's eyes light up with excitement. "Could be
a great comeback story. Teagan Williams hasn't picked up a
racket in over a decade. It's newsworthy."

"I can already see your mind spinning, but you should stop.
Teagan hates the press after they crucified her. She would
never actively seek their attention. Limit the exposure I receive, okay? I don't want to spook her."

"If that's what you want, I'll honor it. Maybe you should
spend more time together, though. It could help you figure
out where things stand. Who knows, you could even play
doubles."

"Doubles?"

A light bulb goes off in my head. If we were forced to play
together, Teagan couldn't get away from me so easily. Our
make-out session showed me I only have to light a spark to
make her come alive in my arms.

What would she do if I ramped up her competitive streak?
Would it bring out her fire and send her to my bed?

There's only one way to find out. I'm headed back to Arizona.

Seventeen

Teagan

"I kissed him," I tell Lyric when she calls me two days later.

At first I wasn't going to tell the Gems because I feel stupid for being weak, for allowing my body to take over my common sense.

Dominic hurt me badly in the past. It took me years and a lot of therapy to get over his desertion and the loss of my tennis career. My confidence was shaken to its very foundation. I had already felt unworthy of love because of my strained relationship with my father. Having Dominic leave only reinforced those feelings. But after a few weeks of having him back in my life, I'm falling under his spell.

"You kissed Dominic?" Lyric inquires. "When?"

"On Saturday."

"And I'm just hearing about it? Why did you keep it a secret?"

"I was embarrassed. I didn't want the Gems to know. I'm supposed to be the one who has it together." *Except when I don't.*

"Teagan…" I hear the censure in Lyric's voice. "You don't

always have to be strong or put up a front with us. We love you and support you, regardless. Now tell me, how did this kiss with Dominic come about? I thought you were giving him a wide berth?"

"That was the plan, but he keeps coming to the country club. He senses I have a weak spot for him and he's exploiting it."

"C'mon, Teagan. I know how you can be when you're determined, but maybe there's a part of you that doesn't want to avoid him."

I suck in a deep breath. "I suppose you could have a point. I didn't exactly shy away from playing tennis with him."

"Teagan, being on the court is like foreplay for you and Dominic. I'm not surprised one thing led to another and you guys sucked face. You have a complicated past with Dominic. One that was never fully resolved. You were so keen to break up with him after your injury. You never found out what you could have been without tennis."

"All we had was the sport."

Lyric coughs loudly. "I call bullshit. You were madly in love with Dominic. It's not surprising you'd have a soft spot where he's concerned. I guess my question for you is, what comes next?"

"Nothing. I pushed him away and told him it was a mistake."

"Was it?"

"Lyric! You remember how I was after our breakup. I was devastated."

"I haven't forgotten the pain you endured, especially when I couldn't do anything for you. I was in San Francisco with my own struggles as a Black ballerina in a white ballet ensemble."

"You did what you could. But I—I can't go backward."

"Then don't," Lyric states. "Go forward. You're both different people than you were twelve years ago. You've changed. He could have changed too. Who knows, you might discover you have more in common than you ever did before."

"Or I can find out he's the exact same man he's always been who will run when the going gets tough. I'm not sure I want to risk it."

"Life is all about taking risks. I believe you told me that when I fell in front of thousands of people in that auditorium. You told me my life wasn't over and I could make new dreams. You can too, Teagan. See where it goes with Dominic. I'm not saying you have to jump into the deep end of the pool with both feet, but take baby steps."

"I'm afraid of getting hurt."

"I get it, honey. I was scared too when Devon and I met in Aruba and then again when we restarted our relationship in Memphis. But I also know you've dated all these years but have never gotten serious with anyone."

I hear what Lyric is saying, but I'm not sure I'm ready to jump off the cliff—because I doubt Dominic will catch me if I fall. All I can do is make the best out of the situation, be professional on and off the court until I pull Williams & Associates from the brink of disaster. Despite my mixed feelings about Dominic, I can't afford to mess up this tournament for the country club. They need his star power and I need the leads I'm getting from spending time with the club members. Somehow, someway, I'll push down this attraction that's been unearthed after being buried over a decade.

I can do this, right?

I have to.

★ ★ ★

When Saturday and another committee meeting roll around, I'm ready. I've decided not to play today and come dressed casually in an off-the-shoulder palm-leaf maxi-dress with an empire waist. I've pumped up my hair with a bit of mousse and added light makeup, pink lip gloss and hoop earrings. I'm feeling good until I walk into the room and see the committee has a guest.

Dominic is chatting with Charity and Mitzi, who're hanging on his every word.

"Good morning," I say when I reach them.

There's a chorus of good-mornings, but the only one I care about is Dominic. He's eating me up with his eyes, like he wants to take me to the nearest broom closet, hike up my dress and have his way with me.

I swallow the lump in my voice. "I'm surprised to see you here," I say, not bothering with pleasantries.

He doesn't get to answer, because Charity jumps in. "Dominic has graciously agreed to volunteer on our committee. Can you believe that?"

My eyes laser focus on his, but all Dominic does is shrug and give me one of those dazzling smiles that show off his pearly-white teeth. Damn, even his teeth look good.

"That's wonderful," I respond, when I feel the exact opposite. I want him gone, not fluttering around me like a butterfly.

"I had a little free time," Dominic says, "and figured this is a worthy cause."

"We can use all the hands we can get," Mitzi replies, patting Dominic's arm. She's shameless in getting a feel of his generous biceps. I mean, his serve can go one hundred sixty miles per hour, one of the fastest in the industry. Not many men can keep up with him, let alone fight it out over multiple sets.

Charity recognizes how tense I am because she pulls Mitzi away, leaving me glaring at Dominic.

"You're looking absolutely ravishing today," Dominic says.

My eyes narrow. "Don't try and charm me, Dominic. I'm not one of these infatuated women."

His expression turns flinty. "As I recall, you weren't feeling that way last week. Matter of fact, you couldn't get enough of me."

"I would have hoped you'd be a gentleman and not bring it up."

"I'm no gentleman," he says with a smirk. "My presence will ensure you step up your game, so I think we should continue to practice together."

Charity interrupts my reply by calling the meeting to order. I find a table with only one seat remaining and take it before Dominic can sit next to me. It doesn't matter because I can smell the spice-and-cedar scent that's synonymous with Dominic.

Charity goes over the last meeting's minutes and, after getting approval, moves to the next agenda item. Fundraising is going well but is not as high as they would like. Dominic raises his hand and offers to reach out to several of his high-profile tennis colleagues for donations. Charity preens with satisfaction while I want to jump across the table and strangle him. Instead, I bite my lip until I taste blood.

Don't let him get to you. I give myself a pep talk, but he's being so solicitous, I want to scream. Then Charity's next suggestion really makes me want to do just that.

"I was thinking. I know everyone loves to shine on the

singles tournament, but wouldn't it be fun if we included a doubles tournament?"

"That's a great idea," another committee member concurs, and soon everyone is agreeing.

"I know exactly who our first couple to sign up should be." Charity plants her gaze on me conspiratorially. "Dominic and Teagan! You've both played professionally. It could be a big draw."

I'm about to say *Absolutely not* when Dominic jumps in and says, "I'm in. How about you, Teagan?" He throws down the gauntlet knowing I *have* to pick it up to save face in front of all these women. "I'll even train you myself," he adds for good measure.

I can feel the color draining out of my face and my mouth feels like cotton so I don't respond. Charity takes my silence as acceptance and continues talking as if I've already said yes. "That's great, Dominic. Thank you so much for being a team player."

I don't hear the rest of the meeting. How am I supposed to keep Dominic at a distance if I have to play in a tournament with him? Dominic is responsible for this fiasco, and I will waste no time telling him so, once Charity concludes the meeting. Before the other women file out of the room, they tell me how lucky I am to work with a player of Dominic's caliber. As if I don't know. I've watched the ascension of his career from young upstart to seasoned veteran with seventeen Grand Slams under his belt.

"I suppose you're happy with yourself," I say, folding my arms across my bosom, glad the room is empty and I can speak freely.

"I'm not exactly upset if that's what you're asking. Perhaps we can finish what we started the other day."

I shoot him a dirty glare. "That's not going to happen."

"Ha!" He throws back his head with a laugh. "Keep telling yourself that, Teagan." He starts for the door, but I rush in front of him.

"I mean it, Dominic. The other day was an anomaly. It was…"

Dominic's dark eyes meet mine. "Tell yourself whatever will make you feel good, but I know what it was."

"And what was it?" I taunt.

"Lust. Passion. Heat. Everything we do well together, Teagan. And I look forward to a repeat."

My breath hitches in my chest and I quickly move aside, allowing him to leave. All I hear as the door closes behind him is Dominic's laughter.

Why is it so easy for him to look at what happened between us as lust and sex? It was much more complicated than that. Our history is layered with hurt and betrayal. I can't *not* remember the past, but when I'm in his arms it all melts away.

If only life were that simple, but it's not.

Eighteen

Dominic

My decision to show up at the Phoenix Country Club's Desert Smash tournament committee meeting was impulsive. I wanted to see Teagan again and push her buttons. I knew she would sweep what happened between us under the rug. I won't.

She hates me for having left her all those years ago, for having the career she's always wanted. And me, well, I've hung on to my anger toward her because she gave up on us too easily. Because she's quick to believe the worst about me. I made a mistake listening to her father. I thought I was doing the right thing, but now she hates me for it.

Telling her won't change things. It won't take away the past. It is what it is. All we can do is move forward. I thought that's what I was doing. I've been living my life, winning championships and Grand Slams, because it is what I was born to do. Yet I can't deny that having Teagan back in my life, even in small ways like walking beside her on the trail or playing a match with her on the court, has lit a spark in me I haven't felt in a long time.

I feel *alive*. Everything seems a little bigger and brighter. For a long while, I've been disenchanted with my life. Not that I don't love the game—I do—but I've achieved everything I set out to do. I've broken records and established myself as the GOAT while my love life has languished, never moving forward with any woman because those women are not Teagan.

I came to the meeting to volunteer. I knew she wouldn't be able to deny my entry or my existence. The tournament needs me. Could they find another tennis star? Sure, but not this late in the game. The Phoenix Desert Smash is less than two months away, which is to my advantage.

I suggested the idea for doubles to Charity before the meeting started and she loved it. Having Teagan as my partner means this excitement and exhilaration won't go away. Maybe these feelings are what I need to prepare myself for the French Open at the end of May, and until then, I can allow myself this moment.

And if that includes having Teagan back in my bed, so be it. I *want* her. I know she wants me too, but she's fighting it. Training with me will bring our attraction to the forefront, and she'll have to face it, face me, head-on. I welcome it. There have been other women who've satisfied my needs, but there is something about Teagan that's special, unique.

She spoke to my soul, and I've never let another woman get that close. I'm not sure I can let *her* get that close again because it hurt too much to lose her. After our breakup, I lost a couple of big matchups. My coach told me to get my head out of my ass.

But I felt Teagan's pain. I knew she wanted to be in my position and I was sorry she wasn't, but I shouldn't be punished for the rest of my life for achieving the glory denied to her. What I can do is ensure the Phoenix Desert Smash tournament is a success, and if that means I get to spend time with Teagan in the process and fuck whatever this is out of my system, then I'm down. Right now, she's like a fever in my blood, and it won't break until she's mine again in *every way*.

After the meeting, I don't stick around. Instead, I drive to Bliss's high school for one of her track meets. She's fast and best at sprints, especially the one- and two-hundred-meter dashes. I can't wait to see her in action. I don't often get to make her meets because I'm on the road.

Justice texted me earlier that he, Mom and Ciera are already on-site. I park my Bentley Bentayga SUV beside Justice's BMW X7 and hop out. I'm nearly to the bleachers when several fans approach me asking for an autograph. I scribble my name across journals, T-shirts and miscellaneous items people produce on the spur of the moment when they see a celebrity.

Eventually, I make it to the bleachers. Mom waves at me from the upper row and I climb the stairs. She wraps me in a hug when I arrive. "Dominic, I'm so glad you could make it. Bliss will be too."

"If I'm in town, I'll always try and come. Hey, kiddo." I look down at Ciera, who is on her iPhone snapping pics, videos or whatever Gen Z does these days. As usual, she's in a skimpy crop top showing too much flesh for my taste and baggy joggers while her long mane of weave flows to her ass.

"Hey, Dom," she says absentmindedly. I give her a kiss on the top of her head and give Justice a one-armed hug.

"Hey, bro," I say. "Did I miss anything?"

Justice is smartly dressed in trousers and a polo shirt. I assume he plans on working on his new business venture by talking to some athletes after the event. "Naw, the meet hasn't started yet," Justice responds. "Where were you?"

I frown. "Uh, I had some pressing business to attend to." I take a seat behind him on one of the bench mats Mom brought.

"Does this have anything to do with Teagan?" Justice's brows rise.

"That name is a blast from the past," Mom says, jumping into the conversation. "When did you run into your ex?"

I didn't want this to be public knowledge, but I didn't know Mom was listening. "A few weeks ago."

"And you didn't mention it?" Mom inquires. "I always liked that girl. She had a lot of chutzpah, reminded me of myself. It was such a shame when you guys called it quits."

"She doesn't feel that way," I reply. "She's not a fan of mine."

"Can you blame her?" Mom asks. "You've gone on to achieve great things. I'm so proud of you."

Her words bring a smile to my face. "Thank you, Ma."

"I tell anyone who'll listen who my son is," she continues, and that's when she loses me. "They can't believe it. They say I don't look a day over forty."

I laugh. "Do they now?" I have no idea who *they* are, but go along with her.

"Sure do." Then she points to the field. "Look, look, there's Bliss." She yells out Bliss's name, which causes my sister to glance up. I see her face turn red with embarrassment, but Mama is oblivious. "That's my daughter," she says to the woman by her side. The woman smiles politely and they engage in conversation, leaving me and Justice to our previous one.

"Sorry about that," Justice whispers. "Didn't know Mama was listening."

I shrug. "It's fine. I'm hoping the press doesn't pick up on Teagan and I being in the tournament together. That didn't go too well the last time."

"Then I suggest you keep things between you on the q.t."

"You're probably right." I didn't exactly do that the other day when we made out on the court where anyone could have seen us and snapped pics.

Justice inclines his head to the track. "Race is starting."

I love the thrill of competition, and seeing Bliss thrive in this atmosphere is rewarding. If anyone can follow in my footsteps, it's my baby sister. Hell, she'll go even further because she has smarts behind her too.

I wasn't an F student, but I also didn't love school. I'd much rather have a racket in my hand hitting balls than be stuck in some classroom indoors. Eventually, it got to the point I had to be homeschooled by tutors because there wasn't time for me to train with a normal school schedule. I'm happy Bliss loves school, but seeing her smoke the competition fills me with pride. With her speed, she can get an athletic scholarship.

After the track meet is over, the family and I wait for her outside the school. "Way to go, Bliss." I pick her up and swing her around.

She shrieks. "Dom, put me down. I'm not eight anymore."

I laugh, but do as she asks. "You'll always be my baby sister."

"Great job, little bit!" Justice gives her a squeeze.

"Thanks, guys." Bliss blushes. "I'm not used to having the entire family on hand, even you, Ciera."

Ciera gives a wave from the column she's posing against while taking selfies and talking about the event on TikTok.

"How about some lunch?" Mom asks. "I imagine you're starved."

"I would love to, but some of the gang—" Bliss turns behind her where I see several young girls are standing "—decided to go out for burgers. Is that okay? I know y'all came out for me and I truly appreciate it."

"Go have fun with your friends," Mom replies, and swats Bliss on the bottom. Bliss rushes off to the group.

"Me too," Ciera adds. "No offense, but I see some friends I know." And without another word, she departs. Justice isn't far behind, leaving us to talk to some athletes.

"What do you say, Mom?" I turn to her when it's just us. "You game for lunch with your son or is that not in style anymore?"

Her face instantly brightens. "It absolutely is."

"Good. Lunch is on me at your favorite spot."

Mom claps her hands with glee. "Well, if you're buying, then I know just the place."

Of course, she picks the most expensive restaurant in town, but I don't mind; I'm in a great mood today. I'm proud of my family and what I've been able to do for them. I'm sorry it came at the expense of my relationship with Teagan. But if I had to do it all over again, I would make the same choice—except this time, I would have a heart-to-heart with Teagan so she understood I was between a rock and a hard place with no way out.

But if she had known, would she have understood?

Or would she have expected me to give up everything to stand by her side? I guess I'll never know because I made a choice.

The right one for me, but the wrong one for Teagan.

Nineteen

Teagan

The next morning, I'm happy to lounge around in bed. Sundays are my favorite day. It's one of the few times I allow myself to sleep in. Usually during the week, I'm up and out of bed to work out, have breakfast and get the day started at the office or a house showing. However, today I allow myself to indulge in my luxurious California king bed and sumptuous one-thousand-thread-count silk sheets. It feels decadent. I deserve some downtime.

I try not to think about yesterday, how I was blindsided by Dominic's appearance at the committee meeting and Charity's suggestion for a doubles tournament and partnering me with Dominic.

Dominic Fletcher is my Achilles' heel. As if on cue, my smartphone pings with an incoming message.

Dominic: Are you free this afternoon?

Me: Why do you ask?

Dominic: I'd like us to train to get you ready for the tournament.

Me: I don't need your help.

Dominic: Don't cut off your nose to spite your face.

Me: Don't lecture me. You're not the boss of me.

Dominic: Then grow up. Meet me at 1:00 p.m.

There's not another message. I seethe with fury because, damn him, I know he's right. Once the tennis press gets word of my involvement in the tournament, all eyes will be on me. They'll be waiting to see me fall flat on my face because it will reinforce their negative image of me as an angry diva.

I can't let that happen, *not again*.

But training with Dominic is fraught with danger. As much as I wish the opposite, I'm not immune. He's dynamic and captivating. The husky sound of his voice, the deep rumble of his laugh, the way he commands attention—it all appeals to a place deep within me. I'm afraid of what it means, what could happen to me if I give an inch and let him close.

But what choice do I have?

Do I tell Charity and the other members I won't play? It will raise their suspicions and get me on their bad sides when I'm eager to earn new business. I have to do this to save Williams & Associates, but maybe for myself too. Maybe if I play with Dominic, I can work out all this pent-up anger and finally get closure.

Yes, that's the answer.

Throwing back the covers, I head for the shower.

I'm not scared of him.

He should be scared of me. A woman scorned.

I arrive to the court in a flattering tennis dress with a deep V-neck that has the appearance of a skirt, but with built-in shorts underneath. Something tells me Dominic is going to go hard on me so I don't bother with my hair and cover it with a sun visor.

I texted him back earlier that I would meet him at the club, and he's waiting for me in the lobby, but he's not alone. He's signing several tennis balls. He glances up as I approach.

"I'm almost done here." He takes several photos with country club members before striding over to me.

"If you're done with your entourage, can we get to work?"

He snorts. "Glad you decided it was in your best interest."

"I don't have many options," I reply, and head toward the double doors that lead to the outdoor basketball and tennis courts.

Dominic matches my stride as he did on the trail. "Why not?" he asks. "You could choose to walk away from the tournament."

"I can't." I pause my steps and turn to him. "And before you ask, I'm not going to share why. I'm here, so let's do this."

"Fine with me, Teagan. Prepare for an ass kickin'."

My mouth drops open, but Dominic merely walks ahead of me and I follow. It sets the tone for the day because every time I think I'm doing something right or gaining traction, Dominic capitalizes on my weakness and goes in for the kill, garnering another point.

He wipes the mat with me on the first match, which leads

me to believe he was going easy on me the last time we played, allowing me to win a game.

"The claws are really out," I say when we pause between sets, and I guzzle down an entire bottle of water.

Because of his popularity, several club members have gathered outside our court to watch, much to my chagrin. It's bad enough to have my butt kicked, but it's worse with an audience.

"What do you mean?" Dominic asks, wiping a bead of sweat off his forehead and placing his racket on top of his bag. Once again, he's barely sweating while sweat drips between my boobs. I'm thankful this dress makes my breasts look good. More than once, I've caught Dominic's appreciative gaze. If I have my way, he'll never get a chance to touch, taste, lick or suck them again.

Is that really what you want? Wouldn't you rather have his head right between them while he works magic with his fingers between your legs?

I smother the thoughts and respond to his question. "You were going easy on me last time. You're not today."

He cocks his head to one side and regards me. "My kindness wasn't appreciated so I'm giving you a taste of what my other opponents get, in the hopes you'll rise to the occasion."

"I will."

"We'll see." He tosses his sweat towel on his bag and picks up his racket. "Set two. Bring it, Williams. It's time to see what you're made of. Or are you all talk?"

My eyes turn into slits and I don't answer. Instead, I let my racket do the talking and send him a dynamite serve over the net. It has to be going at least a hundred and twenty miles per hour. Dominic, however, easily masters it and sends it back in my direction.

"Ah, that's the Teagan I remember," he taunts. "I want to see more."

We rally for several minutes until I need a break. I screw the top off the Gatorade I brought with me and drink generously.

"Enough of a break, Williams. Let's get back to work."

I glare at Dominic across the court. "Don't be an asshole, Fletcher."

"Ouch." He shimmies his shoulders. "Calling me by my last name, you must be really angry, *Williams*." He comes toward me to half-court and I walk over and meet him. "Use that fire in your belly to show these people—" he glances around the court where a crowd has formed "—who you used to be. You're the great Teagan Williams, world-renowned for her backhand. It's still there." He points to my chest. "Use it!" He backs away. "Your serve."

I really want to climb over the net and do what, punch him in the gut or jump into his arms until he catches me, grips my ass and allows me to plant a big smooch on his incredibly full lips?

Instead, I walk back to my position and use the anger toward him to make this last game a good one. This time, I have Dominic on the run and I love it.

I win two points until we're tied at deuce. Whoever wins the next two points wins this third game. Dominic fools me on the serve. I move toward the center line, but there's wicked slice on the ball that sends it to my right. I try chasing it down, but I can't make it and go sprawling across the court.

"Fuck!" I hear Dominic's curse and then he's leaping across the net and coming to my aid. I'm embarrassed and quickly pull myself up to the seated position. "Are you okay?" Dominic asks. "Are you in pain? How's your knee?"

"I'm fine," I respond. "Just a bit embarrassed." I glance to the crowd, who are staring at us with unabashed interest.

"I'm sorry. I shouldn't have pushed you so hard." Dominic's face is contorted with regret and I can see how upset he is.

Without thinking, my hand comes up to cup his cheek. "Dominic, I'm not injured. My meniscus is fine, okay?" You'd think I'd be the one stressed about the fall, considering I was hurt and ridiculed by the media when I fell off the pedestal they'd put me on. "If you can just help me up..." I start to say, but before I can finish, Dominic reaches underneath me and lifts me into his arms. "Dom-Dominic, put me down."

He shakes his head. "No, I want you checked out. I want to make sure you're okay." He's about to reach down for my bag when Charity comes rushing onto the court.

"Teagan, what happened?"

"I lunged for a ball and missed. I'm fine. I'm capable of walking, Dominic." But he's not listening to me; he's already moving to the court exit. I see the stunned and jealous faces of several women as we walk past. "Charity, can you grab my bag?"

"Of course." Charity rushes to grab it from the floor. I'm so embarrassed. I don't want to see all the stares. What are they thinking? Probably that I can't hack it, going up against the GOAT, but they're wrong. I was making progress. Dominic was right; with a little bit of practice, it'll come back to me.

Just now, though, I can't think straight. I'm in Dominic's arms again. He's carrying me as if I weigh nothing. Despite how sweaty we both are, he still smells divine: earthy and manly. My mouth waters and my core throbs in my damp panties.

Dominic walks right out of the club and I see his car sitting at the front entrance. They gave him a reserved spot meant for the chairman of the club? The valet quickly rushes to get his keys. Dominic waits at the door of his Bentley Bentayga SUV. Once the valet opens it, he places me inside on the front seat. Charity is right behind him and hands me my tennis bag.

I have enough time to say "Thank you" before he closes the passenger door with me inside.

I mouth "I'll call you" to Charity as he rounds the driver's side and climbs into the vehicle. He turns on the engine and the car roars to life.

"Dominic—" I start, but he interrupts me.

"Not now, Teagan." He hits the speed dial on the car's phone display. I see the name Dr. Maverick come up on the screen. "Hey, Doc, it's Dominic."

"Hey, Dom, how are you?"

"I'm fine, but my girl was injured playing on the court and I'd like you to have a look at her. Can you come by my place?"

His girl? Since when? Dominic and I haven't been together in nearly twelve years. He has no right to act like I'm his.

"Sure thing. I can be there in an hour," Dr. Maverick responds.

"Great. We'll be there." Dominic ends the call, then hazards me a glance. "Put on your seat belt."

For safety purposes, I buckle up, and then I turn to him. "I don't appreciate your high-handedness, Dominic. I'm perfectly capable of taking care of myself and *walking*, I might add. There was no reason for you to act like the hero in front of everyone. Once again, I look like a complete fool."

"Dammit, Teagan!" Dominic slams his hands on the steering wheel. "Do you have any idea the absolute fucking terror

I experienced witnessing you go down?" The censure in his tone makes me stay silent. "I've been pushing you all day and I thought I caused you to get hurt. I did what I—"

"Should have done the day I was injured?" I finish the sentence for him.

The fear I see lurking in his ebony eyes is real. He is truly worried about me. I don't know what to do with this, with these feelings he evokes in me. One minute he's taunting me and pushing me on the court. The next he's a hero, lifting me into his arms as if I'm important to him. It's difficult to make sense of it all.

We both stay silent for the remainder of the ride to his house. I fumble in my purse for my phone. There are several texts from Charity asking if I'm okay. I let her know I'm fine and I'll call her later. It seems surreal to be coming to Dominic's home.

Dominic pulls up to a gate and punches in several numbers, and the wrought iron opens to reveal a mansion, much bigger than my slice of paradise. He proceeds to the garage, and backs the Bentley in before shutting off the engine. "We're here."

"I kind of figured that," I reply, and unbuckle my seat belt. I've barely opened the passenger door before Dominic is right there.

"Are you okay to walk?" he asks.

"Yes," I say through clenched teeth.

I don't want to argue. I just want to get through this so I can get back to my car at the club. He's stranded me at his home without any transportation. I exit the vehicle and follow him out of the garage. He disables the alarm and I walk inside. I stand by the door, unsure of what to do next.

He strides past to the adjacent kitchen then returns to hand me a smartwater. That's when I realize I'm dying of thirst.

"Thank you." I screw off the top and drink liberally. When I'm done, I glance at him. "You realize we need to talk about what happened."

He moves his neck back and forth from left to right. It's an action Dominic takes when he's agitated. "Do we have to?"

I laugh. "Ya think? You completely overreacted to the situation. I fell. People fall all the time on the court."

"You're not just anyone to me, Teagan. You never have been, and therein lies the problem," Dominic says, facing me.

I suck in a deep breath. I want to respond, but the doorbell rings and I imagine it's the doctor Dominic contacted unnecessarily.

"Excuse me." He leaves me in the corridor and walks to the front door. When he opens it, an elderly man with stark white hair comes forward carrying a medical bag.

I fill in Dr. Maverick on everything that occurred. He looks me over and asks me to complete a series of tasks with my knees and my ankles. The entire assessment takes about fifteen minutes. When Dr. Maverick is done, he gives me a clean bill of health.

"From what I can see, Ms. Williams, you have no broken bones or sprains. Should you feel any soreness or tenderness in the morning, I would suggest taking some ibuprofen for inflammation and icing the area. If it persists, then I would see your primary physician."

"Thank you. I'm sorry you were called here for no reason."

"It's better to be safe than sorry. Besides, from Dominic's tone, I sensed he was worried about you."

"Can you tell him I'm okay and I'm free to go home?"

Dr. Maverick smiles warmly. "Absolutely." He leaves the

room and several minutes later, I hear the chime of the front door. When Dominic returns, I'm already on my feet.

"As you can see, I'm perfectly healthy." I motion up and down. "I didn't need this level of care, but I appreciate you going the extra mile." There, I said what I needed to say. Now we can squash this. I move toward the doorway, but Dominic isn't budging.

"Teagan…"

I don't like the way he says my name. It's too intimate, too personal. "I need to go, please…" I try to push past him, but he grasps my arm, forcing me to stop moving. I glance up at him and the heat in his eyes is unmistakable. I lower my head, unable to stand the fire raging inside me at his touch. "Please…"

"Please what? Don't care about you? Don't want you? I can't do any of those things and I'm tired of pretending otherwise or making up excuses to be near you. I want you. Right here and right now. Look at me and tell me you don't want the same thing."

I can't lie. So I keep my gaze on the floor, but then Dominic lifts my chin, making me meet his piercing gaze.

"What's it going to be, Teagan? Am I going to drive you to the club? Or are you going to stay here and spend the night with me? Because I know what I want. I want to bury myself deep inside you and make you remember how good it was between us."

My body tightens at his bold words, but can I take the leap? Can I forget the way this man hurt me and accept the pleasure I can find in his arms again?

The answer is an unequivocal yes.

Before I stop myself, I stand on my tiptoes and throw my arms around his neck. "I want you too, Dominic."

Twenty

Dominic

Finally.

Hearing those words is like music to my ears. I pull Teagan's head back so I can look at her. Her breathing is hard as she gazes up at me through her lashes.

She's finally mine to take however I want.

I crush my mouth to hers.

I've been dreaming about this ever since I first saw her again at the cocktail party, but the reality is so much better. I devour her, invading her mouth with my tongue. She mewls with pleasure and I love it. My mouth is filled with the taste of her.

Teagan quivers in my arms. My hands glide down the satin of her shoulders to her back, bringing her closer to the erection straining against my shorts. We move against each other, kissing and moaning like sex-starved wild things. I know I need to slow things down before it's over too quickly. My lips move from her mouth to brush across her cheek until I find her earlobe and gently close my teeth around the tender flesh. Her breath hisses out and her arms tighten around my nape.

"I think we should move to the bedroom," I say, lifting my head. "Otherwise, I'm going to have you right here."

She smiles up at me. "That's a good idea." She jumps up and wraps her legs tightly around my waist. Then she's pulling my head down so she can kiss me hard. It's heavenly.

I climb the stairs straight to my bedroom, confident and in control. As I set her down in the center of the room filled by my massive California king-size bed, all I see is desire in her eyes. It's real and not going away anytime soon. I reach for the shoulder strap on her tennis dress, eager to see her body, but Teagan stops me.

"How about a shower first," Teagan suggests. "I'm all hot and sweaty."

I don't care. I'll take her any way I can get her, but if it'll make her feel more comfortable, I'm game. I grab the hem of my T-shirt and lift it over my head. When I do, I notice Teagan's eyes darken with appreciation.

"I'd forgotten how ripped you are," she replies unabashedly.

"I aim to please." Toeing off my shoes, I swiftly pull down my shorts and briefs in one fell swoop until I'm standing naked in front of her. She lets out a whoosh when she sees how aroused I am.

"Damn!" She licks her lips. I can't wait for them to be on me.

"Are you going to stand there admiring or am I going to have to undress you myself?"

She shakes her head. "Not at all." She reaches for the straps of her dress and pulls them down, baring her breasts to my gaze. They're round, plump and will fit perfectly in my hand.

I step forward and take one brown nipple into the heat of my mouth before she can finish undressing.

Teagan gasps and stumbles, but my arms tighten to support her so I can lick and suck. Lust shoots through me when she begins chanting my name over and over.

"Dominic… Dominic."

I plant my legs wider so she can settle between them. She rocks back and forth against my dick, and I grind my pelvis harder against her. Her pupils dilate, and there's no denying how much she wants me, shower or no. With her dress at her waist, I push aside her thong until I find her wetness while switching my mouth to her other breast so I can bestow it with the same attention as the first. I nibble, nudge and graze with my teeth while exploring her sex.

"You're so wet for me, Teagan," I say, sliding between her folds.

Her eyes drift closed as I tease her with soft strokes of my finger, back and forth until she says, "More…"

I give it to her by adding a second finger, spreading her wider and thrusting faster, deeper and more rhythmically to the pulsing of her flesh and swelling of her bud. I can tell she's close because she's stretching her legs wide and riding my hand. My dick is so hard it hurts, but I grit my teeth as my heart hammers in my chest. I want to be buried deep inside her as she comes, but I want to give her this. Her body arches and bows against my hand as I play her like a maestro with my fingers.

As the sensations take over, she screams and her body goes taut until she's shaking in my arms.

"Oh, god!" she breathes. A sigh of satisfaction escapes her lips. "I think I needed that."

I needed it too. I like Teagan stripped of all the essentials. She's naked, hot and ready to explore this sexual hunger between us. The sooner we can sate it, the sooner I can move on with my life. Maybe settle down one day. There's just something about Teagan that draws me to her. I relish sparring with her and waiting for her pithy comebacks.

Now she looks down at my still-hard dick. She reaches for me, but I shake my head. If she so much as touches me right now, I'm going to come.

"How about that shower?"

She smiles. "My thoughts exactly."

Twenty-One

Teagan

I shimmy the rest of my tennis dress and thong off until I'm as naked as Dominic. I grab his hand as he leads me into his large en suite bathroom. The massive rainfall shower has overhead sprays and wall units. He turns on the taps. While the water is heating up, he brings his mouth down over mine, pulling me into a drugging kiss.

I'm still dizzy with pleasure after that incredible orgasm he gave me. The thrill of his touch undid me.

Logically, having sex with Dominic might not be the best decision, but when have I ever been rational when it comes to him? He's always pushed my buttons and vice versa.

We part long enough for Dominic to pull me into the shower. The water cascades over us, and he reaches for the bodywash. He pours a generous amount into his large hands before placing them on my shoulders, back, arms and breasts. He works his way lower across my ass, caressing every curve as he goes, until he can slip between my thighs. I cover his hand with mine as his fingers work their indelible magic. I lean backward against the cold tiles while my body heats up to a fever pitch.

We make love to each other with our mouths while Dominic brings me to a second swift orgasm. He soothes me by giving my pussy a light tap, but that merely makes me ready for more. I reach for the soap bottle and get a generous dollop so I can wash and caress him. My hands slide up and down his broad shoulders, across his wide chest with whorls of dark hair and rock-hard abdomen. His hands go still as I pay homage to his body. I add more soap to my hands and kneel so I can wash his butt, thighs and legs, but not the part I'm aching to taste. His dick is proud and erect and waiting for my mouth.

When I finally place my soapy fingers over his erection, he lets out a low growl and swells even larger. I gently stroke him up and down until he's all clean. Glancing up, I see Dominic's eyes are aflame.

"You don't have to…" he starts to say, but I bend my head and lightly stroke him with my tongue.

"Don't play," he warns.

I chuckle softly and open my mouth wide to accept all his thick and hard dick. His thighs become rigid as I slowly bob my head up and down his length. His hands run through my short hair, not to stop me, but to encourage me. My grip becomes firmer. Faster.

"Teagan…" I hear his barely leashed groans as his pelvis pistons. I grab hold of his thighs and take him as deep as I can without gagging. My eyes water as his hands grasp my head and he keeps me where he wants me, fucking my mouth. I hear his hoarse cry as he gives up control, giving me everything, coming down my throat.

Afterward, he pulls me to my feet and leans sideways against the tiled wall, letting water sluice over him. His breathing is deep and rapid as he seeks to recover. I lick my lips, taking in every salty drop of him.

"Taste good?" He looks at me with rueful eyes.

I nod, punch-drunk because I don't give head to just any man. They have to be special, and Dominic has always held a unique spot in my heart.

"I think we're clean enough," he states, and turns off the taps. Before I know it, he's picking me up and grabbing a towel off the rack. Within seconds, he's dropping me down on his bed, dripping wet.

I scramble away, but he catches me and takes great pains to dry me off. I'm aching with desire, and Dominic knows it. He tosses the towel away and claims my mouth in a probing kiss. My back presses against the pillows as I take all his warm weight on top of me.

It's been twelve long years since I've felt Dominic, and I'm starving with the need to be fed. His hands and mouth roam the entire length of my body, worshipping and arousing me with equal measure. Eventually, his widespread hands move firmly up my calves to my knees and then thighs to bring himself to my core.

"I need a taste, Teagan. I can't wait. I have to…" Then Dominic buries himself between my legs.

I didn't realize I was holding my breath, but I am. The first lick of his tongue makes me want to scream, not in agony, but in pleasure. He's gentle at first, but then gradually increases the pressure and the pace. He hooks my legs over his shoulders and settles between them so he can eat me out. When I buck, he places a hand on my abdomen and the other lifts my buttocks until I'm completely at his mercy. All I can do is lie there and take all the heady delight he's delivering with his mouth and tongue.

Tension rises and I can feel myself reach the edge. My focus slips away until there's nothing but the firm stroke of his tongue, the suck of his lips, the nip of his teeth and the grip of his fingers on my hips as he takes everything, allowing me to hold nothing back. The edges of my vision darken and I can only see him, *feel him.*

"Don't fight it. Give in and let go," Dominic orders. "I want to taste you."

And I do. I buck and scream, crying aloud as sensation after sensation hits me. Dominic keeps sucking me until my body becomes rigid and I lie limp.

When I open my eyes, I find myself draped across Dominic's tall frame. Our legs are intertwined.

"Hey." He pushes away the damp hair on my forehead. "You okay?"

I nod. I don't think I've ever come that hard in my entire life except maybe with him, only him.

"Yeah, just need a rest from the day and your voraciousness." He smiles. "Are you complaining?"

"Hell no. I believe that was only the appetizer and I'm waiting for the entrée." I spread my hands across his chest. When I do so, his dick springs to attention as if it too was waiting for the main event.

"Well then." His head motions to his nightstand. There are several magnum-sized condoms lying on top. "How about you take one of those and let's finish what we started?"

"With pleasure." I reach for one and use my teeth to open it. Then I slide the protection over his swollen dick.

"Are you ready to ride me?"

I nod wholeheartedly and sit up so I can straddle him, lowering myself onto his hard length. My body welcomes him, accepting him without fear, reluctance or pretense, like it knows this was meant to be. The moment of physical connection is so strong, yet tender, it takes my breath away. I feel so full, so full of *him*.

I come alive and roll my hips experimentally.

"Yes…" Dominic moans underneath me. He grasps my head and his mouth fastens on mine, his tongue searching. Flames of desire shoot over my skin. I need more.

I lift and take him deeper. My senses reel at the impact of being with this man. I try to control my breath, my movements, but Dominic's hands grip my waist and move me while simultaneously thrusting deeper, higher, harder, faster. I jerk my hips to keep up with his rhythm. He cups my nipples, first one and then the other, pinching them until shards of pleasure reach my groin. I'm hovering on the edge of a precipitous cliff, but I'm powerless to stay away.

Instead, I crash headlong into the waves below and find myself carried into a state of bliss. I hear Dominic's roars of pleasure as he pumps into me. I fall forward into his arms and he catches me, gathering me close as tremors shake us both.

When we're both lax, he eases away and disposes of the condom. Then he returns and cocoons me in his arms. I know we can't stay like this forever, but in an alternate universe, we could.

I awaken with a start. It's dark out and at first I don't recognize my surroundings. Then I look over and see Dominic's sleeping figure. Jesus, what have I done?

Had the best sex of your life?

No, no, no, I've made a complicated situation worse by going to bed with Dominic. He's supposed to be enemy number one. Instead, my brain is muddled. I can't think straight. I need to get out of here so I can figure out how best to proceed, but how am I supposed to do that? Dominic drove me to his place. My car is still back at the club. Worse yet, I don't have anything to wear other than a sullied tennis dress from yesterday.

He has to have something I can put on.

Slowly, I edge myself out of his grasp and off the bed. I glance down and he's still sleeping soundly, which means I can make a clean getaway without any messy morning-after feelings or regret. I look around for my dress and find it, along with my thong from last night. Picking them up from the floor, I head to what appears to be Dominic's closet. I tiptoe inside and close the door. I turn on the lights and quickly find a pair of joggers and a T-shirt. Both are too big, and I have to tie the T-shirt in a knot at my waist and roll up the joggers to my ankles. When I'm done, I ease out and pray Dominic hasn't awakened.

Thank the lord, he's still sound asleep.

Quietly, I make my way out of his bedroom and downstairs to the living room where I left my bag. My cell phone is still sitting on the coffee table and thankfully has enough juice to call a rideshare. I pray for a quick departure. Luckily, a car is only five minutes out. I wait until the absolute last minute before rushing out the door. The chime jingles announcing the front door is open, and I quickly shut the door and race to the gates. There's a side door, which I use to exit, and I hop inside the car waiting for me.

I don't dare look behind me because I'm certain if Dominic wasn't awake before, he is now. He won't be happy about my abrupt departure. I know it's unfair, but last night was a revelation for me. I need time to sort through my emotions before I can deal with his.

One thing is for certain: fallout is sure to follow.

Twenty-Two

Dominic

As I sit here going over my finances with my accountant, Peter Jordan, my mind drifts back to when Teagan sneaked out of my house in the wee hours of the morning. I awoke to the chime of the door alarm. In my haste to be with Teagan, I'd forgotten to set the house alarm, but I guess that was a good thing because it gave Teagan the chance to sneak out without bothering to say goodbye or offering a thank-you for the multiple orgasms.

Am I a little bitter? Hell yeah!

I'd hoped after we both let down our guards and acknowledged our attraction to each other, she would spend the entire night and morning in my bed.

I was wrong.

She couldn't get away fast enough and that infuriates me. She's always saying I took off when the going got tough, but she did the exact same thing. I'm not perfect, but I can admit the truth when it's staring me in the face. We're not over yet—

not by a long shot. She can run away all she likes, but this thing pulsing between us isn't going to die out after one fuck.

One incredible fuck.

"Dominic?"

I blink Peter into focus. "Pardon, what did you say?"

Peter chuckles. "I know numbers aren't very exciting, but you did call this meeting. You wanted to know how much capital you could invest in your brother's venture."

"That's correct."

"I would suggest setting up a corporation or limited liability company to protect you personally from any liability," Peter says, "but otherwise, you're liquid enough to supply a sizable investment. But it's still risky with a start-up company."

"True, but Justice is family."

"Which is why I never recommend loaning to family." When I start to speak, Peter holds up his hand. "But be that as it may, a fifty-fifty split would be in your best interests. Give you more say in what's happening."

"Noted. How soon before we can cut a check?"

"As soon as the ink is dry on the agreement," Peter responds.

"Excellent." I rise to my feet. I'm excited to have the means to help Justice achieve his dreams. My entire family has shown their personal support for me all these years, coming to my matches. It's the least I can do to help my little brother fulfill his destiny.

I leave Peter's office feeling hyped. It's the first time in a long time I've been excited about something other than being with Teagan. I do get a certain amount of satisfaction from supporting and participating in several charities, but lately I've been needing more to make me want to get out of bed each morning. I need a new fire in my belly, and helping Justice get his business off the ground is a great start.

I call my brother and give him the good news.

"You're really in?" Justice asks.

"Yes," I respond. "I'm ready to see this idea come to fruition."

"Thanks, Dom. Your trust and faith in me is everything," Justice replies. "And I have my first client. Remember the runner I talked with at Bliss's meet?"

"Yeah, what about her?"

"She and her family are interested in signing up with my agency. Her coach thinks she has Olympic potential, and who knows? With the right representation, I might help get her there by getting them money for coaching, travel and entry fees into various competitions."

"Sounds great. I look forward to hearing more. My lawyer will be drafting up an agreement outlining the investment. But you should have your own lawyer review it as well."

"Already on it. A friend of mine from college is a contracts attorney and will review it for free. I look forward to receiving it," Justice replies.

"Let's celebrate with drinks once it's signed."

"Deal."

I end the call, feeling good, but there's one thing still hanging over my head.

Teagan.

After she left, I thought about not reaching out; she left and obviously didn't want to revisit our night together. However, the next day I worried about her knee and wanted to make sure she was all right, so I texted her. I needn't have bothered.

Me: How are you? How's your knee doing?

Teagan: Good. The knee is fine. Dr. Maverick called to check on me.

Me: Glad to hear it.

I hoped for something more after my response, but got nothing. It's not every day you sleep with your ex from twelve years ago and she has nothing to say. Her cavalier attitude irks me. I intend to call her out on it, so I decide to do a little digging of my own. Over the years, I've kept my distance, never checking to see what happened to Teagan even though I yearned to do so. But I had to cut her out, exorcise her from my life, in order to keep my head in the game and my eye on the prize of supporting my family.

But now? I've achieved what I needed to achieve. I can have some time for myself. Maybe have a committed relationship one day. Perhaps even a family. In another lifetime that family might have been with Teagan.

I want to give her a piece of my mind, but I don't chase after women. Never have, and I'm not about to start now.

Teagan and I are doubles partners for this tournament, and she won't be able to avoid me for long. We need to practice this weekend because time is running out. If Teagan knows what's good for her, she'll show on Saturday for another session. And when she does, I'll make sure she pays for walking out on me.

Twenty-Three

Teagan

I've been grappling with what took place between me and Dominic. It's been nearly a week and I have no answers.

It's crazy the effect he has on me. I've tried to keep this all inside, but then I receive an SOS call from Wynter requesting a FaceTime with the Gems ASAP. I drop what I'm doing at the office and close my door to find out what's going on.

Soon, all five women's faces pop onto my phone. Lyric is in the studio. Egypt's in her chef's coat in the kitchen. Shay is in a complex pose at her studio while Asia's background indicates she's at the jewelry store. It's so great to see all the women at work, except Wynter. There are tears in her eyes.

"Wynter, what's wrong?" I don't like seeing any of the Gems upset.

"I'M PREGNANT!" she announces with a smile, and then holds up the pregnancy stick showing two blue lines.

A chorus of congratulations echoes on the phone. "That's

wonderful, Wynter," I say. "I'm so happy for you. I know how much you and Riley wanted this."

"We did," she replies, grinning from ear to ear. "And we've thoroughly enjoyed trying for this baby."

"I bet." Egypt winks into the camera. "Y'all was getting yer freak on. How long has it been?"

"A few months," Asia responds on Wynter's behalf, "but it only takes one good swimmer to hit the mark. If you recall, that's how Blake and I ended up with Ryan."

"Oh, we remember." I laugh. Asia didn't have a clue she was preggers until Wynter's bachelorette trip to Vegas. I knew something was suspicious when she wasn't drinking. "Do you know how far along you are?"

"Six weeks," Wynter replies. "I know I should have kept it to myself until I'm out of the first trimester, but I couldn't. You're my family."

Wynter's comment makes me feel loved, and then terrible. I haven't told any of the Gems I slept with Dominic days ago. Maybe if I tell my truth now, they can help me make sense of what's happening.

"I slept with Dominic!" I blurt out unceremoniously.

"Excuse me?" Asia asks.

Egypt narrows her eyes. "When?"

"On Sunday."

"Sunday?" Lyric exclaims. She starts counting on her fingers. "That was five days ago."

"I'm sorry." I lower my head. "And I'm sorry, Wynter, for stealing your thunder."

Wynter chuckles softly. "Oh, girl, I couldn't care less. You best spill the tea before the rest of the Gems cut you."

Her comment makes me laugh. Only these women can make me feel better without even trying.

"Well, what had happened was…the tournament decided to do doubles, and Dominic and I were paired. The game got heated. He was kicking my ass and I tried to make a comeback and found myself sprawled on the hard court. He jumped over that net so fast and before I knew it, I was in his arms and he was taking me to a doctor at his place. After the doctor left, well, sparks flew and…"

"The panties went flying?" Egypt offers.

"Something like," I respond. "The next morning, I snuck out of his bed, and I haven't seen him since. Tomorrow, we're supposed to practice."

"You left good dick?" Asia inquires. "Why on earth would you do a thing like that?"

"Because I'm confused. I don't know how I ended up here."

"Yes, you do," Shay jumps in. "I'm going to say what everyone else won't. You ended up in Dominic's bed because you've never dealt with your breakup. So much was left unsaid between you. You have unfinished business. But until you talk it out, fuck it out or whatever, you'll still feel unsettled."

I stare at Shay in disbelief. I expect Egypt or Asia to give me such a forthcoming speech, but not Shay. She's usually more laid-back.

"Well, I declare," Wynter states, fanning herself. "Who knew your one-night stand would cause such heated debate. But I'm with Shay, Teagan. You owe it to yourself to find out how you really feel about Dominic."

"I know how I feel," I snap back. "I hate him."

Egypt snorts. "Hate and love are the opposite sides of the same coin. You need to talk to the man. Clear the air."

"What will that solve? It won't change things. He still left me," I respond.

"You pushed him away too," Lyric says quietly.

I glare at Lyric through the phone, but she doesn't look away. She stares right back at me. Ever since she's been with Devon, she's found her voice, and I respect that. "I hear you," I respond.

"So you'll talk to him?" Asia inquires. "Who knows, you might find you can meet somewhere in the middle. And guess what? You'll have good dick in the process."

I roll my eyes. "I can't with you, Asia." But all she does is smile knowingly with a got-you look. "I appreciate all your advice and I'll take it to heart. And Wynter, I couldn't be happier for you and Riley. I love you."

I end the call and lean back in my chair. The Gems think I should hash it out with Dominic, but will he talk to me after the unceremonious way I left? I haven't spoken to him all week. He at least had the decency to check in on me to make sure I was all right, but what did I do? Nothing.

He probably hates me.

Or does he?

I can't forget the way he looked when he leaped over that net and rushed to my side. There was genuine concern on his face. Perhaps there's more with Dominic that I need to explore, but I won't know until I talk to him. He probably thinks I'll chicken out and won't show up tomorrow, but I've never been a coward.

Or I'm usually not, except for last week. That was an isolated incident.

I'll face Dominic and accept whatever scorn is coming my way. I've always been much stronger than people give me credit for. I endured all the hate the press dished out and turned it around. I made myself into a business owner, afraid of no one.

I'll do the same this time. Bring it on, Fletcher.

Dominic is already on the court when I arrive the next morning. He's playing with the same partner I'd seen him with last time. From the sweat stains on his shirt, he's been playing awhile. He's focused on the game and doesn't notice me. It gives me time to watch his footwork. He's light on his feet, but not like he used to be. Yet what he lacks in speed, he more than makes up for in his serve and the power behind it. The ball has to be going one hundred thirty miles per hour. It's impressive and I can't help but admire he's only gotten better with age, on and off the court.

Back in the day, he was dynamic and intense. After being sheltered by my father for so long, I wasn't prepared for the impact of him. He changed me, and I don't know if I've ever been the same. As if he senses me, he pauses and turns around to face me. The censure I see lurking in his eyes might make other people cower with fear, but I know Dominic. I know how to get to him.

I walk toward him. "Good morning," I say breezily, and slip past him to the other side.

His mouth quirks as if saying, *Really, that's all you have to say after a week of silence?*

He doesn't return my greeting and instead turns to his partner. "Thanks for coming in so early. I needed to work out a few things."

"I always love playing with you," the young man replies before sauntering off.

I pull out my racket and a tube of balls from my bag and wait for Dominic to rail at me. When he doesn't, I'm surprised.

"You ready to play?" Dominic asks.

I nod. "Yes."

"Let's do it!"

The rest of the morning, our games go well. I'm slowly starting to match his pace, but definitely not his stamina. We take a break after each game so I can catch my breath and grab a swig of smartwater. Instead of taunting me like he did last week, Dominic is decidedly measured. I miss the way he was before, all fire and spirit. It's how we've always been together. I don't like this version of him. He's clearly watching me from across the court, but not speaking.

I didn't come to the court dressed for attention like I did last week. Today I'm in a simple lightweight, high-rise tennis skirt and tank top. To get a reaction out of Dominic, I pull the tank over my head to reveal a collared longline bra with open back and a deep V underneath. When I do, Dominic's eyes damn near jump out of his sockets. Something passes through his eyes that I don't recognize and before I realize what he's done, he's ripped his shirt off and tossed it to the ground to reveal his bare chest.

My mouth waters. His pectorals and abdomen are chiseled, showing off his eight-pack. I'm certain someone from the club will say something about him being shirtless, but will they? It's Dominic Fletcher.

"I believe it's my serve," Dominic states, and this time he volleys.

He's got me on the run and he knows it. I chase it down and lob the ball over his head to the back court. He retrieves it and continues our rally, firing balls at me from all angles. I have no choice but to adapt. He's definitely getting me back for last week. I'm running all over the court.

When it's my turn to serve, I hit an ace, serving the ball down the court. He hits the ball short on the return. I want to cheer that I finally got something past him, but my joy is short-lived because he gives it to me tenfold until I eventually tire.

"Are we done here?" Dominic asks after we've played the requisite number of games.

"No," I respond, lifting my breasts. When I do, I notice his eyes catch the movement. "Are you ready to give up?"

"I'm not the one who ran last week," he states, turning his back on me.

Finally. He's not the automaton he's been all morning. He's upset about how I left; we're getting somewhere. He picks up his T-shirt and puts it over his head. I hear several women sigh and glance behind me to see once again we have an audience watching our every move.

"I'm not the only one who leaves," I respond hotly. "If I recall, your career was important and you said you weren't going to let anything stop you from getting to the top." I recite a line I'll never forget reading in one of his interviews after my epic meltdown was caught on-air.

He spins around, his eyes shuttered as if I've mortally wounded him.

I want to take back the words. "Dominic…"

"Not here…" he growls, and shuts me out by turning his back and walking away.

I grab my bag, about to follow him, when Charity comes onto the court. "Teagan, it's so good to see you back on your feet. I was afraid you might have gotten injured after last week's tumble, especially with the way Dominic reacted. But now—" she glances at his retreating figure "—you're back. Is everything copacetic between you two for the doubles tournament?"

"Yes, it is. Thanks, Charity, for checking in on me." I give her arm a squeeze and push my way through the crowd of onlookers and toward the locker rooms. Once I've showered and dressed, I head to the valet. "Has Mr. Fletcher left?"

"I'm sorry, ma'am, he has. But he often comes to practice on Sunday mornings. You might catch him then."

"Thank you."

As I climb into my Mercedes, I feel defeated. I was going to take the Gems' advice and talk to Dominic, but I couldn't resist getting in one last jab. Why does he bring out the worst in me?

Should I go to his house? And say what?

I thought once I saw him today, I would know what to say, but I don't. I only know how to spar, argue and get under his skin.

There's a part of me that wants to return to the moment when he held me in his arms as if I was something special, something to be treasured. No one has ever made me feel that way except him. When the world turned against me after my public downfall, I felt adrift. I learned the hard way, amid sneers and jeers, that I had to love myself because no one else would. I picked myself up, dusted myself off and reinvented myself.

A part of me says I don't need Dominic. Yet there's another side who still wants him. I don't know how to make both halves fit.

I'm so deep in my thoughts that I don't notice Dominic's Bentley sitting outside my house until I pull up next to him.

How did he get my private and unlisted address?

He's Dominic Fletcher. He probably has people who can find out confidential information.

Slowly, I exit the vehicle. "What are you doing here?"

"It's time we talk, don't you think?" he inquires. "Or would you rather have our private lives be fodder for the public again?"

I roll my eyes and don't answer. Instead, I stride to the front door and punch in a code. I open the door and he steps into my abode. After turning off the alarm, I walk to the kitchen. All of a sudden, I'm very thirsty—or maybe it's the fact that Dominic looks all kinds of delicious dressed casually in jeans and a black button-down with the sleeves rolled up. I make for the fridge. Pulling out a Fiji, I drink the entire bottle and then turn to face him.

"I didn't leave you," Dominic states.

I sigh. "Do we have to relive the past?"

"If you're going to throw it in my face every time you get a chance, then yeah," Dominic says.

"We're going to have to agree to disagree."

"You pushed me away!" Dominic asserts. "You were in your hospital room and you told me to go, that you didn't need me."

"And you listened to me?" I ask incredulously. "I was hurting. I'd just lost everything."

"Of course I didn't. I understood that, but..."

"But what?" I press, wanting to know what he was going to say.

"Does it matter?" Dominic states, skirting the topic. "You're determined to think the worst of me. After everything we meant to each other, how can you think that? I *loved* you."

His words are like daggers to my heart. *Loved*, past tense.

Is it possible I love him still?

Is that why I'm struggling with all these feelings?

"I'm sorry," I say. "I was messed up. My father made me feel as if tennis was my entire life, that I had nothing to offer anyone without it. My entire psyche was wrapped up in that identity and I didn't know how to cope without tennis, without you." My admission is pulled from my inner depths and I lower my head. Tears roll down my cheeks. "And then I see you going on to do great things like win multiple Grand Slams. It broke me. You broke me."

When I glance up, Dominic is in front of me. He tips my chin up so I meet his gaze. "I didn't want that then and I don't want that now, Teagan. Do you think any of this is easy for me? Seeing you again has stirred up a hornet's nest I'm not sure what to do with."

"So what do you suggest?"

"I don't know, maybe see where this goes?"

I sigh. "I was crucified in the press and everyone at the club is already interested in our sessions. It's only going to get worse as the tournament draws near."

"So we stay away from each other?" Dominic inquires. "That hasn't worked out too well for us, has it?"

I shake my head. "I don't suppose it has, but if we do this, it would have to be low-key. Perhaps we need to get whatever *this* is out of our systems until it fizzles out, like it probably would have years ago." I don't know if I believe that, but I have to preserve some dignity.

A smile spreads across Dominic's dark features. "If that's

what you want, then I'm down." His arm encircles my waist and pulls me closer.

"Me too."

Seconds later our mouths are hot and fused together. My fingers attack the buttons on his shirt. I all but rip the garment from his body, tugging it down his muscled arms. Eager and needy, my fingers make contact with the familiar hair covering his chest, and his own impatient fingers tug at the hem of my cotton T-shirt. We break our kiss long enough for him to strip the fabric from my body. Then he's unclasping the front of my bra, freeing my breasts, full and firm. His gaze is bold, brazen, then he takes possession of my breasts with his open mouth.

He lifts me off my feet and places me on the large island. I reach for the snap on his jeans. Once it gives way, I begin an urgent attempt to lower the zipper. He beats me to the punch, pushing his jeans down his thighs and shucking them and his boxers off, but not before producing a condom.

"You just happened to come with one of those?" I ask as he dons the protection.

"Not one, but several," he replies. "It pays to be prepared."

He pulls me to the edge of the counter and enters me in a swift, firm thrust. I gasp as he pushes his way inside, filling me inch by delicious inch. I wrap my legs around him and his palms grip my waist, allowing him to control the movement. My nails scrape down the hard muscles of his back and he melts me from inside with each hard stroke. He reaches between us to find the swollen flesh of my clitoris, then places his thumb on my nub and makes slow, lazy circles until my eyes glaze over and I scream out his name.

But he's not done yet. He grabs ahold of me, walks us a

few steps to the nearest wall and rests my back against it. His eyes are heavy-lidded with desire. He seals his mouth to mine again and slides me down to go fully inside me again. His movements are slow, but I want more and rock my hips. He increases the pace. It doesn't seem possible that I can be chasing another orgasm, but I am. I grab his shoulders and fling my head back. Dominic nestles his face between my breasts and nibbles.

"Yes…yes…" I'm so close to another mind-bending orgasm, but I want him here with me.

I tighten my legs around his waist and buck in his arms. He captures my lips then slides his tongue in and out, mimicking our bodies. I can feel his release building too. Just as my entire body stiffens, his climax strikes and he thrusts into me one final time. We clutch each other for several long moments until I'm limp. Somehow Dominic keeps me upright until he can swing me into his arms.

"Where's the bedroom?"

"First door to the left," I murmur as I surrender to the inevitable.

Dominic and I are lovers again.

Twenty-Four

Dominic

I didn't expect to find myself in Teagan's bed. But I'm happy the passion that exploded between us a week ago was no fluke. The fire burns as hot as it did when we were younger. Maybe more so now because we know what we want and how we want it. Teagan is more vocal. She's a grown-ass woman in full control of her sexuality, and it's a turn-on. I love her self-confidence.

We spent the rest of yesterday in bed pleasing each other. It was thrilling, but exhausting. We fell asleep somewhere around dawn, and I'm just now waking up. The clock on her nightstand reads 10:00 a.m. When was the last time I slept in like this? Even though I've been on hiatus, my body's alarm wakes me up around 5:00 a.m. telling me it's time to shower and get on the court. But today? I'm so content lying in her arms that I've lost track of time.

Teagan looks peaceful and utterly adorable. The issues that have plagued us about our past don't seem quite so insurmountable when she's in repose, but I know this truce won't last. This is an illusion, a moment out of time, until reality comes knocking at our door. The tournament will be over soon and I'll have to go back on the tour circuit. Meanwhile, Teagan will return to her life.

The media has no idea about our renewed interest in one another, and she wants to keep it that way. I wince, recalling again that she blames me for not standing by her after the shitstorm when she accosted me at the US Open twelve years ago and lambasted me in front of everyone for leaving her. Neither of us had any idea my mic was still on after giving an interview earlier that afternoon. Teagan lit into me for being a liar and insincere about my feelings.

She said I never loved her, which wasn't true. It's because I loved her that I walked away and listened to her father. And she let me. Teagan didn't fight for me either, yet she puts the blame all on me. She doesn't know what her father did. I'm not about to tell her and blow up her world. That's why what's between us now can be nothing more than a temporary ceasefire.

But until it's over I'll enjoy every moment.

Later that afternoon, after another round of erotic sex that's sometimes slow and other times fast and hard, we make our way downstairs to her kitchen, where I watch Teagan's skills behind the stove.

"If I recall," I say, perching myself atop one of her tufted bar stools in my jeans, "you didn't even know how to boil an egg."

Teagan laughs. "I remember that. I tried making you some protein and the eggs were still runny."

"Yeah, I couldn't even fake eating them no matter how much I tried," I respond. "When did you learn how to cook?"

"After everything went down, I was in a bad place. I didn't know where I was going and spent a couple of months with Egypt after she finished culinary school. She cooked for me and—" she flips over a vegetable omelet in the small skillet with little to no effort "—I learned some basics." She sprinkles some cheese over the top, folds the omelet in half, then slides it on the plate in front of me.

"This looks delicious," I say.

"Why, thank you," Teagan says with a flourish and a bow. Her silk robe drapes open, giving me a tantalizing view of her round, pert breasts. I can't wait to have them in my mouth. In the meantime, she rises and heads back to the stove to finish making her omelet. Once hers is done, she joins me at the bar, but I've already demolished mine.

She chuckles as she tucks into her meal. "Someone was really hungry."

"Because someone wore me out," I reply, "but I'm not complaining. Now that I'm refueled, I'm ready for round two."

"As much as I appreciate your enthusiasm, perhaps we could find another way to burn some energy."

My eyebrows quirk. "I'm listening."

"Get your mind out of the gutter, Dominic. I thought we could play. As you've said on multiple occasions, I need practice if we're going to win doubles at the tournament."

"We'll win," I state confidently.

"That's easy for you to say," Teagan replies. "You never stopped playing. I did."

"Why? You loved the game." I remember the times Teagan practiced for hours before and after training sessions.

"Loved," she responds, "past tense. Once I could no longer compete, I couldn't bear to play or watch a game."

"And now?"

"I'm remembering how much I enjoyed it, how it kept me on my toes, how alert I have to be to react to my opponent. I didn't realize how much I missed having tennis in my life."

I'm pleased and give her a broad smile. "I'm happy to hear that. You were and *are* a gifted player. Don't let anyone stop you from pursuing your passion."

"What about you? Do you still love the game like you once did?"

"I do, but it's evolved over the years. I still love the sport, but I feel as if there has to be something more for me. For so long, my life has revolved around tennis. I need another outlet. I have my own clothing line and that's been fun, but the thing that's brought me the most joy off the court has been starting my own not-for-profit organization, Fletcher Cares."

"But…"

How can she know there's a *but*? We haven't been together in years. Yet somehow Teagan has always been able to read me.

"I need other challenges. I suppose it's why I've agreed to support Justice in his new venture. He wants to run his own sports management business to help junior and college players who don't get the same access to resources like we professionals do."

"I love that idea, Dominic!" Teagan sounds as enthused as I do. "And here I thought you were just a pretty face." She strokes my jaw. The gesture is light and teasing, but I feel connected to her, like I used to when we were together.

I push down the nostalgia and pull her out of her seat and in between my legs. She comes willingly, and I lean forward to kiss her neck. Her head lolls backward, giving me greater access, and I suck on her sensitive spot. Her knees seem to weaken, but I hold her up, circling my arms around her waist and bringing her closer to my mouth.

Teagan moans and I push aside the silk robe to reveal one of her delicate shoulders. I lightly nip at the skin and she cries out, clutching my thighs. If I don't stop this now, we'll be back in bed and not at the court, which is what Teagan wants. I force myself to pull back and when I do, she's shocked. I'm surprised too, but I am capable of putting my needs on hold to help her.

"You wanted to practice," I say. "If I don't stop now, you'll be on this countertop."

A blush creeps up her face and I can see her remembering how I devoured her on this very surface.

"I think that's a good idea," she says. "Let's go."

Getting this opportunity with Teagan to bring closure to our past is unexpected, but now that it's here, I don't intend to waste a single minute.

I hope the truth about why I really walked away from her never comes out.

Twenty-Five

Teagan

I don't know if it's regularly being back on the court or whether it's being back in Dominic's bed again, but the last few weeks with him have been idyllic. We've spent every night together. I'm enjoying all of it because I know this won't last. As soon as the tournament is over, Dominic will go back to his life and I'll go back to mine.

Sometimes I waffle. Getting involved with him again isn't the best idea. It'll be hard to get over him, just like it was all those years ago. Then my mind tells me, no, this is closure. When it's over, I can move forward with someone else, someone who wants to be in a committed and loving relationship. And who knows, maybe I'll end up down the aisle like some of the Gems?

We've tried to dial back the heat and passion between us at the country club, but it's hard. Dominic and I are passionate players. However, we both agreed to keep our relationship undercover because the last thing I want is for the press to get a whiff we're back together. The problem in the past, Daddy used to say, is that I play with too much heart, but that's my style and I doubt it's going to change. I'll keep my composure today on the court as much as I can, but that will be hard because Dominic was deep inside me just hours ago.

We drive separately to the club for an extra Monday session because we don't want anyone to get the idea we're together. However, we're still drawing attention. Bystanders consistently form a crowd around my favorite court, number seven. I guess word has gotten out, and people want to see Dominic play on the weekends. I nod at several folks as I walk onto the court. Dominic is already there.

How does he manage to beat me every time? He has to be as exhausted as I am after that marathon session in bed.

"Good morning." He smiles knowingly from across the net.

"Morning," I respond.

"You ready for a workout?" he asks.

"Are you? Because I'm raring to go." We've come to the court on random weekday afternoons when everyone is getting off work and gotten in some extra games to ensure I won't embarrass myself as Dominic's partner in the tournament.

Dominic gets into position in the back court. "Ready whenever you are."

An hour later, after another intense game, Dominic comes over and shakes my hand. We have an audience so we play it cool. "Good game. You're improving."

"Thanks to you."

He doesn't release my hand. "No, it's because of you and your innate ability. This is a refresher course, nothing more. Okay?" When I nod, he lets go.

"So, what are you doing later?" I ask.

"I'm meeting Justice. The lawyers have drawn up the documents and are ready for us to sign."

"Good luck. I know how much this means to you both."

He gives me a dazzling smile. "Thank you. I'll call you later." He turns on his heel and walks away. I will myself not to watch. It's hard, but I do it. If for nothing else than to test myself, prove that I can endure him leaving because there will come a point one day soon that he will.

After a quick shower and change of clothes, I hop in my Benz and drive to my office. I'm feeling good until my display reads "Dad."

My father doesn't often call. I've been a disappointment to him since I didn't live up to my full potential. I press the talk button. "Hey, Daddy."

"What's this I hear about you playing tennis with that Fletcher boy again?" he asks, no preamble. And how did he find out? Does he have spies or something?

When I'm silent, he asks again, "Well? I'm waiting, young lady."

I don't owe him an explanation. I'm a grown woman and I can do what I want. So why do I feel as if I've done something wrong? "What about it?"

"So you admit to seeing him again?"

"Yes."

Why is Daddy harping on Dominic? I know he was never a fan, but that was twelve years ago. Is he harboring resentment toward Dominic because of how he treated me?

"He's headlining the Desert Smash tournament," I answer. "And somehow I was talked into doing a doubles match with him. It'll be fine."

"I don't think so," my father responds. "Do you remember

how devastated you were? He abandoned you and left you to face all that bad press."

"Do we have to talk about this, Daddy? It's in the past." Where I want to keep it. Hearing all this negativity after Dominic and I have been intimate again is too much. It's not like I can forget what happened. I've chosen to move on so I can have the pleasure I've found in Dominic's arms, if only for a short time.

"Those who forget the past are destined to repeat it."

"I'm not a young ingenue player on the cusp of stardom. I'm a real estate agent, Daddy. No one cares what I'm up to."

"He's a Grand Slam champion, Teagan. The press will always be sniffing around him, and if you're playing tennis again, let alone with him, it's bound to get picked up. What then? I won't be able to come to your rescue."

"I don't need you to, Daddy. I'm perfectly capable of standing on my own two feet. I can look after myself." I was nineteen back then and completely crushed by losing my career and my man at the same time, but I'm not that young woman anymore. I'm stronger.

"That's good to hear, but I'm warning you about that man. He's not to be trusted, Teagan. Don't listen to him or believe a word he says, you hear me?"

I know not to argue with my father and I reply, "Yes, Daddy." However, I'm curious why he's so adamant I stay away from Dominic.

Does he know something I don't?

And if so, what is it? What is he hiding?

"Good girl," he responds. "When are you coming over for dinner? Your mother and I haven't seen you in weeks."

"I've been busy, Daddy."

Busy in bed with Dominic, the man he wants me to stay away from.

"Too busy for your parents? That's nonsense. We'll see you next Sunday."

I sigh in defeat. When he gets into one of his dictator moods, nothing I say will appease him. "Okay. I'll be there."

I end the call before he can make any further demands. I should be used to his behavior, but I'm not. I would give anything to have a normal father-daughter relationship. I guess that's not possible considering he acted as both my coach and my agent for so many years. It skewed how we talk to each other, and even though I'm no longer playing, our relationship never returned to something resembling normalcy. I doubt it was ever possible really because with my father, it's his way or the highway.

When I make it to the office, Amanda greets me. "Good morning, Teagan."

"Good morning. How are you? How's your mom doing?" Amanda's mother has been in chemotherapy and it has taken a toll on the young woman. I sent over a care package as well as had some healthy dinners delivered.

"I'm okay. Mom is hanging in there. She's truly appreciative of everything you've sent. They've gone a long way. Some scented bodywash, lotions and candles may not seem like much, but after losing her hair it made her feel better."

"I'm so glad." I walk over and give Amanda's shoulder a gentle squeeze. "If there's anything else I can do, let me know."

"You've been more than generous by giving me time off to take her to chemo."

"Anytime."

I head to my office and resolve to give my own mother a

call. I have been a bit preoccupied with Dominic the last couple of weeks and need to do better. When I arrive at my desk, I see Brett has left this month's projections. If we close on the Walther deal and another sale that's dragged for months, the agency will finally be in the black and I can breathe again.

My investment in joining the country club is paying off not only professionally, but also personally. If I hadn't joined, I wouldn't have reconnected with Dominic.

Being with Dominic again has reignited feelings I'd kept undercover. It's forcing me to deal with emotions I hadn't wanted to address all those years ago. I had been on the cusp of womanhood and fell hard. I didn't know how to handle the heartbreak when he didn't feel for me what I felt for him.

What does he feel now?

Lust. Desire. I know he feels those because he's unable to control his physical response to me. His dick gets hard if I'm within a few feet of him. I've been enjoying our sexual encounters, and am not ashamed to admit I'm a slave to this white-hot chemistry between us. But if I'm honest with myself, it's not just the sex. I've gotten to know who Dominic is now. He's not just the GOAT. He's a warm, kind and giving man who cares about his family and has supported them for years. His charity organization, Fletcher Cares, does wonders for the community by helping less fortunate children find their place in the athletic world. Then, I see how he's supporting Justice on a new business venture even though he doesn't know what the outcome will be. He isn't the selfish, spotlight-stealing man I thought him to be. He's so much more.

I'm falling for him all over again.

Houston, we have a problem.

Twenty-Six

Dominic

"Sign here," my attorney, Craig Garrett, says.

Justice and I arrived at Craig's office an hour ago to finalize the partnership paperwork, and I have the check from Peter for the down payment. I know Peter had reservations about me investing such a large sum, but Justice is family. He's always had sound judgment and a good head on his shoulders. Plus I reviewed the prospectus and am confident in his idea and his ability.

However, upon further thought, I did talk to Justice about changing the percentage. If I'm putting up the lion's share of the investment, I should be entitled to 50 percent of the business. Once it begins making a profit, Justice will pay me back 5 percent, allowing him to have majority share. He thought it was fair and agreed to the revised terms. His attorney reviewed the document and Justice's signature is already scrolled on one side of the agreement.

"Will do." I scribble my signature on several pages. When

it's over, I rise to my feet and offer my hand. "Congratulations!"

A grin spreads across my brother's face. "Thanks to you," Justice responds, pulling me into a hug.

"I believe in you and know you can do great things." Once he releases me, I turn to Craig. "Craig, thanks for getting this done so quickly."

"Of course. Anything for one of my favorite clients." Craig smiles.

I laugh. "I bet you say that to all your clients."

"Absolutely not, because I don't bring this…" The door to his office opens and his assistant rolls in a cart carrying a bottle of Dom Pérignon and three glasses. Craig walks over and pops open the bottle. The cork flies into the air, and Justice catches it.

"Nice touch," I say as Craig pours champagne for each of us and hands us each a flute. I hold up mine. "Cheers."

The three of us clink glasses and take sips. I don't bother finishing mine since I'm driving. "You ready to head out?" I ask Justice. He wants to show me the location of the offices of Fletcher Sports Management.

"Yes, sir. Thank you, Mr. Garrett." Justice shakes Craig's hand. "Appreciate you."

Justice and I walk out of the office, and my brother is walking a bit taller and more confidently than I've ever seen him.

"Feeling good?" I ask, placing a reassuring hand on his shoulder.

Justice nods. "You've no idea. I know you agreed, but until the paperwork was signed, I didn't know I was still on edge. It's why I didn't sign the lease at the office building until I was certain it was a sure thing."

"Well, we can do that now."

"That's the plan. You coming with me?"

"Absolutely. I want to share this moment with you," I reply. It feels good to help him achieve his goals. I realize I want to help other people do the same.

We take the elevator down to the garage and hop into our respective vehicles. I follow behind him so he can lead the way to his new office. In the meantime, I dial Teagan.

Ever since we've become lovers again, she and I have spoken or texted every day, like we did all those years ago. There's no reason to act as if we don't want each other. Instead, we take pleasure from each other night after night. It's crazy to think the woman who haunted my dreams is back in my bed, though most times we stay at her house to keep the press off the scent. We've picked up where we left off. It's surreal because I know we haven't addressed the underlying issue between us, which is trust. Instead, I'm burning out whatever this is between us so I can move on with my life.

What life will you have without her?

Since Teagan and I have been together, I haven't felt the discontentment that's plagued me the past year. I'm lighter, happier and not weighed down by expectations and the constant struggle to win and stay on top. Being with her makes me see how life could be after retirement. It makes me want more, maybe a family and children someday. Up until now, I've never allowed myself to think too far into the future. I've focused on my next immediate goal and how to achieve it. Life has always been about the game, and nothing else could rank higher.

Maybe that's not true anymore.

"Hello?" I hear Teagan's voice through the car speaker. "Dominic, are you there?"

"Yeah, yeah," I say. "I've signed the paperwork. It's official. Justice and I are partners in Fletcher Sports Management."

"Congratulations, Dominic. That's wonderful. Justice must be over the moon," Teagan replies. "I remember when I first opened the doors of Williams & Associates, it was a heady feeling."

"He's pretty stoked," I say. "We're on our way to the office building to sign the lease."

"Exciting, isn't it? And after? I thought you might like to do something fun."

"I'm game for anything that includes you out of your clothes."

She chuckles. "Actually, I was thinking we could go roller-skating. You remember how much we used to love it."

"I recall otherwise. You were quite skilled while I could barely manage to stay upright."

"Are you chicken, Dominic Fletcher?"

"Of course not," I respond. "Tell me where and when."

We arrange to meet later that afternoon at a skating rink in her neck of the woods, and I continue behind Justice until eventually he pulls into the surface parking lot of a beautiful office campus with a towering water feature. I park and stand in front of the precast-concrete five-story building in Scotts-dale surrounded by walls of glass panel windows overlooking a retention pond.

Justice walks up beside me and glances up. "Come on. Let me show you inside."

He heads to the double doors and holds one open, allowing me to precede him. The two-story foyer is impressive with its high ceiling, modern furniture, tasteful artwork and sleek dangling chandelier. I follow him to the bank of elevators and he presses the button for the third floor.

Once we arrive, Justice exits and opens the glass doors. He walks me around the large floor plan with bright white walls. It has space for reception, perimeter executive offices, conference and break rooms, and can accommodate a few low cubicles for future sports agents.

"What do you think?"

I glance around the suite. "It's great, Justice. You've thought about everything."

"I have a vision."

I walk over to him and pull him into an embrace. "Yes, you do, and I'm proud of you, bro."

Afterward we discuss meeting up on Sunday at family dinner to tell everyone our good news. Maybe Teagan can join me.

Where did that thought come from?

Teagan is not my girl, though at times I feel like she is. We're supposed to be kicking it and working through this heat between us so we can both move on. So why does my heart say something else? It's not like Teagan has said she wants more. She knows I have to get back to the tour, and whatever *this* is won't go beyond the tournament. That's what I have to focus on. I remind myself it's a casual affair, nothing more. It can't be—not if we can't resolve the issues of the past—because without trust, a relationship won't work.

A couple of hours later, after I've gone home to shower and change, I meet up with Teagan at the roller-skating rink. She has no idea I called ahead. Since it was closed until early evening, I rented it out for the rest of the afternoon. It will be just the two of us.

When I arrive, the manager is there to greet me. "Mr. Fletcher, thank you so much for the business," the young brunette states enthusiastically.

"No, thank *you*. I know it was short notice."

"I'm glad we're able to accommodate you." She grins broadly. "We don't get celebrities of your stature in a place like this."

"Is everything set up like I asked?"

She nods. "I've got Pandora playing your music mix, the strobe lights are going, so all you need is your skates and your girl."

I glance down at my Movado watch. "She should be here any minute." Just as I'm saying the words, Teagan's Mercedes GLE SUV pulls into the empty parking lot.

"I'll be inside," the manager replies, and heads back through the sliding doors.

Teagan gets out of the car and glances around as she approaches wearing jeans and an off-the-shoulder T-shirt. She looks sexy. All I want to do is take her back home and ravish her.

"Perhaps we can't get in. I didn't think it would be closed."

"Naw, it's open." She walks toward me and tips her head back so I can kiss her. She tastes like honey and vanilla and I eagerly explore her lips. She opens to my invading tongue, allowing me entry. I deepen the kiss and within seconds it turns hot and feverish, tongue sliding against tongue.

It's Teagan who puts her hand on my chest and pushes me away. "Dominic. We're supposed to be skating not making out."

I laugh. "Can't we do both?" I give her a wink and we head inside.

"The place is empty."

I smile broadly. "Yep, I reserved it for the rest of the afternoon."

"You did?" She seems genuinely surprised by my thoughtfulness. How can she forget I've always tried to put other people's needs above my own?

"I did. Let's go get our skates." We walk over to the manager, who is waiting for us at the counter. We get our skates and head to the nearest bench to lace up.

"Oh my god, I can't believe they are playing our favorite songs. I don't suppose you had anything to do with that?" Teagan asks with a smile.

I shrug and continue tying my skates. When I'm all done, I stand up on wobbly feet. It's been years since I was on roller skates. I hope I don't fall. I can't afford any injuries before the tournament or the tour. Perhaps this wasn't a good idea after all.

Already suited up, Teagan grabs my hand and leads me toward the rink. "Don't be scared. I've got you. Trust me."

Those are dangerous words for both of us, but I accept her hand and she leads me onto the rink. She skates backward and I move forward toward her.

"See, it's so easy. It's like riding a bike. It comes back to you."

I laugh nervously. "If you say so."

She moves alongside me and together we whirl around the rink. As we practice, I can feel the tension ease away. It's because Teagan brings out a youthful side to me that's been missing for a long time. I used to have fun instead of being serious and focused. It's a hard habit to break when my entire world has revolved around tennis.

Eventually, she lets go of my hand and, because I'm confident on my feet now, I follow her lead. I'm not about to try any fancy moves, but I don't mind watching her sway her hips to the beat of Usher's "Yeah!" song. I don't how long we glide before Teagan motions for a break with her hands. We slide off to the exit and head to a table where the manager has graciously laid out snacks of beer and nachos. Ordinarily, I would never be caught dead eating junk food. My body is a temple and it's all about putting in the right superfoods, but occasionally you have to let loose. Today is one of those days.

"That was fun," Teagan says, out of breath. She reaches for the pitcher of beer and pours us each one in the plastic cups provided.

"Thanks." I accept the cup and, after a toast to good times, take a chug. It's cold and refreshing. "I have to agree with you, that was a blast. I think the last time I skated was with you."

Teagan's eyes glass over. *What's she thinking about?* But she doesn't say. Instead, she tips back her cup, finishes the rest of her beer and rises to her feet. "How about one more round?" There's a faint edge to her voice.

I'm silent for a moment, but then place my cup on the table. "Sure thing."

I can tell when she's pushing me away. Her eyes become cool and distant. Her face turns into a mask, much as it did the first time we saw each other after all these years. I know there's a warm, passionate woman behind that front. Does she think I don't sense the change?

Instead of pushing her to express emotions she doesn't want to share, I let it drop. I don't want it to spoil the day because later tonight, I intend to make her surrender and unleash all the passion lurking behind those caramel brown eyes.

We enjoy the rest of the afternoon skating and eating snacks. Since we drove separately, Teagan decides to meet me at my place later. Whatever was bothering her earlier appears to have evaporated. She's in good spirits when she arrives. I would hate to have our short time together be over when there's still a few weeks until the tournament. I know we've got issues to address, but they can be put on the shelf until after this chemistry between us has razed us both to the ground.

We leave a trail of clothes from the front door all the way to my living room. When she reaches the couch, she lies backward against the cushions with her entire body naked. She's mine for the taking.

It takes a moment for my mind to spring into action. "What do you want, Teagan?"

"I want you to make me feel good."

"Oh, believe me, I intend to do that." I lower myself on top of her and cover her mouth with mine. A low moan of need escapes her throat, but I'm not going to devour her tonight. I'm going to take my time. Seduce her.

I lean forward and brush my mouth over the side of her neck. Her skin is soft and warm. I kiss my way to her throat while I run the backs of my fingers lightly over the curve of one breast.

Teagan shudders at my touch, but I don't stop. I gently brush my fingertips back and forth across her nipple until she twists on the cushions.

"C'mon, Dom, don't tease me."

"Oh, babe, that's the best part." I close my mouth around

one of her nipples, applying pressure while my other palm cups her other breast.

She lets out a gasp as I erode all her control with gentle pulls of my mouth. I tug and bite one nipple before moving on to the next. I can feel her surrender, but I don't stop sucking until she begins to shake.

"Yes," she moans. "Oh, god, yes."

I love that I can make her come just by sucking her breasts, but I want to taste her. So before she can climax, I head lower, past her abdomen, to her pussy. She's dripping wet, and I bend down and explore her with my tongue.

Teagan cries out and clutches my head. I use my hands to hold her thighs firmly apart and pin her to the sofa. I hold her there so I can lick her with firm, deep strokes. I lash at her with my tongue and when I reach her swelling bud, I suck on it hard. Her entire body shakes, and she writhes on the cushions. My hands tighten in place, and I stay there until she flies apart and says my name over and over like an incantation.

Primal satisfaction courses through me, but instead of seduction, all I can think about is being inside her.

Teagan must want the same because when I look up, her pupils are dilated and glazed. "Dominic, *please*."

I move up her body until her hands tighten around my dick and guide me home, easing me inside her hot, slick flesh. Our gazes meet and she shudders as I push deeper inside her. The moment is intense, and she looks up at me with wonder and satisfaction.

I drive into her and feel her inner muscles grip my dick tight like a vise. She pulls my head down and kisses me. I thrust my tongue inside her mouth as my lower half thrusts too.

Her thighs clench me at the same time her pussy does, and I drown in pleasure of the best kind. *Will it always be like this?*

I drive into her harder and faster. Our echoed gasps bounce off the walls and vaulted ceiling. I'm so close, but not without her. I reach down between us and tweak her clit. She explodes, which causes my own orgasm to hit. I roar out my release and collapse on top of her.

It takes me a few moments to gather myself and shift so I don't crush her, but I realize I wasn't just making her feel good. It was for me too. There's always been this connection between us that transcends the physical. I can't articulate what it is, but I know Teagan is different from every other woman, for me. On a deep level, I feel like she's mine.

Has always been mine.

I shudder to think that when this affair is over, I'll have to go back to the beige, bland world of lonely days and even lonelier nights without Teagan's fire and passion.

Twenty-Seven

Teagan

I should be nervous as I drive to my parents' home for Sunday dinner, but surprisingly I'm not. Could it be because Dominic has turned my world topsy-turvy? My mind is completely scattered. The last couple of nights, he's refused to let me sleep away from him. Not that much sleep is happening. He's been insatiable and vice versa. I've always had a high sex drive, but Dominic doesn't just match it; he exceeds it.

It shows me how powerless I am to the intimacy we share, but that's not all. I accompanied him to a Fletcher Cares event where he gave out clothes and sneakers to underprivileged youth. I can see how important it is to him to help others, and I was touched. Maybe I misjudged him. He can't be this amazing and still be the jerk who hung me out to dry with the media.

We're supposed to be competitors who like to fuck, but our relationship has become much more than that. I'm scared at how much he's come to mean to me in such a short time.

It was the same way all those years ago. I was enthralled by him. Unfortunately, nothing has changed.

I can't fall victim to his charm again. Can I?

Dammit. It's too late. I already have.

I daydream about him all the time. When we're not together I want to be with him or call him just to hear his voice. But our relationship is on a road to nowhere. He hasn't stopped being a world-renowned tennis player, beloved by all. I'm a pariah, a black sheep in the industry. And that's fine. I don't need validation from the tennis community anymore, but I've put myself back in the line of fire with this tournament and by getting involved with Dominic again. This is bound to blow up in my face. What then?

I can't go running back to my parents; that's for sure. My father made that very clear. Not that I want to. I relish my independence too much and don't want to go back to the days where Daddy ruled the roost. I wish Mama would wise up, but he's her husband and I gave up long ago trying to get her to change. If she wants to be under his thumb, so be it. I don't have to listen to what he says. I tell myself that over and over and all the way up the doorstep.

I lose my nerve a bit when my father answers the door. "Hey, Daddy." I smile politely.

This time I made sure to come in a dress, a vibrant magenta sheath with a square neck and cap sleeve.

"You look lovely, Teagan." I'm surprised at his words because my father usually doesn't compliment me about anything I do. It's always been hard to please him, except when I played tennis. It was the only time I felt he was remotely proud of me. "Come with me to the study."

"What about Mama? I'd like to say hello."

"You can do so after we talk." My father grasps my elbow, leading me toward his study. Once inside, he shuts the door.

"Is something wrong?"

"Did you heed my advice about Fletcher?"

I'm not about to tell him I've done the exact opposite or that we've been fucking like rabbits. "Of course."

He eyes me suspiciously. "Why don't I believe you? That boy has always had a way of turning your head. I remember how you were with him, chasing after him like a lovesick schoolgirl."

His words cut deep, but I suppose that's his intention. "What's the point of this conversation, Daddy? I heard what you said before."

"Did you? Because Fletcher is no good," Daddy says. "He's not the man for you. He's a great tennis player. And had it worked out between you two, then you would have been an unstoppable force, but you're in different places in your lives. You don't mesh."

"I'm well aware of it." I know Dominic is out of my league. He could have any woman he wants, but he doesn't want them. He wants me, *every night*.

"Are you? Because Jackson Bowens told me he saw you two at the roller-skating rink a few days ago."

"Are you having me followed?" How else would he know about our daytime date? *Why is my father so adamant Dominic and I not spend time together?*

His eyes narrow. "You admit you're still seeing him after I told you not to?"

"I'm a grown woman, Daddy."

"Don't you sass me, young lady." His voice rises several decibels and he points his finger at me. "I won't have it!"

Suddenly Mama rushes into the room. "What's going on, Russ? Why are you shouting at Teagan?"

"Stay out of this, Olympia! It's between me and Teagan."

"She's my daughter too," my mom replies, "and you seem to forget that." Her outburst shocks both me and Daddy into silence. "I won't have you yelling at her."

"It's okay, Mama." I don't want any trouble for her later by sticking up for me. My father can be vindictive. He might take away her cell phone or car keys to prevent her from contacting me.

"No, it's not! It's your life," she says to me, then turns to my father. "If Teagan wants to see Dominic again, what's the harm? I've always thought he was the love of her life."

Mama's use of the word *love* hits me square in the stomach. *Love.*

Is it possible that's the ache I've had for so long? That somehow Dominic has filled that space? It can't be. I can't be in love with him *still*. But hearing the word sends me reeling. These feelings can't be put in a box again not to be opened for another twelve years. I need to think about this. Assess it.

"I have to go," I say.

"But you just got here. Where are you going?" my father asks. "To see Fletcher?"

"And if I were?" I taunt, turning back to glare at him. "It's not the end of the world. He'll leave in a few weeks and go back on tour. Nothing will change."

Except me.

I'll be forever changed because once again I'll have lost him. I rush toward the door, but all I hear as I leave are my father's last words.

"Don't believe anything he says. He's a liar."

I want to know what he means. Or is he just scared Dominic will hurt me and leave like he did last time? I wish I knew. I don't have a crystal ball any more than he does.

But I fear I'm headed for a fall.

The Gems' weekly FaceTime call comes just as I'm leaving the house. I pull over to join in, even though I thought I'd be missing this one due to dinner. I'm dying to unload and hear some good news about what's going on in their worlds since I can't seem to figure out my own.

"Gems, I'm so relieved to see you," I say as soon as I see their beautiful faces.

"It's good to see you too, girlfriend," Lyric replies. "How's life in Arizona? You been getting up to any mischief with a certain you-know-who?"

"I'm dick-whipped," I announce unceremoniously.

"Whew, chile." Asia fans herself. "You act like this news is surprising. We all saw this coming."

Meanwhile, Egypt is having a coughing fit. "You have to warn a sista when you're going to talk dirty. I wasn't ready and was sipping on a new Long Island tea I debuted last night at Flame."

"I know it's been years," Wynter replies, "but Dominic set you afire back in the day. I can only imagine with age and time, he's matured like a fine wine. I know Riley sure did." She snaps her fingers.

"Ugh," Shay snorts. "Please remember you are talking about my brother. Some things have to remain a mystery." She places her hands over her ears and several of us burst out laughing.

"Sorry, Shay," Wynter apologizes, and red stains her cheeks. "I was just keeping it real."

"And sometimes real can go so wrong." Asia laughs.

"Hey, hey, I've got a serious problem here. Besides the sex, I think I have feelings for Dominic. Strong feelings I thought were dead and buried six feet under. Well, surprise, surprise. They are still there—alive and kicking."

"Maybe his coming back to your life now is a good thing?" Lyric replies. "It'll help you figure out once and for all if he's the one."

"He's absolutely *not* the one," I respond. "How could he be if he could abandon me during my time of need that easily?"

I keep telling myself what Mama said can't be true, so I fall back on my old argument for why we can't be together.

"Did you talk to him about the past like we suggested?" Shay inquired.

I remain mum. No, I didn't talk to him. I've been too busy having the best sex of my life to want to ruin it with our differences.

"I see." Shay rubs her jaw. "So that would be a no."

"Don't judge me," I respond. "It's not as simple as having a conversation."

Egypt's brow furrows.

"Shay is just calling a spade a spade. You're enjoying getting your swerve, but Teagan, the jig is going to be up soon. Dominic is going back on tour and you won't have resolved anything if you're not honest with yourselves."

"Egypt has a point," Wynter adds. "You can't bury your head in the sand."

"Maybe I'm happy with the status quo."

"Really, Teagan?" Lyric asks.

I'm blowing smoke up their asses. "I'm sorry," I reply. "I'm scared. I don't know if I can go there again to that painful time of my life. I've moved beyond it."

"Have you?" Shay asks. "Or are you still stuck in the past? If you can't talk to Dominic, talk to a therapist. They've done wonders for me and my mom."

"How is your mother doing?" I inquire. Mrs. Davis has battled with her mental health over the years.

"Quite well," Shay said. "She's happy and healthy and seeing her therapist as often as she needs. We've even had some sessions together—me, her and Riley—to make peace with the past. She had no control over her condition, and I can't be angry about that. I've also been talking to Colin about the possibility of children one day."

"Are you guys getting hitched?" Asia inquires.

Shay chuckles. "Not yet. We're taking our time, but all my cards are on the table, and he knows how much I want a family one day. We've talked about my miscarriages, and he's open to IVF, surrogacy and even adoption."

"That's wonderful, Shay," I say. "I know how much it means to you to be a mom someday. And since we're talking babies, how are you feeling, Wynter? This convo can't all be about me and my messed-up love life."

"Baby and I are doing great," Wynter responds, rubbing her belly. "I'm out of the first trimester, so we're breathing a sigh of relief. I'm having bouts of morning sickness, but getting through it. Meanwhile, I've solidified all of Egypt and Garrett's wedding plans, so Operation Forrester Wedding is T-minus-sixty days away."

"Can't wait!" Egypt gives a fist pump at the screen. "I can't wait to make Garrett mine."

"He's been yours since he woke up from that coma and couldn't remember anyone but you," I reply.

"Yes, ma'am." She snaps her fingers. "Just like Dominic has been yours since day one, boo."

"And you Gems have been with me since the start, which is why I want you to join me to celebrate my Real Estate Broker of the Year award."

"Again?" Asia asks. "Damn, girl, how many of these do you have?"

"As many as can line the shelf in my office," I respond swiftly. "So, can you make it? It's two weeks from Saturday."

"Of course, we'll be there," Wynter and Shay reply simultaneously.

"From here on out, I'm going to put this date on my calendar every year." Asia laughs. "But count me in."

"Me too," Lyric says. "I wouldn't miss it. Will Dominic be there?"

I shrug. "No. I haven't told him yet."

"I wouldn't mind seeing dark chocolate again," Egypt says. "Well, I gotta run, ladies, there's an emergency in the kitchen. A chef's job is never done." She signs off and soon so do the other Gems with plans to see each other at my award ceremony.

I'm ecstatic they are coming, but Lyric had a good point that I haven't mentioned the award ceremony to Dominic. He knows what I do for a living, but I suppose real estate has been something just for me that I built after I lost tennis. Could he share it with me? Could Dominic play a bigger role in my life? Do I want him to?

My feelings are mixed up with past hurts. The only way I can make sense of it all is to share them, but I'm afraid of destroying the closeness and intimacy we've regained. I didn't know I needed physical touch until Dominic came back into my life. Now that I have it, I'm afraid of what happens when he's gone.

Twenty-Eight

Dominic

I'm excited to head to Mom's for dinner. Justice and I will be sharing the good news about starting Fletcher Sports Management. We wanted to keep it to ourselves to prevent word from leaking out before the press release. Bless her heart, Mama is a notorious gossip and loves sharing stories with her neighborhood friends. Given the amount of scrutiny Justice will endure and my position in the sports industry, we both wanted to make sure our ducks were in a row. They are, and we're ready to tell our family about our new endeavor.

I'm halfway there when Teagan calls. I thought she was having dinner with her own family. Did she tell her parents about me? If so, how did her father react? He was never my biggest fan. I doubt he would appreciate us getting close for fear I might reveal the truth about what happened. I won't. I made a promise, and I keep my promises. Well, at least one of them. I've never told Teagan about his interference during our breakup or that I listened to his advice to stay away, *back then*. Now is a different story. She's a different person with new dreams and goals.

I answer her call. "Hey, you. What's going on? I thought you were having dinner with your parents."

She sighs. "I was, but that ended rather abruptly."

"Really?" My interest is piqued.

"My father was being a dictator as usual. Warning me to stay away from you. I'm not nineteen anymore. He doesn't get to control me like he does my mother."

"I haven't seen your father in years—what does he have against me?" *You already know. The truth.* Mr. Williams is afraid I'll tell Teagan about him sending me away.

"According to him, we don't mesh because I'm no longer a tennis player. But that's not it..." Her voice trails off and my ears perk up.

"What then?"

"He knew about our skating rink date. It's like he's having us followed or something. I know I'm being overly dramatic, but he was adamant I keep my distance from you, which of course makes me defiant. He has no say over what I do."

I'm glad because I let Mr. Williams stick his nose where it didn't belong once before. But he doesn't get to dictate what happens between us now. Teagan and I do.

"Good. How about you join me for dinner at my mom's?" The words are out of my mouth before I have a chance to change my mind.

"Dinner with your family?" Teagan sounds surprised. I don't know why that should irk me, but it does. *I know we said we're a casual thing, but is dinner too much?*

"Um, yeah, if you're free. I'm on my way there now." I give her the address.

"Are you sure? I mean, we've been seeing each other privately, but this is your family."

"I know, and I'd like you to see everyone all grown up. They were babies when we got together."

"Okay, I'd like that. I can be there in fifteen minutes."

"Excellent, I'll see you then." We end the call.

I don't know why it pleases me that she's agreed to come, but it does. I try not to analyze the *why* too hard, but instead bask in the knowledge that she'll see me in my element. At the root of it all, I'm a family man.

When I arrive to my mama's, Justice's BMW is already parked in the driveway. I exit my Bentley and bring two bottles of champagne. Justice and I celebrated a couple of days ago, but it's time to bring the rest of the fam into the mix. Instead of using my key, since it annoyed Mom so much, I ring the doorbell, and Ciera comes to the door.

She and I may share the same mother, but we look nothing alike. Her skin tone, eye and hair color must take after her father. Her skin is the color of honey, her eyes are light brown and she's got a curvy figure—unlike the rest of us, who run on the long, lean side.

"Hey, Dom." She smiles. "Come on in. Whatcha got there?" She peers into the bags with the bottles of champagne and her mouth forms an O. "Are we celebrating something?"

"You'll see. C'mon." I follow her into the kitchen to find Mama, Justice and Bliss with a man who appears to be a chef, if the black coat is any indication. He's standing behind the stove flipping veggies in a sauté pan. I place the champagne in the fridge.

"You're not cooking tonight?" I ask, giving Mama a kiss on

the cheek. She's dressed fashionably in a patterned silk lounge-wear set. Her hair is coiffed around her lightly made-up face.

"My days of cooking for the four of you—" Mama motions to me, Justice, Ciera and Bliss "—are over. So yes, I hired a private chef. What are you making, Chef Eddie?"

"First course is my infamous mini crab cakes with a little bit of citrus coleslaw. I also have some salmon Wellington bites with cream cheese cooked in a puff pastry until golden brown."

"Sounds delicious," I say, but the chef isn't done giving his menu.

"Appetizers will be followed by a Caesar salad with corn-bread croutons and my homemade dressing. Your mama told me you all like a good steak so I'm making USDA prime Hawaiian rib eye with a pineapple, soy and ginger marinade served with either wild rice salad or chateau potatoes."

"I, for one, am starving," my little sister Bliss states. "I ran thirteen miles today."

"You did?" I inquire. "Why so long?"

"Bliss is running her first marathon," Mama states proudly, "and we're going to be there to cheer her on. Aren't we, Ciera?"

"Yeah, yeah," Ciera says absentmindedly as she plays with her cell phone.

"Is there enough for one more?" I inquire.

Several pairs of eyes stare at me questioningly, but it's Chef Eddie who speaks. "I always make extra. Another serving won't be a problem."

"Thanks, man." I pat his shoulder and whisper to him to place some flutes at the dinner table and bring the champagne in with the first course. Then I head to the minibar in the living room for an adult beverage before the barrage of questions. I'm pouring myself a Tito on the rocks and taking a sip when I notice my entire family has followed me.

"Well?" Mama asks. "Don't keep us in suspense. Who's coming over?"

Justice smiles knowingly and Mama catches him. "Do you know something we don't?"

He shrugs. "Nothing I care to tell. Dom, you going to fill them in?"

I don't have to. The doorbell rings, signaling Teagan's arrival. Her presence will be enough to have their tongues wagging. I rush to the door and beat Mama there. When I open it, Teagan is on the other side, looking beautiful and serene in a magenta dress that hugs her curves.

"Hey, gorgeous." I bend down to kiss her cheek.

"Teagan?" Shock is written all over my mom's face, and Teagan shoots daggers at me with her eyes.

"Hello, Mrs. Fletcher, so lovely to see you again." Teagan hands her a bouquet of flowers and a bottle of red wine. "I wasn't sure what to bring. I figured red was a safe choice."

To Mama's credit, she recovers quickly. "It will pair well with the steaks the chef is grilling. Come on in, it's been too long." Mama pulls Teagan into an embrace, and the women hug for several moments.

"I was just about to tell everyone you were coming," I respond to Teagan's unasked question.

Teagan quirks a brow as they separate.

"He was," Mama responds, "but he was saved by the proverbial bell. Come. You have to meet the girls." She circles her arm through one of Teagan's. I grab the flowers and wine out of her hands. "They're all grown up."

I follow them into the living room. Bliss and Ciera both look at me in confusion while Justice has a smug look on his face. Teagan walks toward my younger sisters. "You probably don't remember me because Dom and I—" Teagan glances over at me "—dated eons ago when you were just babies."

"I wasn't that young," Ciera replies. "I remember you. You were going to be the next Serena Williams."

Teagan nods. "Yeah, unfortunately, it wasn't in the cards."

"How did you and Dominic, um, reunite?" Mama asks, grinning from ear to ear as she sits on the sofa.

Teagan laughs nervously. "I wouldn't say we reunited, but our paths crossed."

"And the rest is history?" Justice offers, coming toward her. "It's good to see you again, Tee. I happen to be taller than you and no longer have a squeaky voice that sounds like a chipmunk."

Justice's lighthearted comments break the ice and the room dissolves into laughter. Soon Teagan sits on the sofa with the rest of the women in my family, catching up on old times. It's amazing how easily she fits in with our small clan.

"It's like she never left," Justice states when he joins me near the bar where I've topped off my drink. I'm leaning against the column, observing Teagan's interactions. She's poised and confident.

"Yeah, feels that way," I say.

"So is this serious?" Justice whispers. "Or are y'all, ya know, just kickin' it?"

I stare down at him for several beats. "The latter. Teagan is content with her life. She doesn't need me messing it up."

In another lifetime, we could have been more, but not now.

Teagan doesn't want to be in my world, a world that castigated her and made her feel less than.

"Is that her talking or you?" Justice inquires. "Because you're the one who can't keep a relationship to save his life. It makes me wonder if you've been waiting for this."

"For what?"

"For Teagan to come back."

Justice leaves me with his revelation. It resonates. *Come back to me.* Is that what I want? What I've always wanted?

For years, I banished Teagan to the far recesses of my mind because I didn't want to think about the connection and passion we shared. I only allowed myself to feel anger. Anger at her for believing I would abandon her when the chips were down. I had to believe those things, didn't I? Because if I didn't, all I'd have left is regret that I never righted the wrong I'd done by listening to her father instead of listening to my heart.

And now it appears as if it was all for naught. Despite the years apart, Teagan is still the only woman I've ever truly wanted. That's a sobering thought. What all could we have had if I had made different choices?

"Dom, come over here." Teagan motions me to her side. "I was telling Mrs. Fletcher that we went to the skating rink."

"He went skating?" Ciera asks disbelievingly.

"I know you might find this hard to believe, but I can have fun from time to time, sis," I reply.

"Ha ha," Ciera snorts.

"Dinner is ready," Chef Eddie announces. "It will be served in the dining room."

As everyone heads there, I pull Teagan toward me and my mouth descends on hers. Like always, we catch fire.

That's what Teagan does; she makes things shift and ignite inside me. I love every slide of her tongue against mine, and when she adjusts the angle of the kiss so I can go deeper, my heart thuds loudly in my chest. Any second, I'll be ready to find the nearest room so she can come apart for me, but we're interrupted by Bliss coughing loudly from the doorway.

"Ahem, dinner is ready," Bliss states. "That's if you guys can pry yourselves apart."

"Get lost, squirt," I say, and bend down to kiss Teagan again, but it's she who places a finger on my lips.

"Dom, we have to go." Then she swipes her thumb across my mouth. "My lipstick is all over you. Your family will know what we've been doing."

I grin broadly. "I don't care."

"I do," Teagan states exasperatedly. "I haven't seen your mom in years. I don't want her to think I'm some—some tart."

I laugh, but relent and give her my hand. "All right, let's go."

We make our way to the dining room and sit in the two empty seats across from Justice, Ciera and Bliss with Mama at the head of the table. Mama says grace and then Chef Eddie brings in the first course along with both my bottles of bubbly.

I stand to my feet while everyone's nibbling crab cakes and salmon Wellingtons and immediately twist the cork off the first bottle.

"What's the champagne for?" Ciera inquires as I ask each family member to hand me their glass.

"You'll see in a moment," I say, and fill my and Teagan's flutes last. When everyone has a glass, I hold mine in the air. "I'm here tonight not just for a family dinner but to celebrate my baby brother's big accomplishment."

"What accomplishment?" Mama asks. Her eyes grow wide with concern. "What don't I know? I have to say, I don't like being kept in the dark about what's going on with you two."

"This is a good one, Mama," Justice responds with a broad smile.

"Allow me to congratulate Justice on the opening of Fletcher Sports Management. Cheers, everyone." I push my flute in the air and we all clink glasses, but my mother doesn't seem happy.

Justice turns to her. "What's wrong, Ma? I thought you'd be happy for me."

She forces a smile. "Of course I'm happy for you, Justice. I want the very best for all my kids, but starting a new company would take a huge capital investment. Where did you get the money?"

"From Dom." Justice smiles at me. "I can't thank you enough for believing in me and my vision."

"You gave him the money?" Mama asks loudly, quieting the entire dinner table. Even Bliss and Ciera stop drinking and nibbling. "You told me I had to stop spending so much, but then you invest in Justice's business? What the hell, Dom!"

My eyes darken and my blood boils in my veins. "What do you care? It's *my money* and I can do with it as I wish. If I want to invest in Justice's business—and he had a damn good prospectus by the way—then I'll do just that. It's completely different than me telling you to curb your spending habits on frivolous shit."

"Frivolous!" Mama spits out. "I use that money to support me and your sisters."

"Oh, here we go." Justice rolls his eyes and I see him give

Teagan an I'm-sorry look, but I'm too incensed by Mama's reaction to let it go.

"Don't you dare try to make me feel bad. You, Ciera and Bliss have everything you need and then some."

"We do, Dom," Bliss interjects. "I promise. It's fine. We don't need anything else, do we, Ciera?" She glances at my baby sister in the hopes she'll help defuse the situation, but Ciera shrugs indifferently. "What good you are!" Bliss turns to me. "We were having such a good time—can't we just get back to that?"

"I don't think so," I reply. "I've lost my appetite." I wipe my mouth with my napkin and stand up.

"C'mon, you don't have to leave," Justice states. "Bliss is right. Stay and let's finish this delicious meal Chef Eddie prepared. It sounds phenomenal."

I glance over at Mama. She's not speaking, but her lip is a thin line showing me her disapproval.

Teagan touches my arm. "Dom, your siblings are right. Don't let this disagreement ruin a great family dinner. Stay."

Her words are like a soothing balm to my frayed nerves. I nod and sit back down. I want to rail more at Mama for thinking she can tell me what to do with the money *I* earned. How is it that both she and Mr. Williams think they have that right?

Teagan pats my thigh underneath the table, and I find myself soothed by her calming touch. But then her hand gets closer to my dick. When she softly caresses me and glances over at me beneath hooded lashes, I realize I'm willing to do anything if she'll keep touching me like that.

I settle down and eat the delicious meal with my family. Mama and I will address our issues in private. But when I get Teagan alone later, I'm going to have my sweet revenge.

Twenty-Nine

Teagan

Williams & Associates closed on two sales this week. Hallelujah! It's been a rough few months, but we're finally making headway. Maybe I can pay myself back for the country club membership, which severely ate into my pocketbook, but was it worth it? Yes. The contacts I've made gave the agency renewed energy. It's either feast or famine in real estate. You have to save those big commissions for a rainy day when there's slim pickings. I'm thrilled for my team, but that's not the only thing making me happy these days.

Dominic Fletcher.

The man I've loved to hate for the past twelve years came sauntering back in my life as if he belonged there. It's scary how easily we've reconnected. Not just on the court, where playing tennis has come back to me as naturally as breathing, but on a personal level. I never expected Dominic to invite me to his family dinner, but he showed me a side of himself that he often hid in the past. He shared his family's flaws. I saw that he has issues with his mother like I do with my parents. His opening up to me meant so much. That's why later, when we went for a drive, passion exploded and we made love in the car. It's like he's stripped away all my defenses, leaving me vulnerable, no place to hide. And no way to deny how I feel.

I love him.

I don't know if I ever stopped loving him, which is why I've never been able to fully give myself to any other relationship. I want to cry and rail because I don't know what to do with these feelings. They can't go anywhere. Dominic is the GOAT. The most famous player in current tennis history. He's still on the circuit and going back on tour, and everything will go back to how it was before. I'll work as hard as I always do, determined to be the best in my own field, but I'll be alone. This time, it'll be harder to forget him because I don't have the anger to hold on to. All I'll have is this unrequited love.

Dominic wants me. Yes. Is he insatiable for me? Absolutely. But love? That's no longer part of the equation, and I'm certainly not about to express how I feel. I have my pride. This relationship is only about closure, giving us the bookend we never had. It's a tough pill to swallow, but there's nowhere for this relationship to go.

We will win this tournament because that's what we do, or at least it's what Dominic does and what I used to do, but training with him has made me believe we can. After the tournament is over, he'll leave and I won't see him again. It's how it has to be, right?

We have no future.

A knock sounds on my door and I glance up to see my mother standing in my office doorway.

"Mom?" I rise to my feet. "Is everything okay?" I don't

often see her outside the family home because Daddy keeps her on a tight leash.

She offers me a small smile. "Yes, all is well. I wanted to check on you. I didn't like how things ended on Sunday."

"Daddy didn't leave me much choice."

She turns and closes the door, giving us privacy. "No, your father has always been a man determined to have his way. And usually, I allow it."

"But you didn't. Why did you stand up to him *for me*?"

"It was high time I did," Mom responds softly. "I've never liked arguing with your father, but he has no place sticking his nose in your love life. If you and Dominic want to rekindle your relationship, more power to you."

My nose scrunches. "You think so?" I would have thought she would be against us, same as Daddy.

"I always felt like you threw in the towel too quickly, Teagan. You both seemed so committed back then."

I shake my head. "You're wrong, Mom. He was my first love, and I thought the sun and moon hung on him, but I was just a passing phase for Dominic."

"I disagree, but ultimately what I think doesn't matter. It's what you think. Do you want to be with him?"

"Yes, but he's a hugely successful tennis champion. And me? Well, I've changed. We don't move in the same circles anymore. I'm a pariah with the press."

"Doesn't mean it can't work. You might face some challenges, but surely you're willing to put in the time for the someone you love?"

I wish I could believe her. I *have* seen love conquer all with the Gems and their relationships. I've seen them overcome misunderstandings, unplanned pregnancies and all kinds of hang-ups, but I don't know, this feels different. It's personal. I'm no longer on the outside offering my advice.

"I hear you, Mama. I do, but I also have to protect my heart. I don't want to get hurt again."

"I don't want that for you either, sweetheart. I want you to be happy, Teagan, and if that's with Dominic, then so be it."

"Thank you." I squeeze her hands. "And I want the same thing for you. You don't have to take sides with me or Daddy."

"Maybe not, but I needed to find my voice and not let your father have the last word."

I'm stunned by her speech. I've always wanted her to speak up, but she always seemed content with the status quo. I think it's why I've always been so direct and outspoken. Of course, it hasn't always served me well.

"Good for you, Mama. Good for you."

After she departs, I'm left to think about our conversation and wonder if she's right. Did I give up too easily in the past and let the man I love get away? Am I giving up now? Should I fight for what I want? And how would Dominic feel if I did?

"We're all set for the charity tournament," Charity says at the committee meeting on Saturday. "I'm so proud of all your hard work, dedication and fundraising efforts. I want to thank you, Dominic, for your personal donation to help us meet our goal of two million dollars as well as those of your colleagues on the ATP tour. We're nearly there."

"My agent has been working on a cash cow and I'm just waiting for word on a big donation," Dominic replies.

"That would be great," Mitzi says.

Of course, Dominic knows people. That's the world he lives in. A world I used to be a part of, but was unceremoniously kicked out of. The memory sinks in my belly like an anchor to the ocean floor.

Once the meeting is over, it's time for Dominic and I to practice. I try not to let the bad taste from past memories disturb us because I've come to enjoy our banter on the court. It reminds me of who I used to be. However, before I can leave, Charity stops me.

"Teagan, don't go."

"What's up?" I ask. My adrenaline is revving up for another match with Dom.

"I wanted to congratulate you on scoring another win for Real Estate Broker of the Year," Charity responds. "It's a high honor."

My brows furrow together. "Thank you, but how did you find out?"

She shrugs. "Oh, a friend of mine sits on the board and mentioned it. Are you and Dominic going together?"

"Why would you think that?"

"C'mon, Teagan. I have eyes," Charity responds. "The two of you have been quite cozy the last couple of months. I mean, yeah, there were fireworks in those first sessions, yet I can't help but notice the antagonism between you is long gone. Am I right?"

I'm not about to spill the beans to Charity, who apparently is a gossip if she already knows about my award. "The camaraderie you sense is from two players who've learned to coexist in the same space, nothing more."

Charity laughs. "All right, Teagan. Keep your secrets, but don't think for a second I believe you and Dominic Fletcher are—" she uses her fingers as air quotes "—just friends." With that, she sashays out of the room.

That's when I notice Dominic was standing directly behind her. How long has he been there? Did he hear what I said about the award ceremony? Is the scowl on his face because I didn't invite him? I haven't integrated him into my world outside of the tennis arena. I suppose because it's mine and it's where I shine.

Is it so wrong to want the spotlight for myself?

Thirty

Dominic

We're just friends?

We're just players who've developed a camaraderie?

Is that really what Teagan thinks of us?

We've become much more than that. I wouldn't have reintroduced her to my family if she was just another side piece, but apparently Teagan doesn't think much of me. She's being honored as Real Estate Broker of the Year and didn't tell me?

Why not? Doesn't she know I'd champion her just as if she'd won Wimbledon?

"Everything okay?" Teagan asks, coming toward me.

I school my features to a neutral expression. I don't want her to know I overhead them speaking about the award ceremony. "I'm fine," I respond. "You ready to hit the court?"

If we're just tennis players with nothing between us, we might as well get to it.

"I am," she replies. "I'm ready to whup your ass."

"You think so," I reply with a haphazard smile. "You realize you rarely beat me. The couple of times you did was a stroke of luck."

"And you're an asshole," she says, turning on her heel. "I'll see you out there."

Ten minutes later, I'm getting in position on the back court. The last couple of sessions I've gone easy on Teagan because of our physical relationship, but I'm not feeling generous today. In fact, I would say I'm downright mad. Mad that Teagan doesn't think she can tell me about what's going on in her life. Why? Because she still doesn't trust me.

She'll trust me with her body, give herself to me in every way imaginable, but she won't give me what I just realized I want most.

Her heart.

I don't have time to think about it more because Teagan wastes no time serving the ball. I crouch and wait. The ball comes fast across the net, bounces once, and I return it with equal fire.

Anger fuels my system and this time I give Teagan the business, treat her like I would any other opponent. We rally a bit and she almost manages to hit a ground stroke, but I stay alert. She tries using her backhand, since it was her best stroke when she played on tour, but I attack the net and meet the ball.

There, I've won the first game. Teagan goes to her bag, pulling out a towel to wipe off the sweat. When she returns, her brow is furrowed and she looks focused. That's fine with me. I'm ready for her.

Now it's my serve. My racket strikes the ball, sending it exactly where I want it to go. I set her up for failure and she manages a decent service return, but it's not enough. She wins a few points in various games, but I take the first set 6–2.

She strides to half court. "I don't need you to take it easy on me, Dominic. I want to get better and if it means losing, then I'll take my lumps. So bring it on."

"You sure you ready for me?" I inquire as we switch sides.

Her eyes narrow as she walks past me. "I was born ready. I can take anything you dish out, Fletcher." I notice she resorts to calling me by my last name when she's angry with me.

"Fine." I toss my towel down and head straight to the back court. "Don't say I didn't warn you."

The next couple of hours, I'm relentless. I break her serve and strike the ball corner to corner—over and over again. I have her running like hell. Part of me doesn't like watching her failure. But the opponent in me won't let it rest. Her hair is plastered to her forehead and sweat glistens on her firm body. I'd like to take her in the shower and wash her clean and then fuck her against the wall until I'm no longer angry that she's kept me in the dark about her career, her life.

I finish her by winning the next two sets.

After practice is over and I'm packing up, I head over to her side of the net, but Teagan shakes her head. "Not now, Dom."

"You know this was just a game."

Her eyes narrow into slits as she glares at me. "Was it? I got the distinct impression you were pissed at me."

"Why would I be angry?" I ask defensively. "Besides, you asked me to be tougher on you."

She stares at me for several beats and I wonder if she realizes I overheard her conversation with Charity, but then she says, "I'm just tired and sweaty and ready for a hot shower. Can we talk later?"

"Sure." I watch her walk off when that's the last thing I want. I want her with me, in my arms and in my bed.

Without my realizing it, feelings I didn't know were still there have resurfaced. Teagan Williams isn't the casual fling I thought she was. I was trying to put her into a role that she would never fit. Because in reality, she's the woman I never truly got over. She's the fire in my blood that has fueled me all these years. I was winning for myself, but maybe I was winning for her too because she couldn't be there to do it herself.

Was my superiority on the court a way to put her in her place? Maybe. Hell, there's no maybe about it. I wanted to take her down a peg or two and I did. The satisfaction it gave me is short-lived. I should have told her that I was hurt by her excluding me from her award ceremony instead of acting like a child, but there's always been a competitive edge to our relationship.

We're two strong-willed, independent people, but there has to be a middle ground. One where we can both win, in and out of bed. I just have to find it. And I will, because Teagan is the woman I want to be with.

"Hey, Dom. What's good?" Scott asks when I join him for lunch at the end of the week. I had to fly out to take care of some business for Fletcher Cares in Los Angeles and decided to stop in. A local charity in South Central had reached out for help and I couldn't say no.

"I was hoping you had some luck finding other sponsors for the Desert Smash…?" I inquire.

"Oh, yeah. I looked into it and there's a big sneaker company willing to off-load some serious dollars if you're playing."

"Of course I'm playing," I reply. "I told you, I'm playing doubles with Teagan."

A frown mars Scott's face. "About that… They're only interested in donating if you're playing singles. You're the star, Dom, not your ex-girlfriend, a washed-up has-been." At the daggers I shoot in his direction, Scott amends his words. "Listen, I'm—I'm sorry. I didn't mean to offend you. I just thought you and Teagan were scratching an itch so you can finally close that door."

I reach for my drink and take a sip and remind myself to count to ten. Once I'm sufficiently calm, I put down my glass. "Teagan isn't an itch I need to scratch. She's more."

"How much more?"

I glare at him.

"Oh, shit! You're serious? Are you two like back together?" Scott whispers.

I glare at him. "We've been together for nearly two months, Scott. And yes, I thought it was just sex, but I've come to realize my feelings for Teagan run deeper."

Scott sits back in his chair and stares at me incredulously. "Wow! This is serious, Dom, but you haven't seen Teagan in well over a decade. It was always my impression you hated her or at the very least were upset with her about how she bailed on y'all's relationship."

"I was angry at her, but time and distance have made me realize we both made mistakes that contributed to our breakup."

"How does Teagan feel?"

I shrug. "That's the problem. I'm not sure. I thought we were getting somewhere the last couple of months, but then I find out she's winning Real Estate Broker of the Year tomorrow but chose not to share the news with me."

"That had to sting."

"Yeah, it did, and I sort of took it out on her by giving her a signature Dominic Fletcher smackdown. She was so defeated after losing, she left the court and I haven't spoken to her since. I've called her a couple of times and texted, but she's been too tired or too busy."

"Sounds to me like she's giving you the shaft. I suppose you struck a nerve."

"Probably. I was just so upset she didn't think she could share her life with me. I invited her over for dinner and to spend time with my family. I thought she could see how much she means to me."

"Showing ain't working, my friend," Scott responds. "You might have to follow through on the telling."

"I will, but first I'm going to the awards dinner. I want to see her in all her glory."

Scott frowns. "Are you sure that's a good idea? She didn't invite you for a reason. She may not take too kindly to you just showing up."

"I can't *not* go. This is a big deal and I want to be there to support her. You'll see. Once she realizes I'm there, she'll be happy to see me."

"I don't think so, Dom, but I've given you my best advice, take it or leave it. What about the sneaker sponsorship?"

"No can do. Teagan and I are a team. I'm not changing that."

"All right. Well, good luck at the ceremony," Scott says.

"Thanks, something tells me I might need it."

Teagan will either be happy I'm there to support her or she'll ice me out like she's done the last week. Then where will I be? I can't start back at ground zero. She will be glad to see me. I just know it.

Thirty-One

Teagan

"You look beautiful, Teagan," Lyric tells me as I prance this way and that in front of the full-length mirror in my bedroom. I'm wearing a flowy off-the-shoulder red organza gown with a V-cut.

"Thank you," I say. She and the Gems came in yesterday before the awards dinner tonight so we could catch up. Since it was a slow day at the office with no showings, I was able to take off early after doing some administrative work.

"Is everything all right?" Lyric asks. "You don't seem yourself. I noticed yesterday, but we were so busy gabbing that I didn't push."

"I'm fine," I reply, adding glitzy chandelier earrings to my earlobes.

"You know saying that word means the exact opposite," she responds.

I glance in her direction and she makes me smile. Lyric looks lovely in a silver-gray dress with a voluminous skirt covered in layers of bedazzled petal flaps. Her auburn hair is parted in the middle and hangs in a long curtain down her slender back. Her look is very 1950s chic. "You look amazing."

"Thank you, but don't try changing the subject," Lyric replies, smoothing her hands down her skirt. "You're not getting away without telling me what's going on."

"Okay, okay." I know she's not going to give up. "I'm a bit perturbed with Dominic."

"Oh, really, what did he do?"

"He wiped the floor with me last week when we were playing." When Lyric starts to speak, I hold my hand up to halt her. "It's not that he beat me. I expect that. He's a champion. It's the reason he did it, as if to punish me for some perceived offense."

"Is that what he said?"

I shake my head. "He didn't have to. I felt his anger and animosity. It's like he wanted to teach me a lesson and I don't know why."

"Did you talk to him?"

"No. I decided to give him some space."

"The entirety of your issues with Dominic stem from lack of communication. You both have to stop being so stubborn and proud and start speaking your truth."

"She's right," Egypt states, unceremoniously barging into my bedroom without knocking. She is radiant in a black satin strapless corset gown with a dramatic leg slit. The gown emphasizes her plus-size curves while her hair is swept to one side in soft waves to her shoulder. She looks every bit a strong Black woman. "You and he have had too many misunderstandings. You could easily squash this, Teagan. So why aren't you?"

A soft sigh escapes my lips because they're right. I'm hiding behind what happened because I don't want to address the elephant in the room—the newly recognized feelings I have for Dominic. Or rather, the *love* I have for him that never went away despite the test of time.

"You're right, there's more to it."

"How much more?" Egypt quizzes.

I don't get to answer because Wynter, Shay and Asia sweep into the bedroom and there's oohs and aahs over hair, dresses and makeup. Wynter is in an elegant, body-hugging black dress with a back-tie halter and a flowing cape. You can't even tell she's pregnant. Her hair is in loose curls and she appears effortless and classic. Meanwhile Shay's killer athletic figure is on full display in a beautiful pink sequin gown. Her makeup is fresh with just a pop of blush and pink lipstick. Asia's petite frame is draped in a gold satin-belted gown with a ruched bodice and asymmetrical strap. A messy bun sits atop her head and she has a smoky eye and mauve lips.

The Gems come to stand beside me in the full-length mirror. I have to say we're a good-looking bunch.

"Are you ready to go collect your second statue?" Asia asks.

"I am."

Egypt eyes me in the mirror. She's not done quizzing me, but is giving me a reprieve for now.

"Good, because the limo has arrived to take us to the ball," Wynter states with a flourish. "Are we ready?"

There's a chorus of yeses and the six of us leave my bedroom and strut out the door like we're fashion models on the runway. It makes me realize just how lucky I am to have friends like these women, *my sistas*, who drop their respective lives to come and support me.

Once inside the limo, Asia reaches for the bottle of bubbly in the ice bucket and pretty soon champagne is flowing, except for Wynter, who opts for water. There are toasts and cheers and the vibe is everything I need, especially when I'm unsure of where I stand with Dominic. His behavior last Saturday grated on my nerves and it made me wonder if being with me is about his competitive spirit. Am I just another point on his scoreboard?

The drive to the Kimpton Palomar Hotel is short. When we arrive, I walk arm in arm with the Gems up one flight of stairs until we come to the mezzanine. There's a small red carpet and a photographer with a backdrop is taking photos of guests and recipients. We stop for multiple rounds of pictures until a masculine voice states, "Well, well, well, if it isn't the infamous Gems."

My face burns hot when I see the owner is indeed the man I've been ignoring the past week. "Dominic?" I ask incredulously, disentangling myself from the Gems and walking toward him.

The other women notice my demeanor and instead of coming forward, Lyric holds them back with her hand.

"Surprise, surprise." He grins and despite my shock at seeing him, his beauty reaches all the way to my toes. He looks resplendent in a navy blue tuxedo with a crisp white shirt. His ebony eyes gleam and his goatee is trim and shapely. His gaze travels appreciatively up and down my figure, assessing me in my gown.

"What are you doing here?"

His face darkens at my curt tone, and he clenches his jaw. "I was hoping you'd be happy to see me, but I can see I misread the room."

"I—I'm just surprised."

"Why is that, Teagan? Could it be because you didn't tell me about your award?" Dominic asks. "Instead, I had to overhear you talking about it with Charity."

That's how he knows. I wasn't sure if he'd heard our conversation and hoped he hadn't. I'll have to bluff this out. "I'm sorry. It's really not that big a deal."

Dominic glares at me. "Really? Is that where you want to go with this? It is very much a big deal because the Gems—" he points to the women behind me "—are here. They wouldn't be if this award wasn't important. Silly me, I thought because we were sleeping together, I might rank a bit higher on the list, that you would inform me, but I guess I'm delusional."

"Why are you so upset, Dominic?" I whisper hotly, moving him away from the crowd to a quiet corner. "We said this was casual. Nothing more. Nothing less."

From the angry look that crosses his expression, I sense I've crossed the line. "Yeah, I guess we were just fucking so what does it matter?"

"Don't put this back on me and act like I'm in the wrong. You set the boundaries from day one. Hell, we both did."

"I'm well aware," Dominic says with a sigh. "Go back to the Gems. I'll get out of here." He's walking away when several people realize who he is and a crowd surrounds him.

"Dominic, can I get an autograph?"

"Dominic, can I get a selfie?"

I watch as the momentum of the evening shifts from me to him. Even tonight, when it should be all about my accomplishments and how hard I've worked to build myself up after the downfall of my tennis career, once again Dominic is stealing the show.

Suddenly, I feel a pair of warm hands on my shoulders. I turn and see it's Lyric. "Hey, you okay?"

I incline my head to the crowd around Dominic. "Would you be? This night is supposed to be about me, but it's turning into being about him."

"Is that really what you think?" Lyric asks. "I get the impression he was trying to surprise you and be here for your big moment."

I turn sideways to stare at her. "You're supposed to be on my side."

"I am." Lyric sighs in frustration and puts her hands on her hips. "But when you're wrong, I'm going to point it out, Teagan. I'm not your yes-woman."

The rest of the Gems come over and Wynter asks, "What's wrong?" She looks back and forth between me and Lyric.

"Teagan seems to think the whole world is against her tonight, including Dominic."

Egypt glances behind me to stare openly at Dominic. "Girl, that man came tonight for you. He has eyes for no one but you."

I don't dare look at him because I'm afraid to. I can feel his dark eyes on me even though I'm facing the Gems. *Did I get it wrong? Am I overreacting?*

"You don't understand. I've had to live in Dominic's shadow the last twelve years. I've watched him accomplish all the things *I* wanted but that were taken away from me. Do you know how hard that was? I've tried to make my peace with the loss, but I am envious of the career he has. I've built a new life for myself, a new career as a real estate broker. One so successful I've been named Real Estate Broker of the Year for the second year in a row. It's a big accomplishment, and I—"

I slam my palm against my chest "—I did that. Not him." I point in Dominic's direction. "And I know it's irrational, but right now it feels as if he's stealing my thunder."

A tear leaks down my cheek. "Come here." Wynter rushes to me and pulls me into her arms. "We can't have your makeup failing before your event. Let's go to the restroom and freshen up." She pulls me toward the bathroom and the Gems follow. I don't bother looking behind me because I can't.

I can't see how much I've hurt Dominic with my words. Or feel the pain and envy of having his spotlight shine brighter than mine.

Thirty-Two

Dominic

Scott was right. I shouldn't have come.

Was it so wrong to want to be there for Teagan at her big moment?

She hates that I came. I can see it in her eyes. She doesn't want me here. I planned on leaving, but I never expected a crowd to form around me. I guess I shouldn't be surprised because I'm a celebrity athlete. I sign a few autographs and take several photos and selfies.

Someone calls my name. "Dominic, wait!"

It's Egypt. The tall, full-figured Gem who, if I remember what Teagan told me, has always been the no-nonsense one of the bunch. Oh, lord. I roll my eyes. I can only imagine she's about to read me the riot act.

She storms toward me in stiletto heels, one shapely leg showing from the black corset gown she's wearing.

"Hello, Egypt," I say when she makes it to me.

"What were you thinking?" she asks exasperatedly, hand on one hip.

"I wasn't," I return.

"That's pretty obvious," Egypt responds, but then she sighs. "But I get why you came."

"You do?" I'm surprised she would acknowledge I'm right about anything.

"You wanted to support my girl. Am I right?"

I nod.

"You're not wrong, but Teagan has never fully gotten over the demise of her tennis career, and seeing you here tonight with all your fans... Well, it just reinforces she isn't good enough, ya feel me?"

"I never thought about it like that."

"Why would you? You're a champion. A legend in your own right. Tonight is about Teagan and what she's been able to accomplish *without tennis*."

I nod in acknowledgment. "I understand."

"Do you? Springing it on her might not have been the best idea, but I don't think you're wrong for being here. Teagan needs all the support she can get from people who love her."

"Who says I love her?"

Egypt chuckles. "You can fool yourself if you want, Dominic—" she comes toward me and pats my arm "—but my daddy didn't raise no fool and I know exactly what I see. You'll figure it out soon enough. In the meantime, don't leave. Stay in the background and don't bring any more attention to yourself. She'll appreciate it later that you're here."

"I didn't plan on leaving."

A smile spreads across her round face. "I knew there was a reason I liked you, Fletcher. You've got balls and you'll need them to keep up with Teagan. Good to see you, but I've got to run."

A whoosh of black fabric and she disappears into the ladies' room. I appreciate Egypt telling me how Teagan feels. It helps me see her perspective. When Teagan approached me earlier, all tough and hard, I'd been offended by her harsh persona, but now I have better insight.

Tonight is about her. I never thought otherwise, but I can see how it might look to have a crowd rush around me instead of her. I'm going to get a drink at the bar and once I'm sure the event has started, I'll quietly creep in to see Teagan take home the win.

Besides, I can use some libation to help digest the word Egypt threw out there like an arrow to the heart.

Love.

I hadn't wanted to admit the feelings I have for Teagan, but if I'm honest with myself, Egypt is right. I am in love with her. I think I've never stopped loving her. I just pushed those feelings aside because it hurt too much to think about how easily Teagan let our relationship go. She gave up on us and it hurt. It was easier to blame her than look myself in the mirror and recognize she wasn't the only culprit in the failure of our relationship. I kept secrets from her. I never told her Mr. Williams asked me to stay away for her own good. I gave in to pressure from him, and from outside forces, to walk away. We were both to blame.

But I have a chance to make things right.

If I leave again because the situation is hard, Teagan will think it's what I always do, but it's not. I've changed. I'm not the twenty-year-old boy who was easily led astray.

I'm a man now and I'm going to stay and fight for the woman I love.

Thirty-Three

Teagan

"You don't have to keep Dominic at arm's length," Asia tells me in the bathroom, "not when it's so clear you want him."

"I'm just not sure I can trust him," I say once Wynter has repaired my makeup. Thankfully, it's only us Gems in the bathroom and I can speak freely. "He shows up to this gala like he has a right to be here and is angry when I question why he came. The next minute, he's cold and unfeeling, like he was on the court last week when he laid into me. But I suppose I know why. He overheard me talking to Charity about tonight."

"And in anger, he acted out and struck back at you," Asia finishes. "Sounds like my toddler, Ryan. However, it also makes Dominic human. He was hurt and acted on reflex. We all do, including you."

I frown. "What do you mean?"

"You don't think you were being a tad overdramatic out

there?" Shay inquires, powdering her nose. Her long, dark brown locks are in a half-up, half-down style.

I laugh. "Me? Be melodramatic? That's Asia's thing." I give the short diva a quick smile.

Asia huffs. "As if, heifer. It's all about you tonight, boo. I got my man."

I roll my eyes. She certainly does, and I can't say I'm not envious that all the Gems have found their true loves. Mine is gone because I sent him away.

"Don't gang up on Teagan in her time of need," Lyric says, even though she too gave me shit for my behavior tonight. She hates conflict.

"Thanks, Lyric." I pat her knee. "I'm going out there to pick up my award and be happy because you all are with me. That's all I need." But even as I say the words, they ring false because I wish Dominic were here to share this moment with me.

"Thank you for this award," I say after I get to the stage to accept the statuette for Real Estate Broker of the Year. "It's humbling to know all the hard work my team and I have done this year is being recognized. But I'm especially thankful for the five women in my life who uplift and encourage me during the difficult times. This year in real estate has been one of those times."

I look at Egypt, Lyric, Wynter, Asia and Shay and give them a big smile. I'm stunned to see they're not alone at the table. Dominic has joined them, sitting beside Egypt. A jolt shoots through me.

He didn't leave? Even when I made it clear I didn't want him here?

He stayed.

"Uh, thank you again to the Phoenix Association of Realtors for this honor." I recover the power to speak and conclude my speech. "Thank you again." I hold up the award and rush off the stage.

My entire table is on their feet applauding, but I can't see the Gems. My vision is focused on one person alone: Dominic. I rush toward him. He opens his arms and catches me. I don't care who's watching, listening or looking at us. I just kiss him.

I'm suspended in time when Dominic's strong, firm mouth covers mine. A wave of relief washes over me that he didn't leave. I angle my head and open my mouth to him. When his tongue touches mine, electricity shoots through my entire body down to where I ache for him.

His hands clamp my waist and pull me closer to match me stroke for stroke. I gasp when I hear a discreet cough from behind us. I'm a bit dizzy when I turn around and see Egypt smiling knowingly and Lyric blushing furiously.

"Might I suggest you two depart for a place more private?" Asia says from across the table. "I think you have an audience."

The blur fades from my eyes and I notice the entire audience is watching us. There are a few phones out recording us.

"I think that's a good idea," Dominic murmurs, grasping my hand in his and pulling me away.

"I'll see you girls later." I wave at the Gems, who are all smiling ear to ear. "The limo can take you back to my house."

"Don't worry about us," Shay says. "We'll find our own way."

I blow them a kiss as Dominic hauls me out of the room.

What seems like an eternity later, we arrive back to his place in the limo he procured for the evening. Thankfully, we've eased the urgency because Dominic positioned me astride his lap inside the vehicle, tugged up my dress, released the fly on his tuxedo trousers, quickly donned a condom and pulled me down on top of him. It felt so good to have him inside me again. The week had been too long without him.

"I'm sorry I can't be gentle," he said, and then he wound his hands into my hair and kissed me hard. I feasted on him as his hips flexed and he thrust into me.

"I don't want gentle."

My body arched and I took all of him. I forgot everything but the power and glory of taking everything he had to give because I was giving it right back. I gripped him hard, clenching my inner muscles until the building firestorm exploded.

I gloried in the fact that I love this man who's always been my soulmate in every way.

By the time we arrived to Dom's, our clothes were righted enough to exit the car, but I was slumped against his broad chest, dazed by the emotions coursing through me.

Now Dominic carries me from the limo and upstairs to his bedroom. He gently places me down on the comforter, and when I look in his eyes, I see something I haven't seen in a long time. Something I never thought I'd see again.

And then he shatters me with his words. "I'm going to make love to you."

He covers my body with his hard, huge one and gives me the softest of kisses before doing just that.

The next morning, when I roll over in Dominic's bed, I'm on cloud nine.

I reach for him beside me and frown when I notice the bed is empty. He's probably making coffee so I fall back against the pillows and relive the past eight hours. The way Dominic kissed me, held me, touched me. It has to be love. The fierce look I saw in his eyes last night was real. I'm certain of it. I haven't seen that expression since I was nineteen. A couple of months ago, I might have downgraded the feelings I experienced. I would tell myself he'd never loved me, but last night *I felt loved.*

Dominic was so tender and passionate in the way he paid homage to my body, like I'd been lost to him for years and we were finally together again. He reacquainted himself with every single part of me, leaving nothing untouched. I surrendered myself to him as if I'd been waiting my entire life to do so. There was something comforting about the way Dominic made me feel safe to be completely free.

He is everything I've ever wanted. I'm ready to share with him how I feel—that I doubt I ever stopped loving him. That he's always been *the one.*

I pick up his tuxedo shirt, slide my arms through and button a few buttons, leaving some undone for easier access. Then I pad down the steps to find Dominic. I can't wait to shout from the rooftops how much I love this man.

I hear Dominic's voice in the kitchen and make my way there, but my intuition makes me pause. I can hear Scott, Dominic's agent, on speakerphone.

"I don't care about any damn posts about me and Teagan," Dominic says. "They can rehash our past all they want—that won't stop us from seeing each other."

That's when I remember throwing myself into his arms yesterday at the gala. Phones were in the air. Whatever! I can't worry about that. I'm about to walk away when Scott mentions the tournament. My ears perk up.

"Dominic, I'm telling you this sneaker company is willing to donate a shit ton of money to the Desert Smash. All you have to do is ditch Teagan and play a solo tournament."

Ditch me? My heart clutches in my chest.

"I've got it all worked out, Dom. All you have to do is agree and they will have the funds wired to the tournament by Monday. You know it's the right thing to do."

Of course it is. The charity gets money and Dominic will be center stage while I will be pushed aside as if I mean nothing. What was last night about then? Why did Dominic act as if he loved me, cared for me—when all along he was planning to stab me in the back?

Or maybe he's not going to betray me. But what does it say that my first inclination is that he would? It means that no matter how much I love him, I don't trust him. Will I ever?

I've heard enough and rush upstairs to the master bedroom. I'm dazed as I frantically look around for my clothes and shoes. This feels like déjà vu, like the first night we made love and I escaped, but this is different. Back then, I was confused about my feelings. Now I've just realized I'm in love with a fucking scoundrel!

My dress is a heap on the floor next to Dominic's tuxedo and my thong. I grab my undies and sweep them up my legs. I need to leave. I call a rideshare and thankfully, there's one seven minutes out. Meanwhile, I need to be dressed before Dominic gets back because I refuse to have this conversation while I'm naked. I'm just fumbling with the zipper when Dominic returns to the room carrying two coffee mugs.

He stares at my state of undress in confusion. "Teagan? What are you doing?"

I glare at him. "What does it look like I'm doing, Dominic? I'm trying to get dressed so I can get the hell out of here."

I can tell my outburst stuns him because he looks taken aback. "Damn, Teagan, I'm getting whiplash from your ups and downs. What the hell happened between the time I went downstairs and now?"

I fold my arms across my chest. "I don't know, Dominic, why don't you tell me? You and your agent seemed to be having a chummy conversation downstairs."

His brow furrows in consternation. "Were you eavesdropping?"

"What if I were? Are you honestly going to stand there and act like I didn't hear what I heard?"

"I don't know what you heard!" Dominic's voice rises. "You couldn't have stayed long because if you heard the entire conversation, we wouldn't be standing here arguing. We'd be back in that bed." He points to his oversize king bed.

"Don't try to snow me," I say, furiously trying to get the zip up, but I can't. I turn my back to him. "Can you please zip me up? I can't go outside like this."

Dominic stares at me incredulously, but then stalks toward me. I feel his hands on the dress, but he's not quick about it. He takes his time easing the zipper up my body. When he's done, I feel his warm palms on my shoulders turning me around. "Teagan, please. You don't know the entire story."

"What I know is that I don't trust you," I spit out, jerking away from him. "Your agent wants you to dump me so you can play solo in the tournament. And why not? I'm just a washed-up has-been. No one wants to see me play. But even if that weren't the case, my first thought when I heard your phone call was that you deceived me. Can't you see? Without trust, *we* won't ever work."

"I didn't deceive you!"

I scoff and roll my eyes. "C'mon, Dominic, who are we kidding? It's about more than the tournament. I don't think I can ever let you have the spotlight without thinking about how you betrayed me in the past. How can I ever trust that you're not going to steal the show or worse, leave me behind?"

"Dammit, Teagan. Why won't you give us a chance?" Dominic responds, rubbing his head with his palm. "You're quick to rush to judgment as if you know everything. You don't. You did this twelve years ago. You were wrong then and you're wrong now."

"Oh, back to that," I huff. "If there's some big secret, Dominic, just tell me. Whatever it is."

"Why should I?" he taunts. "You're obviously not going to believe a word I say. You're quick to appoint yourself judge and juror. Why do you always leap to the wrong conclusions?"

I'm furious at his words. "Are you trying to put this back on me? How dare you? You left me and didn't look back. You went on to have a successful career while I was left with nothing but bad press. How can I trust that you won't do it again? You're asking me to put everything on the line, based on faith, and I'm sorry I can't do that. I don't trust you, and I see that I never will!" I snatch my heels and purse off the floor and head to the doorway.

Dominic is right behind me and catches me halfway down the stairs. "Of course you would run. You accused me of leaving you, but you've never been willing to fight for us either, Teagan." He reaches me and I have to stare up to look at him. Into his handsome, lying face.

"Fight for what?" I say. Tears are streaming down my cheeks. Uncaring, I brush them away.

"For us!" he yells. He's as upset as I am, but I suspect it's because I found him out.

"There is no us," I respond. "There never was."

His snatched breath tells me I've hit my mark and hurt him just like he's hurt me.

"It's always an illusion with you. I set myself up for failure each and every time. Right when I believe—" I stop myself from saying more and rephrase. "It's snatched right out from under me." When I reach his front door, I turn back around. "I'm done with tennis, and I'm done with you."

I open the door and run barefoot to the gate. However, when I use the opener to let in the rideshare car, several reporters accost me on the sidewalk. One of them has a camera and shoves it in my face.

"Teagan, when did you and Dominic get back together?"

"Are you making a comeback from tennis after your fall from grace?"

I turn and glance back at Dominic, who is standing in the doorway of his house, bare chested, wearing a pair of pajama bottoms. The expression on his face is inscrutable, but it's obvious to anyone with a pair of eyes what we've been up to since I'm wearing an evening gown. I push past the crowd of reporters and into the sedan waiting for me. I don't dare look back because I'm afraid of what I might see.

Instead, my head falls to my hands and I cry.

How the hell did I end up here again?

Thirty-Four

Dominic

I'm done with tennis, and I'm done with you.

Teagan's words echo inside my head as if they're on repeat. I watch her pass the crowd of reporters and climb into the waiting car. They know not to enter because there are signs that state this is private property. I dare one of them to attempt it. I'll have them arrested so fast their heads will spin. None try, so I turn back inside and slam the door.

Damn that woman!

Why must she always think the worst of me?

Is it ingrained in her DNA that I somehow have it out for her?

Clearly she didn't listen to my entire conversation with Scott. Otherwise, she would have heard me tell him in no uncertain terms that the tournament will remain doubles. I'm not playing without Teagan. I told him to go back to the sponsor and either they participate or they don't. I'm prepared to make up the difference to ensure the committee reaches their goal. But Teagan *didn't* stay or listen to my side of the story because she has this narrative in her head that I'm a selfish jerk who left her to pursue my own dreams and ambitions.

She's only partly right.

I had dreams of being the best. A champion. But I didn't do it at her expense. I continued my career to help support me and my family. Teagan doesn't want to hear that, though. It's easier for her to paint me as the villain. Then she doesn't have to go out on a limb and acknowledge what's between us. I know what I saw, what I felt, last night.

The look of pure joy on her face when she realized I was still at the award ceremony was real. Egypt was right. She wanted me there despite her reservations. The way she flung herself into my arms in the crowded room told me she was in this with me.

How could we spend such an incredible night together and the next morning she thinks I would betray her and cast her aside for money? I have enough money for several lifetimes. No, her reaction stems from her innate lack of faith in me. It angers and hurts me that no matter what I do, the past still haunts us. If I told her the truth about what happened twelve years ago, maybe then she could see what we could be.

Or she could hate me for having kept it from her for so long.

It's a no-win situation. I lose her every time.

My mind is going round and round when I hear my cell phone ring. I find it in the kitchen where I left it when Scott and I spoke earlier. I swipe right. "Hello?"

"Dom? Have you seen the photos of you and Teagan?" It's Justice.

"Hey, bro," I say. "What photos?"

"They're all over the internet. You two hugged up at some

party and then she's looking disheveled leaving your house and you bare chested."

I laugh because what can I do? The entire situation is crazy.

"What's so funny?"

"All of it," I say. "Reporters were waiting for Teagan outside my house this morning, so I'm not surprised. Those bastards are fast—I have to hand it to them."

"You don't care?" Justice asks.

"Right now, I couldn't care less. Teagan and I argued and she stormed off. Said she was done with me and with tennis."

"But you guys have the doubles tournament coming up."

"Don't you think I know that?" I ask testily, and then sigh. "I'm sorry, Justice. It's not you I'm angry at."

"It's all right. I'm happy to be a sounding board," Justice responds. "I was hoping you and Tee were going to make it work this time."

"I was hoping so too, but now I wonder if we'll ever get over the past. There might be too much water under the bridge."

"I don't believe that for a second, Dom. Whenever you want something, you go get it. Why is Teagan any different? Didn't you say you always regretted letting her get away? Don't let it happen again. Make her see who you really are. Show her the Dominic Fletcher who has supported and lifted up this family. Show her the man who's helping me fulfill my dreams. Show her the philanthropist who supports various charitable causes and organizations."

Wow. I'm blown away by Justice's impassioned plea. I never realized what an impact I had on my little brother. Neither one of us knew our father so I've tried to be an example and a good influence in his life. I'm happy to see I achieved the mark.

"Thanks, Justice. I'll take everything you've said to heart."

And I will.

The question is whether Teagan will even listen to me. She's so hung up on past fears and hurts. Can I make her see all that we could be *together*?

Thirty-Five

Teagan

"You don't have to stay, Lyric. You can go back to Memphis. You have a business to run and a man and little girl who adore you," I say when Lyric tells me she's extended her visit.

We're sitting at the kitchen counter sipping cappuccinos I made us after our walk. The other Gems left on Sunday. They are returning on Friday to attend the tennis tournament. Since she's a wealthy heiress, Wynter graciously agreed to pay for each of them to be there so I would have backup since it's unlikely I'll be playing doubles with Dominic.

A smile spreads across Lyric's lips. "I know I don't have to stay, but since I hired help at the ballet studio, they can hold it down this week. Besides, those pesky reporters are relentless."

Lyric and I went out for a long walk at Papago Park earlier so I could clear my head and finally stop crying about Dominic and everything that went wrong. It was great until it wasn't. At the end of the track, some of the media hounded us all the way back to my car. They seem intent on finding out what's going on between me and Dominic. Apparently, several have shown up to the country club trying to interview staff and club members. I'm told they were booted off the property, but not before someone spilled the beans about our training.

Speculation has been running rampant online, wondering if I'm making a comeback. Why would I after the treatment I received? And if that wasn't enough, one of them had the poor taste to rerun the video of my meltdown. I'm thankful that mental health is more prominent these days because the TV station received backlash virally for airing such a private moment. I received a personal phone call from the chairman, apologizing for the intrusion and stating there would be a public statement as well.

Nonetheless, the attention has made it impossible for me to leave my home, let alone go into the office, because media are camped out waiting to get a sound bite from me or one of my team. The only good thing is that today Brett closed on another country club deal. Williams & Associates is back in the black.

"I really appreciate you doing this. I feel like I'm under siege."

"Have you thought about issuing a statement?" Lyric says. "It might clear things up and get them off your back."

"And say what? It's not like Dominic and I are together. And I'm not returning to tennis."

"Aren't you, though? There's still the tournament."

"Which I'm sure I won't be playing in," I respond. "There's no way Dominic will turn down being front and center, in the spotlight, at the tournament on Saturday."

"Teagan… I'll say this again. You're being much too hard on Dominic. As soon as he realized his mistake at the award ceremony, he pulled back. He's been here with you training week in and week out. Why can't you give him a little slack?"

Because I'm afraid to let anyone in. What has love ever done for me? Other than the Gems and the sisterhood I've built with them, love has been lacking in my life. My father always made me feel less than and not good enough because I wasn't the son he envisioned. And although my mother was around, I always felt as if she was downtrodden and too afraid to show her feelings. As I've gotten older, she's shown me affection, but it was hard-won and a long time coming.

Then there's Dominic. When we met I was so desperate for love, I latched on to him like a lifesaver thrown to a drowning person. When it all blew up in my face, I was shattered and unable to move forward. I confronted him because I couldn't understand why he didn't love me as I loved him. I had no idea we had an audience. The shame and embarrassment from having my emotions shown for the entire world to see caused me to retreat into myself and hide behind my father. He was only too willing to take over and control my life.

"You don't understand," I say, finally answering Lyric's question.

Lyric reaches for my hand. "Explain it to me, Teagan. Sometimes you're closed up like a tortoise. Let me in and share whatever it is you're feeling."

Her words give me pause and I know she's right. I sigh heavily, and the words spill from my lips. "I don't feel worthy of love. If my own father couldn't love me, why would Dominic?"

My words surprise her and she's silent, so I continue. "You've always had the Taylors, Lyric. Amazing parents who love and support you, no strings attached. I've always felt like

I had to earn my father's love and even then, I was never good enough. With Dominic, I thought I had to be his equal. Show him I was worthy to stand beside him. And even though tennis has been out of my life for some time, when this tournament came along, all those feelings came roaring back. He's a champion and I'm a nobody."

"That's not true. You're fucking Teagan Williams, an extraordinary human being, entrepreneur, friend and sister," Lyric replies fiercely, "and I won't hear you speak otherwise."

I squeeze her hand. "You're biased."

"Because I love you. And I think it's entirely possible Dominic does too. I think your fears stem from your childhood and your past, but at some point you have to let those go and focus on the here and now. Dominic wants to be with you or he wouldn't have stuck around for this tournament. He did so because you're a part of it. Why would he steal the spotlight? He's had it for over a decade. Did you ever think he was helping you shore up your confidence?"

"I never thought about it like that."

"Because you're being a negative Nelly and quick to think the worst of him."

"He hurt me."

"Forgive him, Teagan. Forgive yourself so you can be with the only man you've ever loved."

Lyric's advice isn't without merit. Later, when I'm in my home office, I think about what she said. Forgiveness. Is that all it would take to help Dominic and I move forward? It seems so simple, yet hard to do. I've had years to develop the impenetrable shell that protects me from getting hurt again.

My doorbell rings and I glance at the camera to see it's my parents. What are they doing here in the middle of the day?

I'm almost to the door when Lyric appears. "I've got it. It's my parents."

Lyric's mouth forms an O. "I'll make myself scarce."

I open the door. "I'm surprised to see you."

"Hello to you too," my father states with a huff.

"Russ," my mother warns. "Hello, darling." She comes to me and wraps her arms around me. "We've seen some of the news coverage and thought you might need reinforcements."

I smile. "Thanks, Mom. C'mon in." They walk inside and I glance behind them. Most of the reporters have left, but there are one or two still lurking on the sidewalk. "I appreciate you coming by, but I haven't been alone. The Gems came this weekend for my Broker of the Year award and Lyric is still here."

"That's right." Mom smiles. "Congratulations again. I'm so proud of you."

My father tsks and I sense his displeasure at the mention of my successful real estate career.

"Would you like something to drink?" I inquire.

My mother shakes her head. "No, thank you. I was hoping we could talk."

"Of course." I lead them into the living room Lyric vacated and they sit on the sofa while I plop down into an armchair. "What's up?"

My mother looks at my father and then back to me. "Well, we wanted to talk to you about the past, about when you left tennis."

I frown. "Do we have to? Watching the news reports is making me relive those unpleasant memories all over again."

"It's important you have all the facts about what happened back then," my mother says. "Isn't that right, Russ?" Once again, she stares at my father, waiting for a response. I've never seen this sort of interaction between them. Usually, he's in charge and my mom is sitting back as a participant.

"What's going on?" I glance back and forth between them.

My mother coughs and my father suddenly speaks. "After your injury, Dominic came to see you."

"I know and I sent him away." I remember that moment when I learned the odds of me returning to tennis professionally were impossible.

"What you don't know is he came back, time and time again," my father replies. "And I sent him away. I told him you needed to recover and would be better off without him."

"You did what? Wait—what?" I can't comprehend what he just said.

I jump to my feet and begin pacing the tile floor. *He came back? Dominic came back for me?* All this time, I thought he abandoned me, and instead my father sent him away.

"You sent him away!" My voice rises to near hysteric proportions.

"I was doing what was best for you. You were in a bad headspace," my father returns. "You needed peace and stability, not having Dominic flit in and out when you couldn't be a part of that world anymore."

"And of course, you knew best." I can't believe his audacity. "All this time, you let me believe he abandoned me. It was because of that misconception that I confronted him and had a very *public* meltdown. If I had known..." My voice trails off and my breaths come out in short pants. All of this is my fault. I went after Dominic, guns blazing, accusing him of the unthinkable, when it was my father interfering in my life. He set about a chain of events I could never have envisioned.

That's why my father didn't want me to speak to Dominic—because he didn't want his lies exposed.

But why didn't Dominic tell me?

Why did he let me nail him to the cross without defending himself?

He tried and you shot him down each and every time.

He kept saying I didn't know everything, but he never told me the truth. Why not? Shock reverberates through me and my knees turn to jelly.

My mother rushes toward me. "Teagan…" She guides me back to the chair, crouches beside me, and I hear her voice, but it seems to be coming from far way. "Put your head down… let the blood get to your brain."

Slowly, I recover. Heavily, I lift my head.

Regret is etched across my mother's face. "I'm so sorry. We should never have kept this from you, but given everything that's happened, I thought it was incumbent upon us to come clean."

Tears streak down my cheeks. "If I'd known…it would have changed everything."

Dominic and I could have been together. All these years I wasted being angry at him when I should have been angry at my father for constantly controlling my life.

"Why didn't you tell me sooner?" I implore.

My mother's eyes are rimmed with red. "I should have, but I let your father take the lead in this family, in our lives, but not anymore. I realized I have to stand up for myself, for what's right. I couldn't let this continue. I knew we had to tell you the truth. I know I'm not innocent in keeping you from the man you were meant to be with."

"You think that?" I cry.

My mother nods. "If you can find your way back to each other after all these years, then it was meant to be. Who am I... Who are *we*—" she glances at my father "—to stand in the way of true love."

I shake my head in disbelief. "I can't believe this. It upends everything I've thought about Dominic. I've wronged him."

"I know." She nods. "I just hope the truth helps. I understand if you're upset with both of us. Maybe in time you can find it in your heart to forgive us for the mistakes of the past."

Forgiveness. It's what Lyric was preaching to me earlier. It seemed so much harder to do then, but now? Knowing what I do, it changes *everything*.

"I need time, Mom, to process all of this."

"Absolutely. I don't expect forgiveness immediately. I just hope you know how much we love you. Don't we, Russ."

Once again, she gives my father a hard stare. I don't know what's happened between them and I don't care. I'm happy to see my mother has found her own voice.

"That's right," my father says. Even now, he can't say the words *I love you*, but what I've realized in this moment is that I don't need him to say it. There's only one person I need to hear say those three words.

My father glances at his watch. "We should go."

All I can do is nod.

My mother rises to her feet and so does my father. "We'll see ourselves out."

She squeezes my shoulder and then I hear the chime of the front door as they exit. A loud sob escapes my lips. If I got it so wrong about what happened in the past and my father's machinations were behind our breakup, then I incorrectly accused Dominic of wanting the spotlight for himself at the Desert Smash, just like Lyric said. I was wrong like I have been about so many things. Dominic was at the award ceremony for me. He stayed even when I pushed him away. I should have trusted my feelings and my gut instinct that Dominic cares for me, *loves me*. It doesn't have to be one or the other. It's possible for me to have my own spotlight without diminishing his.

Several seconds later, I hear the tap of feet and Lyric approaches me. She's wearing a leotard, tutu and ballet slippers. She must have been practicing. "Teagan, what's wrong?" She wraps her arms around me as sobs wrack my body.

"Everything, Lyric," I cry. "You were right. I was so wrong about Dominic and I've ruined everything."

He must hate me after the horrible things I said to him. I misjudged him time and time again.

Can he ever find it in his heart to forgive me and take me back?

Thirty-Six

Dominic

I don't like drama. Never have.

Which is why I'm perplexed as to what went wrong between me and Teagan. With so much going wrong in my love life, I can't have drama in my family dynamic too. Ever since our dinner, Mama has been short and to the point when I call or text. I know she's upset about my loaning Justice the funds to start up his business.

Tough luck.

She's going to have to deal with it, but I don't want the rest of the family to suffer due to the tension between us. So I decide to meet her in neutral territory at a café Teagan and I like to frequent on the weekends for brunch.

I'm already waiting for Mama when she arrives in a flurry through the front door. She's dressed more casually than normal in simple blue jeans, a white peasant shirt, stilettos and carrying a designer bag. I'm incognito in jeans, a T-shirt and a baseball cap because I was finally able to lose the couple of reporters tailing me since my night with Teagan.

"Mama." I rise to my feet and give her a kiss on the cheek.

"Dominic, I was surprised to hear from you," she says. "I haven't been your favorite person lately."

I sigh because she always plays the victim card and it's time for it to stop. "Listen, I didn't call you here to be your whipping boy. I thought we should talk and clear the air about a few things."

She places her bag on the adjacent chair and responds, "I'm listening."

"I feel like you've changed since I became rich and famous," I say, going straight to the point, "and not in a good way."

Her face contorts in anger. "That—that's not true."

I hold up my hand. "Please let me finish." I'm determined to get everything I have to say off my chest and let the chips fall where they may. I should have spoken up much sooner instead of letting my anger fester.

"Fine." She sighs dramatically and leans back in her chair.

We take care of the formalities of ordering a cappuccino for her and an espresso for me, but then I get right back to the matter at hand.

"I don't feel like I matter to you anymore. I have hopes and dreams that you don't even know about because you stopped asking. It's all about the money and what I can do for you. Me loaning Justice funds to start his business was a good thing. Something I could do with the money *I* earned to help Justice fulfill his dream, and it's an investment I'll earn back, but you turned it around and sullied it by complaining about money. Did you think how he might feel? How hard it was for Justice to come to me, his big brother, for a handout? No, you could only see how it might take away funds from you."

My words must shock her because for once my mother doesn't interrupt me. So I continue. "I will always be there for Ciera and Bliss. I've set up college accounts for them to help them get the best start in life. I would never want them to suffer or endure the poverty Justice and I did. And as for you, Mama, I will continue to support you and ensure you have everything you need, but you're not entitled to be consulted on how I spend my money. Are we clear?"

She nods and a tear escapes her lashes. "Why did you never tell me you felt this way? It sounds like you've kept all of this bottled inside for years."

"I didn't want to hurt you. I still don't. But I don't like the choices you make. I haven't in a long time, but I've done my best for you. I gave up the woman I love to ensure I could support this family. I can't give you anything else. I'm tapped out."

She reaches her hand across the table to grasp mine. "I never expected you to, Dominic, and I'm sorry if you felt there was no way out for you except through tennis. I appreciate everything you've done for me and this family."

"Thank you, Mama." I squeeze her hand.

"Would you be willing to share with me what your new dreams are for the future? Because I suspect, since Teagan has returned to your life, that there are changes coming."

"Well, about that…"

I tell Mama everything that's happened in the past and the present, from start to finish, including listening to Mr. Williams and staying away from Teagan. By the end, I feel relieved after unloading all the hurt and anger. Mama understands and I think finally sees how difficult it has been not only being her son, but also being the sole provider of the family. She promises to do better, and, honestly, that's all I can ask for.

Now I have to figure out how to win back my girl. It won't be easy, but then again, nothing with Teagan ever has been. But when I do win, it'll be worthwhile.

"We should start talking about my retirement," I tell Scott on Friday. He's arrived to attend this weekend's Phoenix Desert Smash.

"What?" Scott's eyes bug out. "What do you mean you're going to retire?"

"I didn't say I was doing so right this second, but my retirement is imminent," I respond.

"What brought this on?" Scott asks. "Is it because of all the heat you're getting with the press rehashing you and Teagan's breakup and her meltdown?"

I shake my head. "It has nothing to do with that. Though I'm not happy to see they would publicize her breakdown. They have no idea what she went through, but I do."

"You sound very passionate about a woman who told you she wants nothing to do with you," Scott replies.

I called Scott right after Teagan's departure to release a message via my publicist requesting that the media consider our mental health before rebroadcasting a private conversation. The statement caused the station in question to stop running footage of Teagan, but not the speculation about our relationship or her return to tennis.

"Yes, I still care for Teagan. And I'm not about to let the press crucify her again. I made that mistake years ago and won't do it again."

"What are you going to do?"

"Get her back," I say.

I remember what Justice said. I have to fight for Teagan. I decided to give her this week to cool down and when she's calm and rational, I intend to tell her what happened all those years ago. How I listened to her father instead of listening to my heart. I'm going to tell her I made a mistake and should have talked to her, fought for her. I want her to know she can have her own spotlight and I would never diminish her. I only want to love her.

"Strong words, but can you back it up?"

"I can and I will."

She'll be at the tournament tomorrow because she's part of the committee and unbeknownst to her, she's still playing doubles with me.

"She may think I was screwing her over and trying to steal the spotlight, but she can't be more wrong. I'm going to prove it to her."

"You sound determined."

"I am. I've let my career and family dictate my actions in the past, but today and all my tomorrows are for Teagan."

A grin spreads across Scott's face. "And your retirement?"

"Will bring us closer," I respond, "but I won't be sitting idle. Helping Justice get his business venture off the ground showed me I'd like to do that for other people. I'd like to empower other diverse people to live their dreams and change the world. I want to start a venture capital company called Dominic Ventures."

"Venture capitalism? That's a pretty bold move."

I shrug. "Maybe, but I'm passionate about helping people."

"Honestly, as much as I hate to lose you as a client, I think it's a great move," Scott said. "Let me know if there's any-thing I can do to help."

"I will, but for now, I need you to limit my future tour commitments and ensure I participate in the Grand Slams and only the most lucrative games."

"You got it. It's good to see you so sure of yourself."

"Thanks, man."

Part of it is the work I've done on my own, but my family and Teagan are also a big part of why there's a need for a change. I haven't been completely fulfilled by tennis in a long time. It's time to spread my wings.

Now all I have to do is convince Teagan.

And *this time*, I'm not giving up. I know what I want, and I want Teagan.

Thirty-Seven

Teagan

Today is the day.

Today is the day I get back the man I love.

I didn't immediately go to Dominic's after my parents left and beg his forgiveness. I needed to digest everything my parents told me. I've been going through what I could say to make Dominic forgive me for the horrible things I've said. I misjudged him horribly because I was so afraid to believe anyone could love me unconditionally. I kept throwing the past back in his face and he took it, letting me harangue him when the truth was much more sinister. My father was controlling my life and I fell right into his hands. I allowed my fears to cloud my judgment.

Because the truth of the matter is Dominic isn't solely responsible for our breakup, but it fit the narrative I contrived in my head to put all the blame on him instead of taking equal responsibility for what happened. I pushed him away, not my father. I didn't think Dominic would want to be with me if I couldn't play professional tennis anymore. I thought he deserved someone better. I didn't value myself or give him enough credit. And when he did return, I assumed he wanted the spotlight for himself, but that's not true.

My star can shine just as bright with him by my side.

I won't make that mistake again.

I get dressed for battle. I opt for a rich crimson Nike tank and flouncy tennis skirt because with all the press coverage, the tournament sold out. I learned from Charity that Dominic didn't accept the money in exchange for a solo tournament and instead donated the balance himself for the Phoenix Desert Smash to reach our two-million-dollar goal—which means our doubles tournament is still on. Everyone will be looking at me so I might as well be noticed. I've paired the tank and skirt with my favorite pair of red Nikes. My hairstylist came over yesterday and did my hair into sleek waves close to my skull. I've foregone makeup because lord knows how many sets we'll endure, but I did add a touch of mascara, some lipstick and lathered my skin with shimmering suntan lotion. The least I can do is look dewy.

"You look great!" Lyric states from the doorway when I spin around. She's wearing khaki shorts, a simple cotton tank and a pair of espadrilles. "How do you feel about the tournament and Dominic?"

"Nervous. Scared. Anxious," I reply. "What if he doesn't want to speak to me?"

"Then you make him listen."

I nod. I have to get through to him because I refuse to lose another decade with him.

"I'm going to head out."

The rest of the Gems are coming midmorning and Lyric

is picking them up in my Mercedes-Benz. So I hired a vehicle to take me to the tournament and it's already idling in my driveway. I wave at Lyric, pick up my tennis bag and walk toward my destiny.

The drive to the club doesn't go as planned and I don't have a chance to talk to Dominic before the tournament. There's a big wreck on the expressway, and I'm stuck in traffic for over two hours. When I finally arrive to the club, the place is a hub of activity. I head to Charity and the rest of the tournament committee to check in and see how I can be of assistance.

"Teagan, how are you, darling?" Charity rushes over to kiss both my cheeks. "I'm so sorry about all the unflattering news coverage. They had no right to air it."

I shrug. "Nothing you can do. We can't change the past."

Charity smiles sympathetically. "No, we can't, but I'm not surprised to see you and Dominic are an item. I knew it!"

"I can't get one over on you," I say, pointing in her direction with a wry smile. "Has Dominic made it?"

"Oh, yes, he's already on the court and making a splash. There's a crowd just to watch him practice hitting the ball."

Of course he would beat me here because he's a consummate professional. I suck in a deep breath and remind myself I can do this. I will get through to him.

"Thanks. I'll make my way there, but do you need any help?"

Charity shakes her head. "Mitzi and I and the rest of the volunteers have it covered. You're playing in front of the world. Go get ready." She gives me an enthusiastic thumbs-up.

I leave the check-in desk and make my way to the courts. My heart beats so loudly in my chest I'm certain everyone can hear it. My palms are damp and I can feel sweat under my armpits. I haven't been this nervous since my first junior championship when my father and trainer were breathing down my neck.

There's a crowd around one fence near the courts showing me exactly where Dominic is. "Excuse me," I say, pushing my way through. At first, I'm met with resistance because they're all jockeying to get a view of Dominic, but when someone realizes who I am, suddenly the crowd parts and allows me to enter.

Lucky number seven. I smile.

Dominic is playing in earnest, slamming his racket against the ball and sending it at least one hundred thirty miles per hour across the court.

"Good morning," I say once he and the hitter finish an intense rally.

Dominic spins around on his heel and instead of being greeted with the frown I'd expected, a wry smile spreads across his full lips. As always, he looks sexy in a simple white tennis top and shorts. "Teagan, so nice of you to finally join us."

His snarky remark makes me laugh because it's classic Dominic. He likes to rile me up before a game.

"Not all of us are programmed to get up at the crack of dawn," I respond, coming closer and dropping my bag. I pull out my visor because the sun is beaming overhead. It's going to be a hot one, which won't make this tournament any easier.

I walk over to him. "Could I have a word with you in private?"

He glances around at the crowd on the sidewalk and already in the bleachers. "Now isn't the right time, Teagan. Can we talk later?"

"I know that," I whisper, glancing behind us, "but it's really important."

"We need our heads in the game and I don't want to argue."

"Please…" I implore.

"Fine." He tosses down his racket and we move farther away from the court. People can still see us, but they can't listen in.

"You're not wired or anything?" I ask.

He glares at me. "No, Teagan. I've been playing all morning. What have you been doing?"

"Trying to get here," I say sharply, and immediately soften my tone. I don't want to fight with him. I want the opposite. "I was caught in traffic on the interstate."

He nods and stretches his neck back and forth. "I'm sorry. I'm just wound a little tight."

"Because of me?"

He looks down at me and his expression softens. "Teagan…"

"Listen, I know I made a mess of things," I begin quickly, "but I wanted to tell you I'm sorry. I'm sorry for every hurtful thing I've ever said to you."

His brow furrows. "Where is this about-face coming from?"

"From the fact that I finally know the truth," I say, looking into his ebony eyes. "I know what my father did."

His eyes widen in surprise. "You do? How?"

"My parents. They told me everything. My father admitted you kept coming to see me after I was injured. Even when I sent you away, you kept coming back." Dominic doesn't say a word, so I keep going. "My father said he asked you to stay away from me because he thought it would be in my best interests if we weren't together. He thought I wouldn't want to be around you and watch you live the dream I could no longer have."

"That's exactly what he said," Dominic responds. "He told me you were better off without me, to leave you to find someone better suited and out of the tennis world. I foolishly believed him. I thought I was doing the right thing when I walked away and left you."

"And I thought it was for the best to push you away so you could find someone better, someone worthy of you."

"Worthy of me? Teagan, you're the only woman I've ever cared about. Why would you think that?"

"Because I've had a lot of fears and hang-ups after growing up in my father's house. No matter what I did, I could never be the son he always wanted. When the accident happened, it was like a sign showing me I wasn't good enough—that I wasn't worthy."

"That's crazy, Teagan. You had me right by your side telling you day in and day out...that I—" His words are cut off by the announcer stating that the tournament will begin in fifteen minutes. When the announcement is over, I look at Dominic, eager for him to finish that sentence.

"That you what?" I press.

Dominic's gaze moves behind me. Our opponents have walked onto the court. He looks down at me. "We need to finish this discussion later."

I grab Dominic's arm. "No, we can't." Something tells me if we don't finish, if I don't get out everything I need to say, I may never get another chance. "I'm sorry I let my fears get in the way of us. You're not the only one to blame for the demise of our relationship. I shouldn't have put all the blame on you."

From the stunned expression on Dominic's face, he's surprised by my words. "You mean that?"

"Of course I do. I'm to blame too. I pushed you away and

gave my father the leverage he needed to break us up and control my life. It was just easy to make you the fall guy rather than face my own shortcomings. I don't want to do that anymore. I want to embrace life, and I hope it's one that includes you. Can you forgive me for all the terrible things I've said?"

The crowd starts to chant Dominic's name and he glances to the bleachers and then back at me. "We should get into position and get ready."

My heart stops. I don't want him to put distance between us, not now.

I grasp his arm. "Tell me it's not too late, Dominic," I blurt out, blocking out all the voices around us. "That I haven't lost the best thing that's ever happened to me."

His eyes soften and my heart finally starts beating again. "Baby…"

Hearing the endearment is like music to my ears. "I can't wait to play tennis again," I say, moving closer to him and placing my hand on his chest, "but more so because I have you on my side. I know you weren't trying to steal the spotlight, and I know you didn't take Scott's offer even though it would have brought the tournament more money. I let my fear take over, but I don't want to do that anymore. Promise me if we win that I get to have your heart."

A broad grin spreads across his full lips. "Now, that's a promise I can keep."

His large palm reaches out and rests on my cheek. The tiny action is a comfort.

The five-minute whistle blows, indicating we should get ready. Dominic and I walk over to our opponents, shake their hands and then move back to our side of the court. I bend down, grab my racket from my bag and inhale sharply.

The moment of truth is here. All the practice Dominic and I have put in will finally reveal itself for the entire world to see. My hand is shaking and I remind myself to calm down.

When I'm upright, I glance up and see the Gems holding a sign: Go Get 'Em, Teagan. I can't help but smile because these women have stood by my side during the best and worst of times. I see Dominic's family too. His mother, sisters and brother are waving Dominic signs.

Dominic and I both move to the baseline.

"Are you ready for this?" he asks.

"I was born ready."

Because this moment means I get to start my life over again and finally find the happiness I seek.

Thirty-Eight

Dominic

She knows.

Teagan knows what happened all those years ago between me and her father. And rather than be angry and rail at me like I suspected she might, she took part of the blame. I can't believe it. She finally sees that I'm not the selfish bastard who walked away from her, but rather I'm the man who never gave up.

When she walked onto the court, looking dazzling in a tennis getup I hadn't seen before, I kept my cool when I felt the opposite. I would have liked nothing better than to crush her in my arms while I plundered the sweet cavern of her mouth. But there's no time.

After months of practicing, the day is finally here to find out if Teagan and I can bring home the win. But we're not just fighting to beat our opponents. We're fighting for so much more.

For a do-over.

For a new start.

One that begins with Teagan and I being open and honest with each other. This time, we will get it right.

I can't wait for the game to begin because I'm going to play my heart out.

Thirty-Nine

Teagan

I crouch down at the baseline and so does Dominic.

We're ready.

This will be a knockdown drag-out fight until winner takes all. For me, it's not about a trophy. My win will be having Dominic's heart.

The opposition wins the first serve. That's fine. Dominic and I have been preparing for this moment. They serve and the ball lands in the corner, right in my backhand's sweet spot. I'm right there to slam my racket against it and send it bouncing far and high across the net. The other team makes a run for it and lunges, hitting the ball back over. Dominic makes it this time, easily tapping the ball.

And so it goes. A short rally until finally we make a point. Then we make another. We take the first set easily 6–3. I'm happy about how we're doing.

"It's going good," I say when we break to have a quick drink and wipe sweat from our faces.

"Yeah, but don't get comfortable," Dominic says. "They could be setting us up. Conserving their energy to come at us hard in future sets. Maintain focus."

"I will." There are local channels and major sports networks on-site, but I block out that the entire world is waiting to see what I do next. Instead, I think about Dominic. Being this close to him is driving me wild. He smells manly and earthy with sweat, and I wish I was curled beside him in bed.

"Stop thinking dirty thoughts," Dominic whispers in my ear because of course everyone is watching us and probably trying to read our lips.

I laugh, wink at him and pick up my racket, getting back into position. He's right. Our opposition comes back strong in the second set and takes it 6–4. I'm glad I didn't completely embarrass myself. I missed a few shots and if Dominic hadn't gotten the others, we'd be in worse shape. The crowd cheers when Dominic hits the ball and boos when I miss a point.

"It's okay," Dominic whispers when I take a swig of Gatorade as we prepare for our third set. "Don't let the crowd get in your head."

"That's easier said than done."

I forgot how loud the crowd can be when you're on the court, but my adrenaline has kicked in. I know what's at stake. I have to win this game. To show to myself I can do it and that I'm ready to win Dominic's heart.

One of Dominic's hands comes down on my neck and he whispers, "Get the ball deeper. They are weak on the left."

When it's my turn to serve, I send it deep in the corner of the service box, but they return it and storm the net. I swing hard and lob them, sending the ball deep and to the left like

Dominic said. Our opposition struggles to run for the ball and falls flat against the court.

It's 15–Love.

It's time to serve again. I lift on my toes and give it a hard swing. They tap the ball but it falls out of bounds. The point is ours: 30–Love.

Serve after serve, we keep giving them the business, but they come back at us until it's 30–40.

It's been years since I played professionally and I feel every moment of this match. We need to get a deuce so we can get back in the game. They serve again and this time I remember to use the backhand Dominic and I have been working on, what used to be my strong point, and it helps.

We're at deuce point, but get two points in a row? I'm not what I used to be. I'm worried about disappointing Dominic, the Gems and all the fans who're sitting in their seats with bated breath.

It's my serve again and it's a fault, so there's another chance for me to get the serve right. This time, I hit across the net and bam, we are one point from the win. We're getting closer to the finish. I can hear the crowd getting louder as if they too smell victory.

I'm ready to lock this in so Dominic and I can finish that talk and finally have the life we deserve, the life we should have had twelve years ago. When it's time for what I hope is the last point of the day, I'm moving from side to side on the court, ready for whatever comes my way. I don't worry because Dominic serves it up. We rally back and forth against our opponent. Each of us chases the ball, not allowing the other team to have the point.

He's just as determined as I am because we're fighting for us.

It's our time.

I see the return from my serve coming toward me. I know this is the make-or-break shot. I jump in the air. My racket smashes the ball and sends it flying across the net. It's fast and deadly. I know the other team isn't going to make it. My eyes widen as I wait for the inevitable.

It finally happens and they fail to hit.

The crowd soars to their feet with thunderous applause, and I fall to my knees.

We won.

We won.

Tears of joy stream down my cheeks and I don't care who is watching. I know this isn't a major. I did this for me. For us. And when I see Dominic's outstretched hand, I take it and rise to my feet. Then, uncaring of who sees us, I jump into his arms, circling my legs around his waist. He catches me and crushes his mouth to mine.

It's everything I've been waiting for.

I kiss him with fearless abandon. The crowd starts chanting our names. When we lift our heads to finally catch a breath, I say the words I should have said a long time ago.

"I love you."

Later, after the tournament is over and we've accepted congratulations from the Gems, club committee members, Dominic's family and Scott, who all showed up and showed out to support us at the country club, it's just me and Dominic.

We're finally alone at my place.

"You did it, Teagan," Dominic states. "I'm so very proud of you."

"Thank you. I've been away from the game for so long I

didn't think it was possible to have a comeback, but I did, because of you and your support."

"No, it's because of you and your innate talent. You're too hard on yourself and don't give yourself enough credit. You're an amazing woman, Teagan. And I've spent the better part of my life being mad at you or loving you."

"Loving me?"

"That's right. I love you, Teagan," Dominic states. "I don't think I ever stopped. No matter how far away I was from you, I never forgot you."

"And I never forgot you, Dominic. You are and have always been the love of my life. I'm sorry about my father's machinations and that I was so quick to judgment. You deserve better than that. I promise that I will spend the rest of my days making it up to you, if you'll let me."

"Let you? You had me the moment I locked eyes with you from across the room at the Desert Smash cocktail party."

"Really? I thought you were mad at me."

"I was. Because you thought the worst of me and weren't willing to give us a chance to see all that we could be."

"I not only see it," I say. "I believe we could have a happy life as long as we're together."

"What about tennis?"

"I understand you're still on the tour. I will support you and stand by your side, just as you stood by mine throughout this tournament."

"And if I told you I might retire soon?"

"Then I'll happily fill up our days and nights showing you just how much I love you."

"Good answer." Dominic lowers his head for the kiss I've been waiting for.

Epilogue

"You were a gorgeous bride," I tell Egypt after her wedding ceremony to Garrett.

She's never looked lovelier than she does in the crepe chiffon dress. The sweetheart neckline highlights her bountiful breasts that I'm a tad envious of while the thigh-high slit is all Egypt. The Sandals location in Curaçao was the perfect setting for them to say their vows. I got choked up when Egypt spoke about how she knew Garrett was her someone special from the moment they met at her restaurant.

"And you were equally as stunning as a bridesmaid, girlfriend," Egypt replies, "or maybe it's because you have Mr. Tall, Dark and Handsome with you." She nods at Dominic, who is looking hot in a black tuxedo suit, pristine shirt, silk tie and gold cufflinks. "Welcome to the family."

"I'm glad to be part of it," Dominic responds. He invited his entire family, mother, sisters Ciera and Bliss, and Justice to the festivities all expenses paid. They are all on the dance floor cutting it up with the rest of the guests. "I'm lucky to be reunited with this beautiful lady." He hugs me to his side.

"I love Black love. You guys have fun tonight and do absolutely everything I would do." Egypt winks.

"I'm so happy for her," I say as she sashays over to Garrett's side and he plants a soft kiss on her lips. Who would have thought several years ago that nearly half of us would be married and the rest happily ensconced in committed relationships?

"Penny for your thoughts," Dominic says, resting his head on mine as I watch the Gems dance with their respective partners. Wynter glides across the floor with Riley. Her baby bump is visible now because she's due in several months. I can't wait to be an auntie again and maybe one day have a family of my own.

Egypt and Garrett are all booed up; Asia and Blake are closer than close. Meanwhile, Shay and Colin are whispering sweet nothings in each other's ears, and Lyric and Devon are slow grinding on the dance floor while Kianna attempts to babysit Ryan, but Asia's toddler is running all over the place.

"I'm just thinking that maybe the Gems have a heavenly angel looking over us because ever since we received our inheritances from Aunt Helaine, each of us have not only achieved our dreams, but we've found love along the way."

"Then I'm thankful to the angel above because she led me back to you," Dominic replies.

"Thank you for loving me, Dominic, and I promise to never take you or our love for granted ever again."

"Deal." And he seals his vow with a kiss.

★ ★ ★ ★ ★

If you liked Break Point, *don't miss these other enemies-to-lovers romances from Yahrah St. John and Afterglow Books!*

Frenemy Fix-Up

Free-spirited yoga guru Shay Davis has only ninety days to get her workaholic former classmate Colin Anderson from work all day to namaste...

Only they both really, really get on each other's nerves.

Soon, though, their sessions are heating up the studio. But as Colin gets closer to achieving his goal, he and Shay both move further away from what they thought they wanted. Before they know it, they'll have to step out of their comfort zones and rethink their own versions of "right"...before their time is up.

Going Toe to Toe

What happens in Aruba, stays in Aruba...

That's what former ballerina Lyric Taylor keeps telling herself. After all, now that the curtain has closed on her ballet career, and with the search for her biological parents stalling, she could use a little distraction. So when a lodging mix-up leads to an unexpected fling in paradise with her sexy bunkmate, Devon, Lyric takes the plunge.

Seven days of sun, sand and plenty of sizzle—and when it's time to go home, their no-strings sitch will come to an end... Right?

But nothing can prepare them for discovering Lyric is Devon's daughter's new dance teacher.